ABOUT SWARM THEORY

It was a time of hippies, heroin, and *All in the Family*. It was a time, in the small town of New Canaan—a fictional town in mid-Michigan— when developers gobbled up farmland and spit out subdivisions.

Against this backdrop, *Swarm Theory's* interlocking narratives reveal the troubled lives of Astrid (a young woman trying to hold her family together), Caroline (Astrid's best friend who has lost her mother to heroin), Will (a soldier struggling to make sense of life after being discharged from the Marines), and Father Maurice Silver (a priest caring for a young man dying of AIDS).

Nothing in New Canaan is quite what it seems.

Swarm Theory is a book that reveals life's amazing contradictions—the wonderful and the profane, devotion and infidelity, understanding and revenge— through stories told from different perspectives. These stories investigate what happens when people come together—whether to do admirable or horrific things. Here, intimates and strangers alike can't help but be intertwined; their unpredictable journeys providing a backdrop for characters complex, honorable, and not.

Swarm Theory reveals our often misguided, dark, and life-sustaining dependency on each other.

swarm theory

swarm theory

Christine Rice a novel

HELL PRESS
UNIVERSITY OF HELL PRESS

For my family, living and gone

"Caged birds accept each other but flight is what they long for."

—Tennessee Williams, *Camino Real*

CONTENTS

I. OBSERVE
Atmospheric Disturbances. 15
Known Issues 33
Exacting Revenge 53
Falling Bodies 69
The Art of Survival 79

II. FORMULATE
Irreversible Acts 85
Common Notions 91
Solid-State Reactions 97
They'll Do as They Please. 107

III. EXAMINE
Striking Disclosure. 123
Swarm Theory. 129
Cloaking Device 147
King of the Lakes 157
Undesirable Interruptions 181

IV. RESULT
Proving Grounds. 197
Kinetic Friction 211
Other than Honorable Intentions 221
Angle of Entry. 239
Initial Encounters 253
Tell Me Something I Don't Know. 265
Tangled Elements 285
Spectacular Diversions. 303

What Will Crush You 313
Ectopistes Migratorious 329
Swarm Suppression 333
This Is How Accidents Happen 349

ACKNOWLEDGMENTS
ABOUT THE AUTHOR

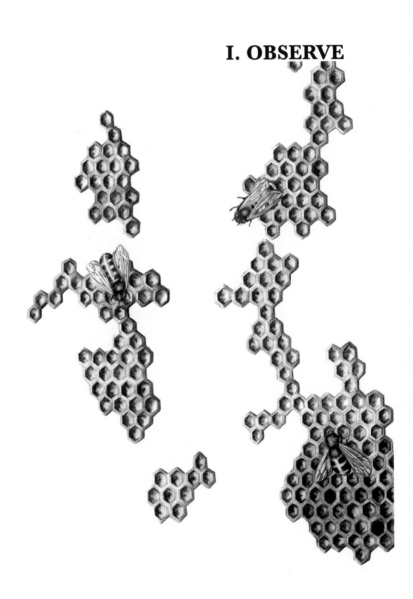

Atmospheric Disturbances

Just before a fight, right out of the eerie green stillness, the atmosphere in our house would shift precariously; the barometric pressure rising, winds whipping, funnel clouds skipping down hallways, rain, sleet, hail, snow filling sinks and cereal bowls.

Every time Dad walked in late (always a bad sign), his well-cut suit smelling of cheap perfume (Mama wore Chanel), or sporting a speck of red lipstick on his collar (Mama wore coral), the ether would churn in a frenzy of screaming and denouncements and, eventually, always, and inevitably, Mama's sobbing.

Tempest. Tsunami. Cyclone. You get the picture. Big or small, it was never pretty.

Because she didn't like the neighbors knowing our business, Mama always closed the windows before the verbal fireworks exploded. If it was one of those calm, clear Michigan nights, just before twilight, as the neighbors dried and put away the last dinner dish or drew their kids' baths, Mama would close windows—in anticipation of Dad's late return—from one end of our sprawling suburban ranch to the other.

This particular spring evening, having just walked in from my cashier's job at my Auntie's grocery, Mama's voice, pitched and hot, hit me before the screen door slapped shut. The smell of warm dough, za'atar, and lemon drew me to the kitchen. Judging from the tone of her voice, it was only a matter of seconds before she'd start throwing stuff. Could be a metal bowl. Or a Teflon frying pan. Apples. Oranges. Onions. Those were her favorite missiles to launch at Dad. She opted for unbreakable items (never glass, too messy) and relatively light (never cast iron).

I'd once suggested she try the crêpe pan, but she'd only grimaced, *That could take his head off.*

Wasn't that the point?

Her back to me, both of them oblivious to their only child, Mama stood at our kitchen island, her hands splayed on either side of a sheet of rolled dough. She always used a juice cup to cut the fatayer dough but, in her anger, she'd lost any sense of finesse and bludgeoned the dough with such force that it looked like a child had gotten to it. She spat choice Arabic insults at Dad. Roughly translated they meant *shit of a dog, dogshit on a shoe, piece of shit* but she possessed an exceptionally creative talent to mix and match those with English standbys. I stood quietly behind her, unable to move, my heart pounding slightly faster than usual. I was used to the fights. Hell, I was used to them but they still tore me up inside.

Dad sat at the kitchen table, tie loosened, the *Journal* opened in a V between his fists, his readers resting at the tip of his angular nose, copper hair slicked back in a perfect wing above his forehead. Cool as usual. A whirlwind of stainless steel mixing bowls, spoons, spatulas, a bag of Gold Medal Flour, a roll of 35-millimeter film, onions, lemons, and bits of dough orbited him as if he'd become the king of a very odd universe.

My folks never acknowledged the chaos swirling around them, maybe because it never touched them. Only me. But I would stand there, dumbly unable to speak, watching the bedlam. By the time it stopped, I'd be drenched by rain, pelted by hail, flattened by their whirlwinds.

From where I stood, I could see the veins on the side of her neck bulging, her thick curls lifting like black snakes. She suddenly picked up the rolling pin and rounded the island to stand at arm's length from Dad.

"I want a divorce."

The frenetic air shifted down the hallway toward the bedrooms only to be replaced by a dark cloud above Mama's head. It materialized suddenly and throbbed above her like a black heart.

Dad merely raised the newspaper closer to his face. It was his kryptonite; nothing could get to him when he read that paper.

"Did you hear me?"

"Impossible."

"Why?"

"Catholics don't divorce, dear." His voice remained calm.

Mama pointed the rolling pin at him like a dagger, "Catholics don't screw their secretaries or their friend's wife."

"Who told you that?"

"About the secretaries or Charlie's wife?" If Dad was cool (and, yeah, he was) it was Mama who didn't miss a beat.

A light rain began to fall and, simultaneously, thunder grumbled, lightning crackled. I leaned on the island and was about to speak when a strange feeling overtook me. Usually I would let them know I was there and they'd stop. But this time felt different. This time something felt truly broken, irretrievable, so I kept quiet.

The rain picked up intensity. When Dad didn't respond, Mama poked him in the arm with the rolling pin. It was one of those old-fashioned heavy ones with red handles and a thick, sturdy center.

"You're getting yourself all worked up about nothing, Leila. Why don't you sit down?"

"About nothing? You son-of-a-bitch."

Dad merely turned the page, flicking the paper as if he'd finished the conversation but, just then, instead of retreating, Mama cocked that rolling pin like a tennis racket and swung it right through his newspaper. It caught Dad on the chin and he pitched backward with such force that his chair toppled over and he hit the floor.

It happened so fast that I thought I'd imagined it. But I hadn't. He lay on his back, blood from his split chin already staining his white shirt, paper still gripped in either hand, as if he'd decided, all on his own, to recline and read the paper.

I couldn't move. As far as I knew, she'd never actually *hit* him. The sight of Dad on the floor like that, glasses hanging off one ear, gave me a sick, twisted feeling.

The rain picked up intensity. Fat drops bounced off the table as Mama leaned over him, her free hand extended but not touching him, as if afraid to make contact. It was like she wanted to rewind time, reel him back, pat his hair into place. Instead of taking her hand, he stayed there until, with one fist still gripping the paper, he rolled over and pushed himself up. He then grabbed her shoulders and spoke very slowly, "Get ahold of yourself."

Mama didn't respond, but I could imagine the look on her face. I imagined she wanted to spit, rip the lapels off his suit, pick apart his cool. When he finally let go, she swayed before sinking to her knees.

Straightening his black frames, he looked up, startled, "Astrid …"

He picked up his chair and put it back in place as if nothing had happened. Walking around me, he grabbed a towel and cleared his throat, "How was your day?"

I could barely see him through the storm.

"Better than yours," I hollered.

He pressed the towel into the cut on his chin to staunch the bleeding, "Yes. Well."

"*Yes. Well*," I repeated.

I walked to Mama, helped her stand, and buried my face in her neck. She felt fragile, her shoulder bones pressing into my cheek, smelling of lemon and spices. I helped her into a chair.

"You're all wet," she said absently, "is it raining?"

She was so beautiful. Even now in her miserable life, without makeup, wearing a print skirt and stained blouse, gray eyes contrasting her black hair, caramel skin pulled taut over high cheekbones. She fought the urge to cry. I could tell because she always ran her tongue under her top lip, over her teeth, and looked up as if she might be able to stop the deluge. Her sadness transferred to me and it tasted of brine at the back of my throat.

I fought to keep my tears in, anticipating Dad's exasperated questions. *What's all the fuss about? Why the tears?* And, while the answer always seemed obvious to me, I could never respond logically, reasonably, in a way he would understand.

The wind calmed, the precipitation stopped but the cloud, like a dark smudge, hovered above us.

"Luke," she pleaded. "Please."

He filled a towel with ice and pressed it to his chin, his words measured but edgy. "Why do you want a divorce? Why can't we go on like this?"

Mama looked at me.

"Astrid's a big girl. She can hear this."

I nodded.

Mama rested an elbow on the table and pressed her fist into her forehead, "You know why, Luke. I can't go on like this. We haven't had a proper marriage. Ever."

"What's *proper*?"

He loved to bait her, didn't believe she'd keep it up, placed his bets that she'd fold the way she always did when I walked in. I suppose it was her way of protecting me. She would go to her bedroom where she might stay for hours, even days. All the same, his cool veneer seemed thin tonight. His eyes kept flicking from me to Mama.

She looked at him, "*Proper* as in I'm sick of you smelling of—" She flapped her hand.

"What?"

"Whores."

His smirk flattened, "What do whores smell like?"

Mama just shook her head. It was more of an *I feel sorry for you* than an *I'm angry with you* gesture. She seemed calm, eerily emotionless, when she said, "I want to get on with my life, Luke. I'm finished with all of your nonsense." She then walked over to him, "I'm serious, Luke. I'm done."

•

Out here, where we live, in the vast inner gut of Michigan, in this former corn field converted to upscale subdivision, I've stood in our family room, palming the picture window overlooking the eighteenth hole of a golf course and, beyond that, miles of farmland, to watch tornadoes in the distance, their swirling tubes scoring the land, until Mama would haul me to the basement where we would sit under the steps, in the unfinished nook where Dad set up a table for my science experiments. We would make ourselves small and compact, her arm wrapped around my waist, my head resting on her shoulder, her hair cascading down my chest.

Her fear wasn't unfounded. Her parents died in the 1953 tornado that claimed 116 lives. She'd been in the car with them after closing their grocery store when the sky dissolved into a murky bruise. If I'd been there, if I'd even been alive at that time, of course, I'd have recognized the signs: the late spring temperature of 78 degrees, a dew point of 71 degrees, and a barometric pressure reading that fell to 28.89 inches of mercury. I'd have been measuring all of it, painstakingly recording it in my notebooks, detecting the patterns. I'd have known that those dramatic readings, combined with the severe thunderstorms, would result in devastation. But I wasn't there. And before they knew what was happening, an enormous funnel cloud—its base a half-mile wide, its top connected to an enormous churning thunderstorm—appeared in the distance.

My grandfather turned east and tried to get to the side of it but it shifted quickly and its girth and unpredictability caused him to panic. Mama said it seemed to follow his every move. He'd turn perpendicular and it followed; he'd turn away, it followed. Eventually, the gusts pushed the lurching Buick Special off the road and he lost control, flipped, and landed in a gully. This is what saved my mother—the car turtled in the ditch. She'd been pinned under the heavy frame, alive in the back seat while in the front seat her parents lay dead, crushed by the Buick's weight.

I'd imagined those moments so many times that I could feel the stillness before the freight-train wind, see the trees twist from the ground like screws, marvel at how the blue sky blossomed in the devastation's wake.

So, yeah, Mama took tornadoes seriously.

Dad, on the other hand, never joined us in the basement. He probably thought he could stop the storm, redirect it with a sidelong glance, snuff it out by sheer will. He was *that* guy. Never flinched. After WWII, he came to the States from Denmark weighed down by medals, saw the 1953 Motorama Corvette in New York, wrote the president of General Motors a letter outlining his plans to improve it, and the rest, as they say, is engineering history.

•

Later, after Mama composed herself, arranged *fatayer* on baking sheets and slid them into the oven, she asked me to pull a black suitcase out of the spare bedroom closet and bring it to her room. I did and settled, cross-legged, on the king-size bed to watch her carefully pack her things. The deep blue spread reminded me of the ocean setting of our annual trips to Florida. We would walk for miles along the shore searching for shells, drive to the Everglades to spy on horseshoe crab and heron, visit Cape Canaveral, go deep-sea fishing.

But my most vivid memory of Florida was when a hurricane slammed into the coast. One day a cool breeze blew off the ocean, the sun baked the sand, and the next, a steely lid of dense clouds blew in on a stiff wind that bent palm trees, frothed the surf, sent water birds inland. Men with boards and ladders appeared and the gentle sounds of the coast were suddenly and urgently replaced by the pounding of hammers.

We drove inland, found a little motel with a sputtering neon sign, and checked in. We bought candles, batteries, board games, cheap paperbacks, water, ice, a big cooler, cheese and oranges, cards, a chess set—everything we believed we needed to ride out the storm.

We put on rain ponchos and ran into the storm, holding hands, screaming into the wind. The wind swallowed our voices, erased them, as if we weren't even there. Even after all these years, I still see, very clearly, the palm trees bending, silver sheets of rain, the pool escaping its cement frame to cascade into the parking lot. These moments marked me not because of the danger, but because I distinctly remember being surprised and relieved that this kind of drama could occur *outside* our home. It didn't matter—not the sting of the rain against my bare skin, not the warnings from the hotel manager or his insistence that we go inside—because there I was, a hand held by each parent, cocooned in a twisted togetherness, the tumult knitting us together, binding us, keeping the storms that tore us apart safely at bay.

•

When she'd finished packing, Mama asked me to drive her to Auntie's. She'd be staying there for a while. The violent system that moved through our house had stalled over the miles of farmland surrounding our subdivision. Silken curtains of dark clouds dropped a steady rain. Trees trembled in violent gusts. Lightning flashed. Potholes became miniature ponds. Heavy-bottomed toads stitched their way across the asphalt.

Mama, upright in the passenger seat, stared straight ahead.

"You okay?" I asked.

She nodded.

It had been a good while since she'd fallen into a *mood* but, naturally, I was wary. During middle school and right up through my sophomore year, her *sadness,* as I referred to it, caused her to stay in bed all day. For the last year or so, though, she'd started eating breakfast, dressing in something other than a housedress, cooking, getting home just before I came home from school or practice. She seemed joyous, as if she'd lost something that had weighed her down, or perhaps gained something that buoyed her now.

Parents are funny things. As an only child, I studied them like apes in a zoo—their whims, habits, moods—and believed it was my duty to make them happy. There was no Child Number Two. Everything fell on me. I simultaneously caused pride and embarrassment, joy and pain, walked the tightrope connecting them, all too aware of the gusts of emotion that could throw me off balance.

During her dark moods, Mama would scream and rant. Not at me, but at the entire world, it seemed. Her mood would darken suddenly and she would focus on something, anything in her line of vision, and glare at it like an enemy, an intruder. I would stand close by, inert with confusion, to make sure she didn't hurt herself. Her face would twist and her voice would rise to such volumes that, after a while, the strings of the baby grand piano would vibrate in tune to her anger. When I was little, I would simply cover my head with my hands, roll into a ball, and whimper until she stopped. Afterward, she would fall to her knees in exhaustion, suddenly turn to me, reach out, and gather me in her arms.

It was always like that. The storm followed by the eerie calm that, I knew, would inevitably roil into another disturbance.

"How about you?"

"Peachy."

"I'm sorry you've had to put up with all of this, all this time. When you were little, we——"

"It's okay." I kept my eyes on the road.

"Let me finish. When you were young, it was easier to hide. But I just can't put up with it. I hope you understand."

Her voice, firm and clear, bore into the center of me. The emotional haze, kicked up by so many turbulent years, was finally lifting and, whether I was ready for it or not, something else had moved in to take its place.

When I was a kid, we would sit on our back deck after a storm to marvel at the startling transformation of the sky from silvery gray to brilliant blue or orangey red. *The rain washes the sky*, she'd say. She was right, in a way. The storms did their job. Knocked all the crap out of the sky. And this latest bout between my parents had done the same: all the dirty little particles of their marriage—the lies, deceit, hurt— blew away to reveal this brilliant reality.

•

I left Auntie and Mama hunkered in front of a *Dallas* episode with a bowl of popcorn. It wasn't too late, about seven, but it was unusually dark. About halfway home, something shifted in the sky yet again—the rain picked up, trees bent, branches snapped. The windshield wipers couldn't keep up with the deluge and I crept along, praying I would remember each nuance of the road I'd traveled so often. After nearly sideswiping a pickup, I turned into the Goynes's gravel drive.

Will, his sister Rebecca, and I had been friends since we were kids. Along with our friend Caroline, we were known as the oddballs of New Canaan, the kids teachers held as examples while our peers teased and taunted us. Who knew why? Looking back, I suppose we didn't fit suburbia's budding cookie-cutter norm. Will and Rebecca, with their creamy freckled skin and black hair—long and lean and awkward—had grown up on one of the few remaining farms that hadn't been gobbled up by developers. Caroline's grandfather raised her alone. My mother rarely socialized with our neighbors, the *Country Clubbies*, as she called them, and had the reputation of being *uppity*. But she'd taken in the Goynes kids after their mother died and Caroline, when her mother left, as if they were her own. So we'd grown up eating dinner together, riding bikes through forest trails to get to each other's houses, stealing wood from construction sites to build tree forts, fishing for carp in Thread Creek.

The ancient black walnut trees lining the Goynes's drive shuddered as I pulled the Monte Carlo up. Nearing the barn, I spotted Will, Rebecca, and Caroline sitting on milk crates inside the open track doors. In the summer, Caroline and I often stopped by the Goynes's farm, after a day of cashiering or, in her case, shelving at the New Canaan Public Library, to make a bonfire and hang out for a few hours before going home.

Will moved the crates aside so I could pull the Monte into the barn. By the time I got out, Will had set another crate out. Caroline got up to hug me. As she pulled away, she stopped to look at me, "You're crying."

At Auntie's, I'd battled my emotions, tried to act nonchalant so Mama wouldn't feel guilty. I didn't want her to reconsider; I knew that she'd stayed as long as she could. All the same, something about seeing her drag her suitcase into Auntie's house terrified me.

When she let go of my shoulders, I plopped down on a milk crate and told them what happened.

Rebecca leaned into me to put her hand on my knee. Caroline stared into the distance as if she saw something no one else could. She could do that—stare like she was looking at something just out of reach. It's what kind of freaked people out about her, I guess. But we were used to it, and I knew that if she thought she could do something to help, she would. But what can another person *do* when you feel like that? I mean, really? What's to be done about it?

The rain hit the gravel drive with the intensity of miniature explosions. Will pulled his hand through his hair, "Wasn't a surprise, though—"

I nodded, shook my head, stopped, realized I hadn't really expected it, then realized I should have expected it and then, just as suddenly, didn't feel like talking about it. They wouldn't push it. They'd let it hang, let me sit there with this uncomfortable new weight, feel the comfort of their company until, if ever, I was good and ready to bring it up again.

"Dark Side of the Moon" sputtered out of a battered silver radio, the static making it sound especially eerie. While we sat there, silent and watchful, the rain turned to hail and, within a few minutes, back to rain. When the rain no longer fell vertically but horizontally, a warning tone cut the silence before the DJ announced that a funnel cloud had been spotted about ten miles east.

I found myself on my feet, digging the keys out of my jeans pocket, "Let's chase it." I made my way to the car.

Will scrunched his lips to one side the way he did when he considered something idiotic, "Or we could go to the cellar."

The girls jumped up, their faces suddenly flushed, "Come on, Will."

Will shook his head like we'd lost our minds.

Rebecca slid into the back seat, "Don't be a wet rag."

I slid behind the steering wheel. "Blanket. A wet blanket."

"Whatever. Come on, Will. Don't you want to have some fun before basic training?"

"Not really. But I'll come along in case you die." Will got up slowly, like a very old man, walked to the passenger's side and slid in.

I threw the Monte into reverse, cranked the wheel, and flew down the drive.

The sky became very still as if all of the energy had been absorbed by something huge and unwelcome. No rain. Just a slight, rustling breeze. I headed east on Perry. Everything seemed normal. The newly sprouted fields, still milky green, unfurled around us as if into infinity. Birch copses lined Thread Creek. Porch lights flickered. Nothing seemed amiss besides the sudden, stultifying stillness and bruised mossy sky.

As we crested a hill, we spotted the funnel in the distance, moving away from us, huge and looming, blossoming like the films of nuclear explosions we'd seen in grade school. It wasn't a twister, the elegant kind that whipped up quickly, an elongated V, only to sputter into nothingness. This mass was terrifying in scale with an anvil top thousands of feet above ground. Bursts of light, probably electrical lines exploding, sparked its gray base. The radio became a long, droning tone punctuated by National Weather Service warnings to take cover, to find low-lying shelter, to stay away from electrical lines. We knew the drill. And we ignored it. I wanted to be close enough to feel the funnel's force but far enough to outsmart it. That's how I was then, a carbon copy of my Dad.

I drove as fast as I could in the rain and wind. Will, Rebecca, and Caroline knew I could outmaneuver anyone or anything, anytime, anywhere. Another quality I'd gotten from Dad. No one said a word but Will white-knuckled the dash and, in the rearview, I caught a glimpse of Caroline and Rebecca plastered together, eyes wide, leaning as far forward as their belts would allow.

We headed toward the column. I felt compelled by it; its destructive messiness, after all, felt familiar.

At times creeks swelled over the road but, for the most part, Perry ran high and straight. As we approached the tube, now maybe a few miles ahead, the rain intensified, trees scattered like matchsticks, their branches stripped completely or bent unnaturally over now ruined fields. Roofs littered driveways, sides of barns bent like aluminum cans, horses ran wild, cows and pigs wandered aimlessly or lay broken-necked in ditches.

The tornado exerted a magnetic force on me. As we approached, the rain fell harder and the winds bullied the Monte. It wasn't a matter of me knowing how to drive. It suddenly became a matter of simply keeping the car on the road. We'd become light and insignificant, like pests, the Monte's V-8 weak against the storm's force, the gentle country we thought we knew now nearly unrecognizable.

Caroline put her hand on the back of my seat, "Let's turn around, Astrid. It's too—"

Before she could finish, the tornado shifted back on itself. I braked and jerked the wheel to the left until the Monte headed west. I knew to travel at a 90-degree angle to the column's trajectory but this part of Perry ran straight and long with no perpendicular roads to escape.

Will turned to look out the back window, his face chalky white, "It's *moving*, Astrid."

I pressed the accelerator. The Monte shook as if it might fall apart. Time slowed. My hands felt slick on the wheel. Every movement and decision became significant. A fist pounded my seat. Someone begged me to go faster. Another told me to pull into a ditch. The thought that we would be swept up by the vortex seemed entirely possible now and the road appeared like a dark, shiny, straight ribbon taunting me.

In the distance, I spotted a stop sign and prayed for a paved road. I slammed on the brakes but had to pick the right direction—the wrong direction could be as disastrous as trying to outrun our pursuer. Tornadoes *usually* moved northwest but they were fickle and could shift any direction. It was least likely to move southeast, though. So at the intersection, I swung the Monte south. Because of the storm's girth, we were still in its path. I'd picked the right direction because the winds, while still tremendous, lost some of their ferocity. The rain picked up, making the road ahead difficult to see. I must have been going seventy when I saw the railroad crossing—too close to slow down. The road rose gently and the Monte bottomed before lifting with that sickening loss of gravity that makes your stomach go all soft and airy. As we hurtled through the air, I imagined the tires continuing to spin, its pistons plunging wildly, everything as it should be except we were airborne. I'd lost complete control. In that moment, my breath held, hands strangling the wheel, I realized that everything I thought I'd known was wrong. This was reality: hovering in space, unanchored, with no one and nothing to pull us back down.

Known Issues

That summer everyone's tongue clicked with the news: Katherine Godrich, Caroline's mother, had come home. During her eight-year absence, the adults' head-turned whispering kept us rapt and inquisitive. Especially clever or lucky children heard her name associated with *heroin* and *addicted* and *men*. Perhaps because of her great beauty, the rest of us let her legend spin, glittering and sharp, to prick our imaginations and fill the empty corners of our uneventful lives. She'd become one of the Flying Wallendas. She danced with the Rockettes. She performed on Broadway.

Undercutting the life we'd carefully constructed for her were the darker facts, the ones we tried to tamp down: the times she'd been arrested, the time she'd shown up at our preschool singing "Me and Bobby McGee" in nothing but a bikini and red cowboy boots, the rumor that a social worker held Caroline's hand as a police officer escorted Katherine out of Mr. Godrich's house for good.

I know now that she hadn't kicked her heroin addiction when she begged her father to take her back. I suppose he did it because he wanted to believe she'd changed, come out the other side, that his tough love had finally won out because after Katherine had stolen and hocked every last piece of her mother's jewelry, after Caroline's birth, after his wife died, after he'd kicked Katherine out for good, he needed to believe in goodness again.

Maybe she'd tried to change. Maybe she'd been trying so hard it nearly killed her. I don't know. I'm an ER nurse now—I see a lot of sick people, people who've done stupid things, who were in the wrong place at the wrong time, who are just plain sick with addiction—but looking back on it, I'll never forget the hungry look in Katherine's eyes. The heroin had bullied her chemistry, mutated her nature, trans-formed her into something, I'm willing to bet, not even she could recognize.

•

Katherine Godrich arranged to take Caroline's best friends—me, my brother Will, and Astrid Miracal—to the carnival that appeared every summer in an abandoned field across from the US 23 Drive-In. She'd called our dad and Astrid's mom to tell them we would make a day of it, send some spending money, not expect us home until late.

It was a Monday in mid-July, one of those still, blistering, humid Michigan days when you pray for a break in the heat or a powerful diversion. The thrill of winning a stuffed animal or seeing a bearded woman or riding a rickety coaster made us beg Daddy to let us go and, even though he couldn't get Mr. Godrich on the phone, he finally agreed. Will and I sat on our porch steps waiting for Mr. Godrich's Buick Roadmaster to pull up our drive and, by the time it did, the ten one-dollar bills Daddy gave me felt slimy in my sweaty palm.

Katherine Godrich flung her hand out the window as she pulled up our long drive, silver dust curling in the station wagon's wake to settle on the black walnut trees' leaves, until she jerked to a stop in the barn's shade. In my young mind, the Janis Joplin incident took daring and guts—something sorely lacking in other New Canaan adults. It had become one of those magical events, a wonderful dream, and the anticipation of seeing Katherine Godrich again nearly made me faint. I wasn't disappointed. Her fashion prowess stunned me into silence. From what I could see through the windshield and then from the back seat where I sat between Astrid and Will, she parted her auburn hair, same color as Caroline's, down the middle and tamed it with a bright orange scarf. She wore a gauzy long-sleeved top, huge white plastic hoop earrings that accentuated her long neck, a peace sign thumb ring, and beaded bracelets that clicked when she moved her arm. I studied her reflection in the rearview, admired the quirky space between her two front teeth and the equally dramatic pause between her eyebrows. Her cheekbones seemed impossibly high, like small cliffs carved below her eyes, and her bowed lips, painted orange-red, contrasted her pale skin. But when she removed the big, dark sunglasses to check her lipstick in the rearview, there was a vacancy in her green eyes as if something had been snuffed out, broken, or gone missing.

It's hard to explain. Kids see things adults don't. Or perhaps we—me, Will, Astrid, and Caroline— were different. Maybe our circumstances forced us to see things others simply couldn't. I'm not sure. Our mother died when Will was fifteen and he took it awfully hard. He'd stopped talking altogether for a while and this, multiplied by the fact that he hadn't grown into those long legs and skinny arms, caused bullies to flock to him. Astrid's mother rarely left the house (except every Sunday for Mass), opting to stay in bed most of the day with a wet washcloth over her eyes. Caroline's grandfather did the best he could (better, really, than could have been expected) the entire time Katherine had been away.

Caroline sat in the front and I noticed that she seemed as curious about her mother as we did, stealing glances at her profile every chance she got. Katherine treated her daughter like an especially adorable pet and kept referring to her as *Sweet Pea* or *Doll* or *Gorgeous* as if she couldn't remember her name. What Katherine lacked in affection, however, she made up in panache. She carried herself like a rock star, had an affected way of speaking, taffied her vowels, and flapped her hand to make a point, "You darlings ready to have fun?"

Turning her attention to Daddy walking toward the car, she adjusted her mouth into a neutral line. His face looked especially drawn that day as he wiped his hands on his thighs before resting one on the side mirror.

Katherine tapped her painted fingernails on the steering wheel and, as if she'd long been accustomed to waiting, waited.

"Long time. How you been, Katherine?"

Katherine nodded, "Good. Real good, Mr. Goynes."

"Well that's good." Daddy smiled and patted the mirror a few times, like he wasn't convinced. "That's real good."

She kept her face forward like she'd spotted something in the distance. "Been working. In Florida. Got some deals going. Real estate."

"Real estate, huh? Well that's just fine."

"Yep." There was an awkward pause and I wished Daddy would walk away but he just stood there, hand on the mirror, biting the inside of his cheek until Katherine said, "Well, nice to see you, Mr. Goynes. I'll have them back before bedtime."

"You do that." Daddy tapped the mirror twice and stepped back to let her pull past, around the big oak and down our long drive. I looked at Daddy, just a speck then, as we turned onto the main road. He stood with his hands in his pockets and, for a brief moment, I felt panicked. I fought the urge to jump out of the Roadmaster and run into his arms.

"Sorry about the air. Busted." She looked into the rearview, "So you're Rebecca and Will."

"Yes, Miss Godrich," I said.

She tapped her fingers on the steering wheel, "You can call me Kat. No need to be so formal."

She drove with her right arm draped over the seat and, every once in a while, would touch Caroline's long hair.

Caroline lowered her voice. "Are you sure Pops said it was okay to go?"

Katherine ruffled Caroline's hair. "Stop being such a worry wart, Caroline."

"It's just—"

"I told him. Last night, after you went to bed. He said it was fine."

"Before he left he told me—"

"Don't worry about it, Sweet Pea." She laughed. "Don't you want to go?"

I couldn't see Caroline's face but watched her rub her left eyebrow with her knuckle the way she did when she got nervous. "Yeah, but—"

"Stop worrying and just have fun." Katherine adjusted the rearview to look at us. "Caroline doesn't know how to have fun, does she?"

It was one of those cheap questions adults aim at kids, the kind that brands you traitorous if you answer. We shrugged uncomfortably.

She readjusted the rearview. "How much money you got to spend?"

Astrid pulled a change purse out of her shorts pocket and pulled out two tens. "Twenty."

"What about you two?"

"Ten each," I offered.

She dropped her hand into the back seat. "I'll hold it for you so you don't lose it."

Caroline shifted in her seat and Katherine shot her a look. "What?"

Caroline looked away as Katherine fluttered her fingers. We dutifully placed the bills in her waiting palm.

Katherine snapped her fingers at her daughter. "You bring any?"

Caroline didn't move. Katherine looked into the back seat. "Can you believe Caroline doesn't trust her own mother?"

Astrid elbowed me and gave me a look that said, *What the?* Will leaned forward like he was about to say something but didn't. It was noon and even with the windows down, the heat felt stifling. I tried to keep from touching Astrid or Will but, sitting between them, and with the way Katherine drove, it wasn't easy. She didn't make full stops and swung the Roadmaster around turns so that the back end nearly fishtailed.

When we got to Saginaw Street, Katherine turned south instead of north. "I need to make a quick stop before we go to the carnival."

Caroline started rubbing her eyebrow again before asking, "Where're we going?"

Katherine didn't even turn her head. "Wouldn't you like to know?"

Caroline turned, eyes wide and frightened, and a wave of fear washed over me. Katherine drove south and got on I-75. She kept chattering about things I suppose should have interested us: the Jackson Five, *The Brady Bunch*, the Osmonds. When "One Tin Soldier" came on WTAC, she launched into a rant about Lyndon Johnson and Nixon and Kent State and Agent Orange and the *righteousness* of war protests. As we passed miles of corn and soy fields, Katherine kept up the rolling commentary and the more she talked, the more frightened I became.

Will bit the inside of his cheek like Daddy. Caroline kept rubbing her eyebrow. Astrid, used to the unpredictableness of adults, just stared out the side window. The landscape changed from cornfields to city streets and, the deeper we drove into Detroit, the more ominous and unfamiliar everything became. Burnt homes and businesses still wore boards over their windows from the '67 riots and, besides a panting dog running alongside the car, the weed-cracked streets were deserted. Only occasionally, we'd see a woman, dark skin glowing in the heat, fanning herself on her stoop. Katherine swung into a ramshackle motel. Its sign—ALGIERS in neon red, the *A* made of two scimitars joined at the top—flickered weakly against the blinding midday sun. The drive curved into a U-shaped motel, a low-slung, single-story red brick building between two three-story structures. An empty pool, its naked sides cracked and bottom glittering with broken glass, occupied a trash-strewn courtyard. A few cars with dull paint and curb feelers rested in the parking spaces.

Katherine pulled into a space in front of the low-slung building, got out, walked around the front of the Roadmaster, opened Caroline's door, and told her to get out. As soon as Caroline did, Katherine reached into her daughter's shorts pocket, grabbed her change purse, pushed her back into the car, and shut the door. "Wait here. I'll be right back." Then she looked around like she'd just noticed where we'd stopped and added, "And don't get out of the car."

She strutted up to number seven in white go-go boots and a mini-skirt, knocked, and disappeared inside.

Caroline turned to us, bit her lip and looked ready to cry. "Sorry—"

"It's okay." Astrid tried playing it cool. "Adults do anything they want."

Caroline nodded vigorously and then whispered as if Katherine might appear at any moment. "Pops and his brother took the Amtrak to visit their sister this morning. She had a heart attack yesterday."

We nodded but even that motion magnified the heat. It all felt stifling, like we would melt into the leather seats.

"As soon as he left she started going through everything—all the drawers and cupboards and closets—and kept asking me if Pops left money anywhere. She got really angry when she couldn't find anything."

Caroline kept looking at door number seven. "I think she's buying drugs."

Astrid, always impatient, said, "Well, she better hurry up."

Will said quietly, "I can start it without the key. I know how. Drive us home."

We'd been driving on the farm ever since our legs were long enough to reach the clutch and hotwiring the old Chevy pickup since the ignition went.

Caroline shook her head. "Not without my mom."

There was no use arguing with that. We knew how Caroline felt. We opened the car doors to catch a breeze but nothing stirred. It seemed even hotter outside. Other than two guys who seemed to be motioning towards us and laughing, one black and one white, both shirtless and skinny, leaning on the balcony railing smoking cigarettes, nothing moved.

In anticipation of the carnival, I hadn't eaten breakfast. "Your Pops ever leave money in the ashtray? Maybe we could buy some chips in the office."

We started rummaging around between seat cushions and on the floor. Caroline found seventy-five cents under the seats. I recovered a penny and Will, a nickel.

Before we got out of the car, Astrid jerked her head up to the balcony that ran perpendicular to the building into which Katherine disappeared. "Those guys are creepy."

I looked up. The sun, bright and glaring, reflected off the men's sweaty skin. They wore dark sunglasses but it seemed as if their eyes followed our every move. We walked toward the motel office. It was shaped like an aquarium; the front walls were glass from bottom to top and a flat green roof extended like a lily pad over the entire thing. As we approached, we spotted a thickly built man reclining in a folding lawn chair. A little red cooler sat next to him with an open can of Stroh's sweating on top. Hooked on the arm of the folding chair was a thickly carved cane. The cane's curve, where the man's hand now rested, had been shaped into the head of a crow. The beak was long and pointed and silver and two large amber eyes shone out of the polished wood. The bottom half of the cane was at least three inches around and embellished with crosses and swastikas and circles and triangles. The bottom third of the cane, the part that touched the ground, was made of a dull, silver-colored metal. The man stared hard and tapped a folded newspaper on his knee as we approached.

Before we could step into the shade, he pointed the newspaper at us. "I'm no babysitter!"

We stopped, not quite sure if he was talking to us. "You deaf?"

We shook our heads.

Caroline spoke up. "My Mom's in number seven and—"

His eyes narrowed. He bit into a thick, soggy cigar and spoke out of the side of his mouth. "Number seven? You think I care? Now get!" He flourished the newspaper at us.

We'd never been spoken to like dogs and didn't know quite what to do. Astrid stepped forward. "We just wanted to see if—"

He dropped his newspaper, grabbed his cane, and pointed it at us. "I said I'm no babysitter!"

Astrid folded her arms. "We don't need a babysitter!"

The man pushed himself up, leaned on his cane, and limped toward us. He was taller than I'd imagined, his chest thick in a once-muscular way. He wore white polyester shorts and his legs were solid and hairy above black socks. A faded tattoo of an eagle clutching the earth with an anchor covered his right bicep. He leaned forward but before he could say anything, the guys on the balcony started yelling.

"Chill, Eddie!"

"What's your problem, man? Leave 'em alone."

Eddie stepped out of the shade. In the light, I noticed how his hip stuck out and the painful way his torso bent slightly to the right. His skin looked yellow and the whites of his eyes matched his sick pallor. He pointed the cane at the guys on the balcony. "You two pieces of dog shit shut the hell up or I'll call the cops!" He stepped closer to us and poked the air with his index finger. "And you—spawn of the bitch in number seven—crawl back to where you came from."

Caroline's bottom lip trembled but Astrid leaned in. "We didn't do anything to you! Why're you so mean?"

Eddie stopped, just for a moment, it seemed, to consider the question.

Astrid grabbed Caroline's hand and turned. "We just wanted to buy some chips."

"Don't got chips."

"We wouldn't want 'em if you had 'em—" Under her breath, Astrid added, "Ugly old man."

We walked across the parking lot, to the end of the two-story building, where an anemic Crabapple offered speckled shade. The huge, V-shaped neon sign hid us from Eddie's view. The VACANCY sign hummed and stopped, hummed and stopped. We squatted in a semicircle, our backs to the stairs leading to the second floor, on ornamental white rocks that seemed hotter than the asphalt. My T-shirt stuck to my wet skin and I wanted water so badly my throat hurt.

Will rarely looked scared, but he did now. I could tell because he picked at the fringe of his cut-off jean shorts and kept tugging the brim of his Tigers' cap. Rusty freckles covered his nose and cheeks. His sleeveless T-shirt revealed the bones of his shoulders and elbows poking beneath his skin. At ten, I was a carbon copy of him—the only thing distinguishing us was my long brown hair.

Astrid squatted to one side of Will, her long legs and arms very pale against a purple jumper, wild black curls askew. Caroline tried to hide the fact that she was crying and kept wiping her face with the collar of her shirt.

"Hey." The guys from the balcony suddenly stood behind Astrid and, from my vantage point looking straight up, the sun outlined them in hot white rings. The white guy, still shirtless and wearing bell-bottoms, pulled a hand through stringy hair. He paused to survey our little party. "I'm JT and—" he ticked his head to the black guy, "this is Skin. Come on up to our room and cool off."

I'd seen hippies on television but never actually met one in person. New Canaan had hippies, harmless high school kids with long hair who protested the war outside City Hall, but these guys didn't seem like harmless kids or laid-back hippies. They were older, the skin of their faces taut and drawn, their pants barely hanging off jutting hipbones, arms so lean and pockmarked that their veins bulged.

Will shook his head. "No thank you."

Skin took a swig from a clear liquor bottle and handed it to JT. "We got Cokes and air."

"No thank you."

Skin's afro looked heavy and wet, like it would break his skinny neck. He leaned over Will. "You a polite little dude, huh?"

JT finished off the liquor and dropped the bottle at his feet. "In't he, though?" He snatched Will's cap off his head and tossed it to Skin who put it on top of his afro. It sat on top of his head like a deformed mushroom until he threw it like a Frisbee at the neon sign.

They suddenly seemed huge and dangerous, smirking and elbowing each other. I wanted to run or scream or cry.

JT lifted his chin. "These your sisters?"

Will swallowed. "Yeah," he lied.

"All of 'em?"

Will nodded.

"What's your name?"

"Will."

"That your old lady went into seven?"

Will hesitated and, finally, nodded.

"Chicks go in there don't come out for a *looong* time."

"If they come out at all," Skin added.

JT leaned over Astrid, fingered her black curls, and lifted her chin with his index finger. "This one don't look nothing like you. You sure she's your sister?"

Astrid jerked her head away.

"Not as polite as your brother, huh?"

Astrid hugged her knees to her chest. A chorus of droning window units filled the air.

Skin stuck a bare toe into Astrid's back. "Hey! He asked you a question." When Astrid didn't respond, he kicked her viciously in the back so that she pitched forward onto her hands. Will, Caroline, and I stood quickly. My chest felt tight, like someone had bound it with rope, and that hopeless feeling, the one that accompanied me during Mama's illness, wrestled the courage right out of me.

JT stuck his hand in his back pocket and, in a flash, a blade sliced the air. He leaned over, grabbed Astrid's arm, yanked her up, and pressed his skinny arm against her chest, the hand gripping the knife hovering just below her jaw. The switchblade's point rested behind her earlobe.

Caroline lunged to grab Astrid's ankles but Skin kicked Caroline fiercely in the ribs to send her sprawling backward.

Blood trickled down Astrid's neck. JT met each of our eyes. "See what happens when you don't act right?"

As JT dragged Astrid toward the steps, Skin pointed a long finger at us. "You cats better come along. Never know what we might do to your sister if one a you leaves."

Caroline pushed herself up. "I'm gonna tell my mom."

Skin leaned over her. "That junkie? She don't give a shit about you. Wouldn'a left you here if she did. Besides, she's higher than a kite by now."

As he turned, Will picked up two handfuls of stones and hurled them at Skin's back. Skin swung around and, in two great steps, grabbed Will by his T-shirt and shoved him against the tree.

Will struggled against Skin until JT pointed the knife into Astrid's Adam's apple, "You want me to cut her more?"

Will stopped.

JT smirked. "Didn't think so."

As we made our way up the steps, I looked down to where Eddie sat, across the parking lot, in the shade, and even though it was a long way away, I thought his eyes flicked up, for just an instant, over his newspaper.

•

It took my eyes a while to adjust to the dimness of the room but the smell of piss and something skunky immediately turned my stomach. Empty liquor bottles, spent needles, strange ceramic pipes littered the floor. Fist-sized pockmarks connected long, gaping cracks in the wall. Skin led Caroline into the room by her arm, followed by JT and Astrid. JT ordered me and Will to stand against the wall next to the door. When we did, JT sat at the foot of one of the two beds and pulled Astrid down between his legs so that her back pressed against his chest. He pushed her legs open with his free hand and touched her crotch. I'd seen dirty magazines in the woods where we rode our bikes, damp and ripped under piles of leaves, with pictures of adults doing things like this but never imagined an adult doing it to a kid. Astrid tried to squirm away but JT pressed the knife into her skin until a steady bead of blood trailed down her neck.

"What's your name?" The black guy ran his hand through Caroline's hair.

"You two—" JT lifted his chin to Will and me, "sit." When we didn't move, he poked the knife into Astrid's neck until we did.

Skin grabbed Caroline's arm and led her to the other bed. Just as he pushed her, face first onto it, the door burst open and Eddie moved toward Astrid very slowly. I noticed, however, that he gripped the silver end of the cane so that the raven's head looked at me upside down as it passed on the floor.

"Hey, Gramps, you're crashing our little party." JT wiggled the knife on Astrid's neck. "Get the hell out—"

Eddie didn't slow down or hesitate. He limped right over to JT and swung the cane into the back of his skull with such force that JT's chin hit the back of Astrid's head with a crack. Astrid scrambled away from JT just as Eddie took a step toward Skin and, swinging the cane back, caught Skin on the side of his head. Skin teetered and, just for good measure, Eddie caught him again in the jaw so that his teeth popped and knees buckled before he hit the floor.

Eddie, muttering something about drug addicts, ordered us the hell out of the room. Astrid and Caroline stepped through the bright doorway but when I turned around to wait for Will, I found him kneeling over JT, lifting his head by his stringy hair, pressing the blade to JT's neck with a trembling hand.

Eddie stood over Will. For a minute, I thought he would bring his cane down on Will's head.

"Let's go."

Will shook his head, and snot dripped onto JT's hair.

"I said, leave it, goddammit." When Will didn't, Eddie leaned over and pressed his thumb into Will's skinny bicep until he dropped the blade.

"Now, get!"

Will dropped JT's head to the floor and stood. Eddie pressed the end of his cane onto the blade until it bent, then jerked his head toward the door. My entire body shook so violently that I could barely walk. As I reached the bottom of the stairs, I spotted Caroline and Astrid standing outside room seven, Caroline's fist raised, ready to knock.

Eddie leaned over the railing and yelled for them to get away from there. He limped behind us, the metal end of his cane pounding the balcony like a drumbeat. When he'd made his way down the stairs, he told Will and me to fetch the other two and bring them to the office. We led Caroline and Astrid, their faces smeared with tears, into the office where Eddie handed Will the phone. "You got someone can come pick you up?"

Will nodded but Caroline sobbed, "But Pops'll find out. He'll make her leave again."

Will held the phone in both hands. "I've been driving on our farm since I was seven."

"How old are you now?"

"Twelve."

"Twelve, huh?" Eddie squinted at Will. "Got the keys?"

Will shook his head. "Screwdriver'll work."

Eddie pointed to a pile of thick phone books. "Grab a couple a' those to boost you up."

Eddie rummaged behind the check-in desk, produced a screwdriver, and handed it to Will. We followed Will to the car where he popped the hood. Eddie watched intently while Will arranged the wiring under the hood then sat in the driver's seat, pushed in the emergency brake, and put the car into neutral. He removed a few pieces of plastic around the steering wheel and then slid, face first, under the dash. It took about five minutes before the Roadmaster turned over.

Will sat on the phone books and adjusted the mirrors. I walked over to Astrid and Caroline, who held each other in a little patch of shade. They looked shocked or stunned or like they didn't really know what had happened.

"Come on," I said as softly as I could. "Let's go."

Caroline stepped forward but Astrid didn't move.

"What about—?" Astrid tipped her head towards room seven.

Caroline didn't even shift her gaze. "Leave her," she said, her hand tugging Astrid's, her body rigid, her voice terrible with resolve.

Exacting Revenge

Caroline Godrich has become obsessed with tragedy: *Othello* and *Macbeth* and *King Lear*, of course.
Her favorite is *Hamlet*. She hasn't read Shakespeare's
later work, but she will because she's smart and has
loads of time on her hands since she doesn't go out
much. That's because of what happened under the
bleachers last fall. It's been a year but she still can't
put words to it or even conjure up what happened.
Maybe she doesn't quite remember what completely
happened after all that whiskey. She does remember
the ache between her legs, what boys catcalled after
her the following weeks at school, some lurid stick
drawings in the girls' bathroom, and the embarrass-
ing fact that, when the school janitor responsible for
locking up the field found her bloodied and naked
behind that pillar, she had shit her pants.

Instead, she focuses on two real-life tragedies in
New Canaan. The first occurred on the sprawling,
inland lake where she lives with her grandfather
and the other at a school long since razed where

her grandfather's twin brothers died. Both tragedies happened in the 1920s, nearly fifty years before she was born and decades before her unwed mother dropped Caroline off with her widowed grandfather.

Regardless, Caroline spends her time pen and inking her imagination. She's strung the drawings on dozens of clotheslines across her grandfather's enormous unfinished attic. There are hundreds of them so that when she opens both windows, the lake breeze animates the pages—like fluttering sails—toward the back of the house.

The first set of drawings shows five troikas drafting a house across the lake one winter morning. She painstakingly researched the event at the library, found photos and eyewitness accounts in the local newspaper. She took great care penning the center horse flanked by others hitched on either side pulling a makeshift sledge, the home's Victorian gingerbread fretwork, turrets, and front porch. Those drawings took time but not as much time as those depicting the house breaking through the ice at the deepest part of the lake, the lake swallowing the horses and, less significantly according to Caroline, thirty men plunging into the icy depths.

The next series of drawings begins with a gaunt, hard-looking man gazing down at his bedridden, morbidly thin wife. His name's Keck. He's a farmer but also an electrician for the young, growing city of New Canaan where he has been commissioned to wire its new school building. His wife's been sick for years. His debt to doctors and hospitals has piled up, his farm has not been successful, and now, on top of all of that, he's being taxed for the damn schoolhouse. Something snaps in him. In addition to wiring the school for electricity, he wires it to explode magnificently.

Caroline sketches these events in painstaking detail. The first shows Keck placing bundles of dynamite in the school's basement. The next depicts Keck connecting the explosives to homemade wires. Another shows children filing in through the heavy oak doors of their new school building while, in the foreground, Keck leans against the dusty front fender of his Olds. Two of those children are Caroline's grandfather's twin brothers. They hold hands because they're just little guys, the youngest of twelve kids, her grandfather being the oldest. This is their first day of school.

The previous night, Keck placed bundles of dynamite in the school's basement, connecting the explosives with homemade wire, threading the wire through a basement window, and hiding the tarry wreath behind a shrub. That morning, he simply fetched the wire, ran it to his car, and attached a coil. The rifle shells, loose and jangling in his pocket, would serve as fuses.

The last drawing reveals a leveled, ablaze schoolhouse, and a man leaning on Keck's car, his face sooty, a bloody gash on his forearm. Caroline captures the terrifying moment when this man realized that Keck wasn't helping, the instant just before Keck reached through the open window of the Olds, plucked up his rifle and, before the man could stop him, fired into the boxes of explosives piled high in the back seat.

•

Caroline moves through town and school like a ghost. She doesn't speak and isn't spoken to. At those times, she's not convinced she exists at all. Her grandfather, Cyrus Godrich, says, "You're an old soul, Caroline." She has the old-fashioned beauty of a young Gene Tierney with her wide forehead, arched eyebrows, apple cheeks, and bowed lips. "A spitting image," he says, "of all the Godrich women."

She absolutely adores her grandfather. And he, Caroline. He loved his wife and daughter but admits that he pushed them too hard. He sees, now, that they weren't as driven as he was. Not as focused or single-minded. And all those miscarriages took their toll on his wife. Why couldn't he see that she couldn't keep up with the demands of the farm? After she died and his daughter left, he sold everything—lock, stock, and barrel, as he said—to the neighboring farm. Wanted to wake up every morning to hear water lapping the shore, walk fifty feet to the dock, hop in his Chris-Craft, and go fishing.

So that's what he did.

•

One snowy November morning, as Cyrus sits at the Big Boy counter drinking coffee and reading about Brezhnev's death in *The Journal*, Billy Vance, New Canaan High School's tall, gaunt janitor, settles next to him. Cyrus slaps Billy on the back and the younger man marvels at Cyrus's strength. He shouldn't be surprised, though, because Cyrus is a solid mass, like granite, known for bringing men to their knees with his handshake. Billy has known Cyrus since he was a boy, when he and his brothers picked sugar beets on the farm. Out of all the boys who worked on the farm, Billy's always been Cyrus's favorite.

Billy apologizes for bothering Cyrus but, really, he's apologizing for not bothering him sooner. He begins, haltingly, to recount what happened: how he had found Caroline long after the stands cleared and, with the help of Coach Haney, assisted her to the bathroom and drove her home. That next week, he'd phoned Principal Bunch and, after nothing happened, he'd visited the superintendent's office. Still, nothing happened.

The coffee and Danish sour in Cyrus's mouth. "So, you're telling me nothing's been done. They didn't call the police. Or me. The boys weren't punished." He recites it like a poem he'd learned long ago.

Billy shakes his head, "I should have called the police but Bunch promised he'd take care of it. And Caroline said she'd die if you knew. I just didn't feel right about it. All of it. I'm sorry, Mr. Godrich."

Cyrus looks at Billy with cool, blue eyes and runs a hand through his thick, white mane, "It's not your fault. But I suppose, now that I know, something's got to be done about it."

•

Her grandfather has been so sad lately. The spring of her junior year, he's been quiet and especially gentle with her as if she's suddenly turned to bone china. He's stopped watching *M*A*S*H* and *All in the Family*. Instead, he's been spending a lot of time at school board meetings or down at the Big Boy having lunch with Principal Bunch and Superintendent Gerald. When she asks him what they talk about, he says, cryptically, "Fishing." When he comes home, in the afternoons and evenings, he stays in his den or in the pole barn tinkering on the only other thing, besides Caroline, he truly loves: his Chris-Craft cruiser.

It's strange, though, her grandfather's newfound interest in getting involved. He'd never been a social man, aside from meetings at the VFW the first Tuesday of the month. He'd always performed his parent/caretaker duties—teacher conferences, band concerts, plays—with a certain resignation.

Caroline is nearly done revising the series of school drawings when it hits her: he's upset about the upcoming anniversary of the bombing. Why not invite a relative of Gideon Keck's to come and talk to her grandfather? Because, even though she's asked a hundred times, he won't discuss his baby brothers' deaths. Maybe he needs to talk to someone, connect, gain some peace. This idea strikes her with such resounding force that she feels giddy.

She finds Harry Keck, alive and living in New Canaan. She writes him a letter, signs it from Cyrus, and invites him to dinner.

•

It's a spring for the record books: cool evenings, steady precipitation. The fragile milky green of new life takes Cyrus off guard, as if he'd never seen a Midwestern spring before. The lake is high and smells of thawing ice, and that green-weediness he's come to love, when he takes Caroline out in the cruiser for the first ride of the season.

It's something they've done for as long as she can remember. This Saturday morning the air bites her bare hands and face as they cruise east toward the flicker of sunrise tipping over the horizon. No one's on the lake yet, not even the fishermen. It's one of those calm, magical, windless mornings with the cruiser cutting the water like skating across ice.

Cyrus stands at the helm with his right hand languidly resting on the windshield. He wears a Tigers' baseball cap and red windbreaker. His face is splotchy from the biting wind. He's tall and solid with smooth skin like the elms by the shore. His hands and shoulders are thick, his back stooped and eternally sore from decades of hard work. He looks to the northern shore and points to an eagle circling high above a pine copse.

From above, the lake resembles a bulging bag cinched at both ends, or maybe the outline of a fetus with a large head, bulbous body, and small feet. Caroline knows this because there's a map of the lake hanging above the couch in the living room. Cyrus bought it when Annie's health started failing, promising the lake would be their escape from the constant demands of their land.

He bought the cruiser in 1963, the year Caroline was born, from the original owner who babied it for thirteen years. He spends winters tinkering with the inboard (which he knows intimately), repairing upholstery, varnishing the cedar decks and double-planked mahogany hull, and hiring a buddy to touch up the golden arrow running along her sides.

"She looks good this year, Pops." Caroline sits on the red leather bucket seat and tries to act like she's not freezing (which she is) because she loves this moment, every moment, every year, with him.

He considers changing his plan. But then remembers, with a thump of guilt so powerful it nearly crushes him, that he stood by dumbly as his daughter fell into heroin, as Annie wasted away. He wouldn't let the men who should have done something about his granddaughter's horrific assault go unpunished. Since Billy Vance told Cyrus about that night when he'd found Caroline, Cyrus has been planning, researching, working for months on the explosive device and remote he'll put in the Cruiser, buying everything with cash (on a road trip to see his sister in Ohio), staying up nights considering every detail. He's bought Bunch and Gerald lunches, coffee, engaged in their inane conversations, and finally lured them with the promise of revealing his secret fishing holes.

And there's another thing. One day when Caroline was at school, he'd made his way, slowly and painfully, up the stairs to his attic to retrieve something or other and found Caroline's drawings of the bombing hung like freeze frames of his nightmares. He'd spent hours looking at them, the horror of that morning again fresh in his mind, marveling at the detail and accuracy of her work.

In the far corner of the attic, a stack of smaller, detailed ink drawings sat on an old trunk. There were no captions, only images. The first few were drawn as if Caroline hovered above three girls and three boys, all wearing puffy coats, hats, and mittens, sitting in a circle. One girl drinks from a bottle while the others throw their heads back, laughing. Caroline sits apart from the group, her eyes wide and bemused. She is not laughing. The next, from a lower angle, shows Caroline with the bottle. Caroline drinking. Caroline making a funny face. Others laughing. A repetition of this scene—only smaller drawings—five times. And then, one dark, dreamlike frame from Caroline's vantage point, of the two other girls huddled, arms around each other's necks, looking at something. In the next picture, the girls turning their heads. The next, the girls stumbling away. The last drawings show Billy Vance hovering over a girl, covering her nakedness with his own jacket, lifting her like a wounded soldier, and then walking away.

Sure, he considers changing his mind. Who wouldn't? But then he looks at Caroline, his quiet, gentle granddaughter, now standing next to him with her face pointed into the wind, hair streaming behind her, and decides it's the only way.

•

It's the Friday night before the Saturday morning Cyrus has planned to take the men fishing and Caroline has been cooking ever since she got home from school. She bought steaks and broccoli and potatoes and tells Cyrus she's cooking him a special dinner. Cyrus knows it's prom night (because Bunch and Gerald have been talking about it) and figures it's Caroline's way of taking her mind off the fact that she's not going.

Cyrus is reading his newspaper and drinking the one beer he allows himself every night, when the doorbell rings. Caroline flashes by in a print skirt, red top, and low-heeled pumps. Because she wears her mother's clothes (she's the size her mother was when she left), Cyrus has that relieved feeling that his daughter just flew by, that she's back and safe.

Cyrus is just pushing himself up from his worn recliner when Harry Keck walks through the door and practically fills the entry. For a moment, Cyrus thinks this could be Caroline's prom date but, as he approaches the enormous, red-headed figure dressed in faded jeans, white shirt, and lopsided tie, he realizes this man is much older than Caroline. A savage feeling rises in him.

"This is Mr. Keck, Pops."

Harry keeps wiping his palms on his thighs, pulls his shoulders around his chest, and seems afraid to straighten to his full height. It's as if he's bowing or folding in on himself, apologizing for being so big.

Cyrus doesn't take his eyes off Harry until Caroline, happier than she's been in a very long time, says, "Harry's great uncle was Gideon Keck."

And that's when Cyrus realizes what's going on.

She adds, quickly, "Well, dinner's ready. Let's eat.

Cyrus tries to make the best of it. He realizes, from the stricken look on Harry's face, that the poor guy thought Cyrus had invited him. And, even though it's a cool spring evening, poor Harry's forehead drips with perspiration. He dabs his face apologetically with the cloth napkin Caroline ironed to perfection and keeps dropping his fork. He doesn't say much until Cyrus mentions the trial of John Hinckley, Jr. and, from that point on, Harry loses some of his self-conscious bumbling and begins to talk.

After dinner, Caroline makes a big deal of serving tea, settling them into the living room, and lighting a fire.

Harry sits on the camelback sofa with his feet planted firmly in front of him. His legs are so long that they get in his way when he leans over to pluck the delicate teacup off the coffee table.

He's started perspiring again and looks comical holding the delicate teacup. Finally, Cyrus says, "I didn't know what Caroline was up to."

Harry nods and looks up from sipping his tea. He's cradling the teacup with both hands like he's holding on for dear life. "I didn't know what to do. The letter was signed by you. Said you wanted to discuss a few things, put a few things to rest. I didn't want to be rude."

Cyrus nods. They sit in silence for a few more minutes until Cyrus gets up to throw another log on the fire. He pokes the lower log with a long iron hook and sparks fly into the chimney.

Harry clears his throat, "I didn't know Keck was related to me until I was in high school. My folks never talked about it."

"How are they?"

"Good. Moved to South Carolina after retiring from GM."

"Send them my best." Cyrus continues poking the fire. He's thinking about what he's about to do. About the intricate plan he's devised. Now, with Harry here, he's thinking about Caroline's drawings and connecting the dots between himself and Gideon Keck and realizing that the reverberations of Keck's actions keep unsettling things, keep rolling across space and time and generations. This poor kid had nothing to do with what happened and, yet, he's paid a price.

Bunch and Gerald have families, too. But they didn't give a damn about Caroline. Why should he care about their kids?

"It doesn't stop, does it?"

"What's that?"

Cyrus turns to Harry, "Even if you do what you think is right. It doesn't change much."

Harry sets down his teacup, "Millage rate goes up every year. That's for sure." He nods, "But you gotta do what you think is right, I suppose. As long as you're reasonable about it."

Bunch's and Gerald's kids are young. In grade school, maybe high school. Cyrus was eighteen at the time of the bombing. His little brothers had just turned six. Burned beyond recognition. After sixteen hours of moving rubble, they finally uncovered their classroom. It's something he's tamped down, hard, his entire life. But he can't forget it, of course, and now, at this moment, it hits him so hard that he feels around for something to steady him.

Harry is up in a flash, stepping over the coffee table, grabbing Cyrus by the elbow, bracing him with a thick arm around his back.

"I'm okay." Cyrus points to his recliner.

Harry settles him into his chair and stands awkwardly next to him, "It haunts me, though. Me and him being related. But I got a taste of killing in the service. And I didn't relish it." He shifts his weight from side to side, "I'm awfully sorry for what happened to your brothers, Mr. Godrich. I should get going now."

Cyrus wants to cry. Instead, he stands to shake Harry's hand.

Caroline appears as they make their way toward the door. She looks from her grandfather to Harry to decipher their moods. They're smiling which she takes as a sign that whatever she'd hoped for might just have happened after all.

•

Bunch and Gerald arrive the next morning in the eerie calm of dawn. Bunch reminds Cyrus of a series of puffy orbs stacked atop each other: pudgy legs, doughy stomach, and round, bald head. He has forgotten to remove the price tag from his new fishing vest and walks unsteadily down the dock in front of Cyrus. He responds absentmindedly to what others say with, *Well, that's just excellent. That's fine.* Or, *Good thought.* Gerald is spindly and walks with a physical lilt. He walks confidently ahead of Bunch, ahead of everyone. He's a leader, after all. That's what he does: lead. And, even though his staff makes fun of him—he boasts that he's descended from the Vikings, that his collie with a severe overbite was sired by Lassie, and that his son's IQ is forty points higher than it actually is—he is convinced they revere him.

Bunch and Gerald stand at the end of the dock while Cyrus removes the boat's cover. It's supposed to be clear and sunny, one of the first pleasant days of spring. Perfect fishing, Cyrus says, because the sun will warm the shallows. The two men turn to see Cyrus lowering himself into the boat. He stumbles, though, and grabbing a seat, leans over in pain.

The two men rush to him but Cyrus holds up his hand, "Just tweaked my back a bit. Been giving me a helluva time. It'll be fine, here, in a minute."

Cyrus tries to straighten but winces. Bunch and Gerald look stricken, as if their trip to the circus has been canceled.

"Well, for God sakes. Of all times for this to happen." He tries lowering himself into the captain's seat but can't.

Bunch is the first to speak, "Don't worry, Cyrus. We'll do it another time."

"But you were looking forward to this. Damn it. Of all times." Cyrus shakes his head, "Of course, you don't need me. You could take her out yourself. Might not find my fishing holes but you'll still have a good day on the lake.

Gerald pipes up, "I'll drive."

Bunch nods vigorously.

"Ever drive an inboard? Know how to start her?"

Uncertainty flashes across Gerald's face but he recovers quickly, "How hard could it be?"

Cyrus blows out the engine and turns the key until the cruiser responds with that deep, throaty growl. He methodically explains each gauge, reminds them to untie her from the cleats, demonstrates how to blow out the engine, engage the throttle, back out of the slip, turn her around, and give her some throttle only after they pass the sandbar. But most importantly, after you drift for a while, don't turn that key until you've blown out the engine because those fumes will spark and they'll be blown to kingdom come.

It's brightening to daybreak, a bluish tint to the air, as they help Cyrus up to the house. As they turn to leave Cyrus warns, "Remember. Take her out nice and slow until you pass that sandbar."

•

From his picture window, Cyrus watches them fumble around the boat. Bunch settles himself in a seat until Gerald orders him to untie the cleats. Their laughter travels up the bank and through the screen door a few feet from where Cyrus stands. He leans over and carefully removes the remote control from the cabinet. He'll have only a few seconds before the boat is out of range. Gerald dons a floppy, tan hat to protect his fair skin while Bunch waves at Cyrus, his open palm moving in exaggerated half moons.

Cyrus waves back. The explosion will be spectacular but not spectacular enough to arouse suspicion.

Everyone knows these engines can explode if you don't blow them out properly. And that's what he'll say happened. He extends his arm, aims the home-made remote like a gun at the back of the boat, and is about to press the button when he feels a hand on his shoulder and the sweet, quiet voice of his granddaughter asking him what the early morning commotion is all about.

Falling Bodies

It had been going on nearly a year when Maurice got the first letter in the mail. It was typewritten and said, simply,

I know about you and Leila Miracal.

No signature. No return address. The lower case "e" looked bitten by jagged teeth. He stared at the words for a long time. Blinked. Reread it. A chill passed over him. He broke out in a cold sweat. The letters didn't make sense. The words buzzed across the paper like irritating flies. He wanted to rip it up and throw it above his head in a flurry of confetti. Rearrange the letters. Transform it into a lovely valentine. Turn time back to the moment before he pierced the bland white envelope with the letter opener's sharp, silver point.

•

The letters became a buzz in the brain, an annoyance, but one he'd come to accept grudgingly. He and Leila stopped seeing each other for a few weeks, broke down, changed their meeting places to throw off the pesky busybody. The busybody, however, was a very good one. Each note detailed meeting times, dates, and locations. And, not insignificantly, warnings to stop.

And then, Maurice received this letter.

I've made the archdiocese aware of
your indiscretions.

Funny thing about this one, though, the "e" was perfect. And the ink lighter. A different typewriter? Or a different person? Did more than one person know about him and Leila? He folded the letter, put it in the breast pocket of his jacket, called Leila, told her to meet him at the Whoopee Bowl. They needed to talk.

On the drive down Dixie Highway, the November sun glowing weakly behind a thick sheet of low-hanging clouds, he recalled that day when, two years ago, his hand against her cheek ignited every nerve in his body. Her perfume smelled of gardenia, making him think of Florida and oceans and heat and white sand and flocks of gulls. That close, he noticed the green of her eyes and the sickle-shaped scar just above her left eyebrow. The morning light through the partially closed shades illuminated a fine layer of powder clinging to her cheek.

She had been sitting in the chair across from his desk, in his parish office, confiding in him, saying she could no longer bear Luke screwing everything in a skirt, couldn't live with him one more day. She wanted a divorce but, being a good Catholic, Luke refused. When she hung her head, Maurice rounded the desk to kneel before her. She took his hand. Held it to her cheek. Her skin was velvet against his palm. When he leaned into her, to rest his forehead against hers, she began to cry. He didn't know if it was out of happiness or fear. He hoped it was happiness. But he never quite knew with Leila. Her moods could swing wildly and were equally intense—tsunami-like, upending. This was it, he'd decided: hold on tight, let it sweep him away, let it fill his lungs and drown him.

As soon as he pulled his face away, she began to tremble. "What are we going to do?"

He felt so lightheaded that he thought she meant right then, "Go to your house?" After all, even though he had tried to deny it, it had been sixteen years since he'd fallen in love with her, sixteen years since he'd first watched her walk toward him during Holy Communion with that wretched excuse for a husband. That first day, so many years ago, she had been huge and pregnant with Astrid, her entire body rich with a layer of seal-like fat. Her breasts stretched the buttons of her blouse and a rhinestone brooch glistened on her lapel. Even though it was a damp spring morning, someone had left the doors open so the Crabapple trees lining the sidewalk framed her in a riot of deep ruby blossoms.

She laughed, "I mean—" She stopped, looked at him, at the pleading in his eyes, and was reminded of a cornered animal. She shook her head as if all men were the same, even him, and answered, "Okay. But how do we get you there?"

Their quickly devised plan included driving two cars to Smith-Bridgman's parking lot where they would park next to the wooded area. When he was sure no one would see him, he would slip into the back seat of her car and cover himself with a blanket. She would then drive to her house, pull into the garage, and shut the door.

He had been to her home many times for dinner, holding out his hand to receive a fat check from Luke for a new playground or community center, but never alone with Leila, never through the back door, never with Leila in front of him, holding his hand, leading him. He suddenly couldn't stand the distance between them and tugged her hand so that she jolted to a stop and wound into him. He rested his thumbs on her hipbones, gently pressed the flesh of her waist and looked down. She turned her face up to him with a mixture of trust and agony that suddenly froze him—he wasn't sure he remembered what to do. He'd taken his vow of celibacy in his mid-twenties. He hadn't broken it in over twenty years.

"What?" She brushed his hair out of his eyes, "Reconsidering?"

"No, I—"

"Luke is in Europe. Astrid's at school."

"It's not that."

"What?"

She sensed his apprehension, "I won't ask you to leave the church for me."

"No, not that."

"What then?"

"I'm not sure if I remember. You know. What to do."

When she laughed, really laughed, she threw back her head so that her hair fell off her shoulders. Then she led him to the bedroom.

•

Snow began to fall—fat, wet crystals that stuck under his windshield wipers—as Maurice pulled into the Whoopee Bowl's potholed parking lot. The high-ceilinged, thin-walled hangar-like building listed dramatically to the left. An absolute jumble of junk hung on the outside and, through the open doors you could find everything from string to circuit boards. All used. Some stuffed into crushed boxes. All smelling of mildew and feeling damp as if the place had its own weather system and a storm could spontaneously erupt.

As he walked slowly toward her, Leila thumbed through a stack of *LIFE* magazines. He never hurried. Not Maurice. There could be a fire and he would take his sweet time.

He was disheveled—even his lamb-chop side-burns looked messy. Stopping behind a ratty stuffed elephant, he tapped its trunk with his forefinger. He closed the gap between them while hooking a thumb beneath his too-tight collar. When he stopped a few feet from her, he finally ripped it off.

He stood on the other side of the table looking distractedly at a tangle of steering wheels. It was a strange place to meet but this was where Maurice came to lose himself. It was far enough away from town that few people they knew would see them and, even if they did, the place was big enough and jumbled enough that, with a step to the right or left, they could separate and be swallowed up by the disembodied hood of a car or a tent stuffed full of sleeping bags.

"Got another letter."

She didn't reply or look up. Just paged through an issue of *LIFE* with Ayatollah Khomeini on the cover.

She began to tremble as if she were made of bolts and screws and wood and everything had suddenly loosened to turn her into a precarious structure. She knew this moment would come. For the last month, she'd woken with a cold squeezing around her heart that she'd deciphered as a warning to walk away before it was too late.

"What did it say?"

Maurice shook his head, "Says he—or she—has told the archdiocese about us."

She considered the implications. There were none for her. Luke had moved out but still wouldn't grant her a divorce.

Maurice was a different story. His congregation, reputation, and livelihood would be thrashed. People from all over the world knew him or knew of him. He was theological royalty, rubbing elbows with politicians and leaders from all faiths. Congregants came from places near and far to Holy Family to hear his sermons because, in those bold talks, he thoughtfully considered every issue relevant to faith including what the church considered sinful or immoral:

abortion, birth control, capital punishment, ordination of women, rights of homosexuals. These words in no way endeared him to some, certainly not to the church hierarchy. Yet people continued to attend his services, eager for more, or perhaps merely eager for the spectacle of his ideas.

"I'll leave the church."

Leila shook her head.

"I will. For you. I'll do it." And she could tell, by his look, that he meant it. It was the same look he had when he had knelt before her and fell haphazardly into her life.

•

The bishop's office, tucked in the church's southeast corner, was too warm. In addition to the radiators, a space heater droned and the morning sun, now rising steadily into an irritatingly cheery blue sky, slanted into the room to illuminate Maurice from the chest down. His collar felt like it was cutting into the flesh of his neck, stopping blood flow. He wanted, desperately, to rip it off.

Bishop Connor, tall and pale as a weathered board, rounded his desk to shake Maurice's hand. His baritone voice belied his lithe frame. Once he had settled himself behind his desk, he scratched his cheek. "Well, I suppose, there's no other way to get started than to just start—" He paused to push his black frames up the bridge of his nose. "This letter I received, it says, well, it claims that you have been having an affair. With a congregant. It says—"

"It's true."

Bishop Connor pulled his glasses off very slowly. "Okay … and, so, just what were you thinking?"

Maurice shook his head and looked down, "I—" He couldn't finish, though, and kept shaking his head while he fought the urge to sob. Until that moment, the image of being defrocked, of losing his position, of never delivering another sermon had been a rumbling on the horizon. He hadn't fully entertained it, kept it locked away, but now, with Bishop Connor looking at him, it suddenly became a landslide threatening to bury him.

Connor replaced his glasses and tried to distract himself while Maurice pulled himself together. He recalled the first time they'd met: Maurice had been just a few years out of seminary and assigned to the struggling Holy Family parish. Connor had immediately admired Maurice's defiant intellect, his wit, his ability to connect with his parishioners, all traits (besides intellect, of course) Connor lacked.

When Maurice gathered himself, Connor began again, "I've known you how many years?"

"At least twenty." Maurice lifted his chin. His collar was strangling him and, again, he fought the urge to rip it off.

Connor sat forward, squared a stack of papers on his ink blotter, moved his long fingers across his desk.

"Her name is Leila."

"Ah, Leila, is it?" And, here, Connor wrote himself a note on a yellow legal pad. "It's not so much Leila—that allegation I could have discredited—but I'm obliged to discuss the other allegations. Peripheral allegations."

He could have asked, *Like what?* But he already knew the answers.

"Your stance on homosexuality. On abortion. On women priests."

Maurice nodded and turned his gaze to the thick, leather-bound books lining the shelves, the plaques in perfectly symmetrical rows behind Connor's head. "It's hot in here. Do you think it's hot?"

"Oh, yes, well, turn off that space heater. My feet. You know how my feet get sitting here all day at this desk. Poor circulation."

Maurice nodded and switched off the heater.

"It's those allegations," he paused, "that vex me."

"Who is this complainant?"

"Ah!" Connor wagged his finger, "Can't say. Anonymity and all that. But the son of a gun carboned every higher-up and their respective brother's uncle's cousin. If it had just gone to me, well, it would have been handled more, well, you know …. But, that son of a gun sure was a thorough one."

Maurice had absolutely no idea who had been watching him. More than once he'd set up clever traps. But no go. He just couldn't figure it out. Over the years, many of his congregants had spoken to him about his out-of-step opinions. And by the end of their conversations, they'd agreed to disagree. That's how Maurice played it. He respected differing points of view—and he knew that most of his congregants felt the same way. Most were conflicted about these issues—that's why he approached his sermons with thoughtfulness and lack of judgment. He knew that he shouldn't disagree with the church, but his conscience gave him no choice. If the Catholic Church were his elder, Holy Family was his immediate family. With his brother and parents gone, the church and Leila had become his entire life. No two people—let alone an institution—agreed on everything. But he'd always fervently believed that disagreements wouldn't pull them apart.

Connor locked his gaze on Maurice, "It's not just breaking your vow of celibacy. As far as the diocese is concerned, that one can't be verified without a confession. She would have to come forward and confess and—I trust she won't do that."

Maurice shook his head absently. He was usually eloquent in his own defense. But the words wouldn't come. He knew that Connor would do everything possible to save him. He just didn't know if he wanted him to.

"I'm trying to figure out a way around all of this nonsense but it's these niggling … these fundamental disagreements with church policy and doctrine are vexing." Connor grimaced, "You know what they say, Maurice. It's not the surgery but the infection that'll kill you."

The Art of Survival

This is how they get you: your whole life they fill you with stories about princes and poison apples and kindly dwarves and animals that chitter secrets in your ear and bunion-inducing glass slippers and just-right ruby slippers and needles that prick and the frog prince and a nice girl falling in love with a beast and, next thing you know, you're in the back seat of a Monte Carlo with him pushing into you and all you're doing is looking out the back windshield, into the blackness above the hilltop, wondering what's next. Not what's next after he pulls out, but what's *next?* What's really *next*, you know? Next for you because, as you've been thinking for an awfully long time, you've gotta get out of here. As that thought hits you full force, his torso pounding against the backs of your thighs and him asking, begging, really, "Can you, can you, can you?" and you not even listening to or, for that matter, feeling him, because the promise of something bigger than his football player love— bigger than this whole town—fills you with possibility and hope and you push his sweaty body off, climb through the bucket seats, pop open the door, and dance naked into the starless night.

"What's wrong with you?" He's hopping on one foot, pulling up his jeans, buttoning his fly. He's got your jeans crumpled in a ball under his armpit. "I mean, really? What is *wrong* with you?"

Below, the lights of town cast a dim glow against the rime of clouds so close and thick that you want to reach up, pluck off a chunk of that marshmallow fluff, and pop it in your mouth. Let it fill you. Instead, you throw your arms above your head and twirl toward him.

He's laughing now, as you grab his hand and dance the way your folks used to dance on New Year's Eve: all arms and knees and twists and claps. You barely feel the cold. Not yet. Not as your bare feet slip on the icy tracks made by countless other pickups and vans and souped-up Chevelles and Camaros. Any other guy, you know, would be pissed. But not Paulie. He's crazy about you. Dopey-nutsy-head-over-heels-in-love crazy.

You know this. You don't take it for granted. Or him, for that matter. But he's dumb as a stick. Dumb. You both know it. He, with a certain resigned sadness. You, like a knife-prick to the rib. He's so beautiful, though, so gracefully stunning when he moves on that football field, the crowd cheering his name as he steps into the pocket, scans the field, assesses every moving part, fakes, twirls, stutter steps, and throws, the slow arc of his hand a ballet as the ball explodes in a perfect spiral. Some day, you hope, his brain will catch up with his body.

●

II. FORMULATE

Irreversible Acts

If you'd asked Leila when she first considered killing herself, she'd have told you it was the day Maurice visited Bishop Connor. Since that day, the idea clutched at the dark parts of her brain, adhering to it, spreading like fungus. And since the grinding wheels of laicization seemed inevitable, the thought of taking her life suddenly became as much a part of her as Maurice's faith or Luke's infidelity. Maybe it had always been lurking there. Maybe she'd nurtured it in those moments when she struggled to put on a cheerful face for Astrid and the world. Maybe she'd tamped it down so hard and for so long that it had no choice but to rear up.

During the first few years of their marriage, when she started catching Luke in lies, his excuses were so sincere, so multi-faceted and well-engineered, she actually believed him. Then she pitied him. And when she couldn't take it anymore, she became furious. When she'd confronted him, he'd pledged to change. No more women. Just her.

And then, at Astrid's first birthday party, her entire family gathered beneath pink crepe paper banners, Luke didn't show up for dinner and, when he finally came in, after playing a late round of golf (so he said), smelling of perfume (not hers), she realized she was in this for the long haul.

He'd be faithful for a few months at a time but he always fell back to familiar habits. Always on the prowl for someone to seduce. Someone new. Someone who was *not* Leila.

She'd started concentrating on Astrid so thoroughly, pouring herself into her only child, that she nearly misread the attention Maurice showered on her. And then, unexpectedly, her life became wonderfully, wholly filled with him. She couldn't doubt him. He'd convinced her of his undying love, his willingness to leave the church. But because she knew that Luke would never divorce her, she believed herself stuck in a hole from which she couldn't escape. And there was the inescapable fact that her entire family—seven brothers and sisters—went to Holy Family. Once the affair was exposed (and it would be), the congregation would turn against her, her family, and Maurice. And because Maurice was lionized, she would be accused of seducing him. She would be blamed for his downfall.

The question Leila kept asking herself was how could she make things right for Maurice? What could she do to make all of the ugliness go away?

•

That afternoon, Maurice watched Cronkite's hostage crisis updates. He was tying a Parachute Adams fly (in preparation for the free time he anticipated) and, as usual, when he did anything around the house, cranked the volume of his turntable. Maybe to fill the silence. Maybe to drown out the fact that his defrocking hearings would begin that very week. Defrocking. Silly term. Were they preparing to rip a dress off him? Defrock. He preferred *laicize*, but a condemned man can't pick his poison. That made him laugh. And as he leaned in close to the fly vise to attach the rust-colored hackle behind a white wing, he began to listen to the tragic opening piano chords of Wagner's *Tristan und Isolde*. After the terrifying opening, a phrase of such dread and trepidation—with its quick upper clef and melancholy lower range filling the little office in his parish home—he was suddenly hijacked by an overwhelming sadness. What had he done? He collapsed to his knees, hands trembling, and prayed that he would be strong enough to endure losing the life he'd known, be strong enough to realize what he had. And, what he had—all he had—was his faith and Leila. He pushed himself up and called her. She'd been distant lately and entirely too quiet, as if she'd entered a reality where he did not exist. They'd quarreled the day before when he insisted she tell him how she felt. In response, she began to cry and, since he couldn't stand to see her unhappy, he lost his temper, told her he needed her to be strong, to trust him, to trust in God and God's plan for them.

Leila didn't pick up. Should he go to her and wrap her in his arms? Did it really matter if anyone saw him?

Finally, after an hour of trying, he let the answering machine pick up, cleared his throat of any emotion and, in his most professional voice, identified himself as Father Silver from Holy Family and asked Mrs. Miracal to please, at her earliest convenience, return his call.

•

Leila loved Walter Cronkite. Stoic. Intelligent. Even in his sixties—those eyes, that smile, the voice. And his signature sign-off: *That's the way it is*. She'd hoped to stay awake until she heard it one last time but swallowing an entire bottle of prescription sleeping pills tends to negate future plans. She was happy that the hostages had been freed and that dear Will Goynes would be coming home. How many days? Four hundred and forty ... something. Or was it three hundred and forty something? Never mind. An incessant buzzing filled her ears and she couldn't hear Cronkite's voice, that velvet voice, so she made her way slowly over the green shag carpeting to the television where Walter Cronkite was saying something about Germany and medical examinations and, once she located the volume knob (God, there were suddenly so many knobs), turned up the volume. Her hands were slimy from something. She couldn't remember what. And then it dawned on her that she'd tried, unsuccessfully, to slit her wrists. Couldn't cut the vein, though, because she was squeamish and drowsy from those pills. Mommy's little ... what was it? Mother's little helper? Rolling Stones. That was it. She loved The Rolling Stones. Everyone loved Mick, but she preferred Keith. Oh, for heaven's sake … someone had attached a fishing line to her brain and was trying to pull it out through her ear. Pull her brain out through her ear! Now that would be a feat. That's something she'd stick around to see. That would be something. Something. Something was ringing. What the hell was it? Ringing and ringing and then her voice far off and happy saying, *Hello, you've reached the Miracal residence. Please leave a message after the beep. Have a lovely day!* And then the ringing. And then her voice. And then the ringing. And then her voice. She tried counting the rings but couldn't with her wrists bleeding like that and her blood feeling like it couldn't reach her brain and she really had to lie down but she didn't want to get her bloody wrists on the furniture where Astrid would sit so she made her way down the hallway to her bedroom and into her bathroom but her lungs wouldn't fill with air, and she'd become very light, a thin paper doll lying on her bathroom tile and the tile was so cool against her paper cheek, so incredibly cool, the way her mother's hand used to feel against her fevered forehead, the way Astrid's hands were always cool and then she heard a voice on the answering machine, Maurice, sounding very stern or frightened, she couldn't tell which, and she let the voice fill her, his voice, the voice she couldn't live without, his voice asking her to call him back, call him back, call him back, what did that mean call him back, because she was much too tired to do that right now, much, much too tired. She would do it in the morning when she woke up and it would be a new day and all this foolishness would be over.

Common Notions

When Astrid walks into the house after ski practice, her skin ripples in gooseflesh. It's dark and, without her mother's usual greeting from somewhere in the sprawling suburban ranch, ominously still. As she turns into the family room, the only light comes from the television: Walter Cronkite detailing the conclusion of the Iranian hostage crisis and listing the names of the freed hostages. It's big news in New Canaan, after all, because her friend, Will Goynes, Jr., is one of the Marines who has been held hostage. But not even Cronkite's voice soothes her. She turns down the volume and feels something sticky and wet on the RCA's silver knob. She rubs her thumb and forefinger together and knows, without consciously knowing, the weight of that liquid, the metallic smell of it, the rich burgundy color of it.

She's turning, now, leaving behind the family room's green shag carpeting, fireplace, and paneled walls, walking briskly through the kitchen, over the foyer's dark slate, down the long hall with every school photo framed and hung, lining both walls, her image watching her, to her mother's bedroom. It used to be her parents' bedroom until her mom couldn't take it anymore and kicked him out. She knows, even before turning into the bedroom that her mother is gone. *Gone* is the way she'll refer to her mother's absence. Never *suicide*. Never *dead*. And only to herself. She'll never say it out loud. She'll never humor the shrinks and counselors and social workers and teachers who try to draw her out. They'll lure her with tempting morsels, dangling guidance and mentorship and happiness and healing, but she'll know they're all full of shit.

She stops in front of the king-size bed, next to the mahogany tallboy dresser that once held her father's socks and boxers and Munsingwear golf shirts and that Mexican mug full of coins and business cards, and feels an overwhelming emptiness. He'd cleared everything out, bit by bit, whenever her mother wasn't home. Astrid would sit on the bed, knees beneath her chin, to watch her boyishly lanky father fill suitcase after suitcase until every last physical trace of him disappeared.

But now she's afraid to move, afraid to turn that corner into the master bath because she sees a trail of blood leading there. She's started moving again and, as she does, something begins ringing and ringing and ringing until she can't tell if it's the roaring of fear or something more familiar but it propels her into the bathroom where she sees her mother's feet and, for an instant, tries to convince herself that her mother's pumps, lying sideways on the light blue tile, her feet crossed demurely at the ankle, look normal. But there's the empty prescription bottle next to her mother's knee and the slime of blood trailing over the sink, down the white cabinet to the floor. She's landed on her side with her head bent abnormally against the shower glass, her eyes open as if she might be looking under the cabinet for a missing earring. Her left palm, with the phone ringing next to it, rests at her thigh. There's a long vertical slit beginning just above the wrist, the blood frothy and dark purple now, edging the vein. It's the vein Astrid used to trace with her pinky finger, the dark one that bisects her mother's narrow wrist. The other arm crosses her chest so that her right palm rests just below her shoulder.

Astrid's trying to process all of it but that ringing is incessant and time has ceased to exist, like crossing into another dimension where everything has happened that she'd always known and feared. She kneels between the cabinet and her mother, with the instinct to wrap her palms around those cuts, staunch them somehow. But the ringing keeps up and that single strand of pearls looks so beautiful against the olive skin of her mother's neck, just falling above her clavicle, her black hair tumbling in corkscrews onto her cashmere V-neck, that Astrid thinks she couldn't possibly be dead. Could she?

She's afraid to touch her but something finally snaps her to and she picks up what she recognizes, now, as the phone and it's Auntie, her mother's oldest sister, whose voice sounds frantic as she asks, "Astrid?" And Astrid manages to say something like, "There's so much blood," and Auntie asks, "Where?" And Astrid says, "On Mama——" but Auntie cuts her off as if she knew all along how she'd answer and, before she hangs up, says she'll be right there, that she'll call an ambulance, so Astrid kneels next to her mother and does what she'd wished she'd done when she'd found her: wraps her palms around her mother's wounds.

The next thing Astrid knows there's pounding on the front door and paramedics rushing down the hallway, knocking her school photos off the wall and, when they get to the bathroom, one of them picks up the empty prescription bottle and says, loud enough for Astrid to hear, "Barbiturates and a razor blade? Jeezus, she didn't leave anything to chance," and one medic tilts her mother's head back and lowers his face to hers and the other fills a vial and prepares a needle which he punches into her mother's upper arm, right in the muscle, and it's this gesture that finally makes Astrid's knees buckle, standing there on the threshold, her hands gripping the door frame until she feels her nails digging into the wood to hold herself up. As quickly as it starts, the flurry of activity ends and the medics push themselves up off their knees. Auntie rushes in and stands with one hand over her mouth, a string of creamy-red Rosary beads looped over her index finger, the other resting on the counter in her sister's blood.

•

That night in Auntie's bed, her old lady snoring scoring the darkness, the event loops endlessly through

Astrid's exhausted brain. She's somewhere between sleep and non-sleep, hovering above herself watching herself dream. Each black and white frame clicks off slowly except for the blood flowing in Technicolor waterfalls from her mother's wrists, deeper and deeper, until it reaches Astrid's legs and feet and toes and sweeps her away in its current. It's viscous as glue and paints her body until everything below her head becomes a swirling kaleidoscope.

She must have drifted off because, suddenly, a far-too-harsh winter sun scorches the eastern windows. Astrid feels exhausted. She feels heavy and sick and wants to rewind everything, go back to the beginning, figure out where things veered off course. If she hadn't gone to practice. If her father had been faithful. If her mother hadn't slit her wrists. The *ifs* threaten to snap the unsteady wire on which her life now precariously balances.

Auntie's bedroom is large with a vaulted ceiling. Dark wooden beams meet in perfect angles above her head. Auntie is already in the kitchen making coffee and toast. Auntie likes her whole wheat burnt and the smell fills even this room at the far end of the house.

Her father is flying back from Europe. He's probably in the air now. The fact that he's flying does not panic her. He's indestructible. He survived the worst of World War II. She's never seen him flinch. He would be the only survivor in a plane crash and blame the others for dying.

She goes over the story she'll tell him: how she came home, how she turned down the volume, how the knob felt sticky, how she ran to Mama's bathroom and found her, how Auntie called the paramedics, how they took her out of the house with a sheet pulled over her face.

She'll tell him all this knowing that her father will ask the one question that's been dogging her since the moment she touched that television: *How did the blood get on the knob? What the hell did she do? Cut her wrists and go watch TV?* Astrid finds herself angry with him before he even gets home because she knows that this fact, in his orderly, engineer's brain, will not make sense. He'll say, *It just doesn't add up, Astrid.* And she'll try, in vain, to connect the dots for him, do the math, explain away that insignificant detail before he'll shake his head in disbelief that anyone could be so emotional, so hysterical, so dramatic. As if he hadn't known her at all.

And maybe he didn't. Maybe that was the answer Astrid had been dreading.

Maybe neither of them did.

Solid-State Reactions

Orion Jones is everything Paulie Ehrlich is not. He secured academic scholarships to the University of Michigan and now teaches high school science. He reads Orwell and Bradbury and Cervantes and Milton. Paulie would think these are the names of boys on the soccer team. Orion Jones has a dramatic swimmer's waist and lean arms with skin so taut and arms so long that Astrid imagines ropes winding around his bones. His hips aren't much wider than Astrid's and his shoulder is the perfect height on which Astrid could rest her head. His dark hair is long for a teacher's—to the angle of his chin—but short enough that he won't get in trouble with the administration.

In a word, *dreamboat.*

This is how Astrid thinks of him which, lately, at the end of her senior year, is pretty much constantly. His beauty has not gone unnoticed by her classmates or, for that matter, the female teachers in the school or the football coach, Mr. Haney, who can often be found twirling his whistle outside Mr. Jones' science lab.

The lab smells of rotting leaves or, depending on the experiment, chemicals. Serious chemicals. There are Bunsen burners and frogs and baby pigs and snakes floating in formaldehyde-filled jars and black countertops and high stools and signs directing students to an eyewash area. Paulie nearly burned down the lab when he accidentally increased the amount of ammonium dichromate powder from 15 ml to 150 ml in his "Chemical Reactions" experiment. Now, Mr. Jones keeps a close eye on him.

Astrid's leaning on the high counter across from the student she tutors. The counter feels cool against her skin and, while Grace works through a problem, Astrid gazes past her, out the open windows. She always sits here, in the back corner of the lab. From here, she watches for the hawk that hunts the school grounds. It circles high above the clump of woods just south of New Canaan High and the open playing fields surrounding the grounds. It's not there today but she spots Mr. Jones in the distance walking the path beside a high, chain-link fence that encircles the track and, inside the track, the football field. Beyond that, there are softball, baseball, and practice fields. Paulie is out there, too. Probably running hurdles or throwing the discus. Mr. Jones has a bouncy, jubilant way of rising on the balls of his feet, a gait that makes him look childlike. When she sees him, a wing flutters inside her gut.

It's unusually warm for April and Astrid wears her favorite T-shirt: the one with the Coppertone advertisement of a dog pulling down a little girl's swim trunks. Grace is so small—her skin a milky white with purple veins webbing the backs of her hands—that she looks the age of the girl on Astrid's shirt. She plays clarinet in the band and, because her chocolate brown eyes bulge slightly, reminds Astrid of the smallest of the preserved frogs floating in jars on a shelf above the blackboard. She's named that one Grace and sometimes, when Mr. Orion's lecturing, Astrid imagines the floating frog playing clarinet upside down in the murky water, a tiny instrument gripped in its webbed hands.

She may look like a frog, but this kid's smart. She's the only freshman in honors physics. Mr. Jones wants her to succeed and since Astrid needs more service project hours she agreed to tutor her after school on Mondays. Grace is smart all right but she has absolutely no off switch when it comes to talking. She talks more than anyone Astrid has ever known. Mr. Jones says it's a defense mechanism. She's small and people assume she's a little kid. Grace has been obsessed with the Kennedy assassination since she was much younger and, not surprisingly, Hinckley's attempt on Reagan has ignited her interest anew to transform her into a flaming ball of facts.

She's veered Astrid's lesson off course again. "So Jerry Parr pushes the President behind the door of the limousine and saves his life. If he'd been standing up, the bullet would have hit him in the head …"

She keeps it up. Astrid's spacing out, thinking of how her mother's been appearing in her dreams to warn her about some vague threat, when she hears footsteps and turns to see Mr. Jones, his bright red shirt popping against the blackboard. When he turns to catch her staring at him, Astrid taps her pencil on the desk, "Let's get back to electron shells." Astrid points to an image of a lithium atom, "The third shell has a total capacity of two times three squared equals eighteen electrons, right?"

Grace's shoulders sag and she nods.

"But electron shells have sublevels. The first sublevel, the s sublevel holds two electrons—"

"Mr. Jones," Grace pipes up, completely ignoring Astrid, "when are we gonna do trajectories?"

Mr. Jones leans on his desk.

"What?"

"Trajectories! When are we gonna do trajectories?"

When Mr. Jones smiles, just one side of his mouth lifts. "Didn't you learn that at science camp last summer?"

He's walking toward them, weaving through the long tables, "Isn't Astrid's lesson interesting?"

He stops next to Astrid, reaches across the counter to pull Grace's notebook toward him, and gazes at her chicken scratch within. His shoulder is so close to Astrid's that she sees stubble outlining his jaw.

Grace is off again. Something about Astrid being an *awesome* tutor, the best, yadda, yadda, yadda, and, then, seamlessly, her words start resembling a newscast—Reagan, bullet, angel, bouncing—and, truly, Astrid wants to shove a cork in her mouth. After glancing at the notebook, Mr. Jones turns to Astrid. They're standing there like that, like an atom with their own little Grace-electron buzzing around them, the edge of his lip curled as if he's about to bust out laughing. Astrid's trying not to tumble into his eyes.

She's pushing away from that privacy they'd just shared, when, suddenly, Grace stops talking.

Mr. Jones notices him first and steps back. Astrid breaks her gaze when Paulie knocks twice on the table.

"Hey," he says.

Shaken, Astrid turns.

Paulie's eyes shift to Mr. Jones who's broken out in a full-blown smile and leans across Astrid to slap Paulie on the shoulder. "Those were *some* hurdles today."

Paulie's dumb, but he's not stupid. "Thanks." He looks sad or confused or heartbroken or a shifting collage of all three. "Ready to go, Astrid?" He's talking to Astrid but looking at Mr. Jones.

Astrid has already extracted herself from between them to shoulder her backpack. "In a minute."

But Paulie just stands there looking at Mr. Jones. The high table separates them and, for a split second, Astrid fears Paulie might suddenly, violently close the distance between them.

Or maybe it's just Astrid's imagination because, after she gives Grace her homework and tugs his shirt, he turns, as if on cue, to snake his arm around her shoulders.

She's been imagining a lot lately. Mama in her dreams. A frog playing clarinet. Orion Jones's eyes lingering on her just a little too long.

Astrid always loved science. Now, though, *now* Astrid thinks she might love her science teacher.

•

Graduation lands on her mother's birthday. Because of this, Astrid feels edgy and tense. There are over five hundred kids graduating, so the school rents a neighboring town's hockey stadium to accommodate the jubilant crowd. Astrid sits in a folding chair, in the front row (she's valedictorian, after all) and, even though they've covered the ice surface with wood, an icy chill seeps through the soles of her pumps. She can't see Paulie but knows he sits stoically somewhere in the middle of the rink.

She can't see her father, either, but he called from the airport to say he'd be there. She doubts he's sitting with her mother's family. They blame her death on his philandering.

He's been so busy with work, with the rollout of a new vehicle, that he hasn't been home much. Not even in the months following his wife's death. But that's just fine with Astrid. He'd never been around much. Why should Mama's death change that?

Behind red and black bunting and "BOBCAT PRIDE" banners, a flashcard lineup of adults wax eloquent about "accomplishment" and "following your dream" and "hard work" for so long that, when the principal finally announces her name to deliver the valediction, Astrid feels exhausted. A few parents in the audience stand and clap a little too fervently. Astrid wants to throw something at them and scream, *Sit down. I didn't kill myself. I'm just the daughter.*

Everyone's staring expectantly. She scans their faces and there, in the teacher's section, among the gray hair and bowed backs, is Orion Jones. When he sees her looking at him, his eyebrows raise the way they do when he's waiting for an answer to one of his questions.

Her heart thumps unnaturally and an image of Mr. Jones's face appears in front of her like a teleprompter. He's right in front of her, leaning in, about to kiss her. She can smell the deodorant soapiness of him and feel his soft, almost feminine lips on hers.

She leans toward him and feedback causes everyone in the front row to cover their ears. The sound focuses her, but the note cards feel damp in her sweaty palm and, just before she begins, she realizes that ninety-nine percent of the people in that auditorium know only two things about her: she's the valedictorian of one of the biggest graduating classes in her school's history and her mom offed herself. She tries to push this away. Simultaneously, she tries to push away the thought that *that woman*— Mrs. Shield—is in the audience and that her stepson is also out there beneath the sea of mortar boards. She has successfully blocked them out until this very moment.

If she'd known, she would have also tried to block the fact that Coach Haney stoked the rumor about her and Mr. Jones to Paulie's less restrained football buddies. A few of them are dumb cows, more than willing to swallow the swill Coach Haney offers, and they gossip like chattering birds. After all, Astrid doesn't hang out with them or their cheerleader girlfriends. *She's uppity. She's smart. She turns down invitations to party. She hangs out with that cornchip Caroline Godrich and other complete losers. She's a bitch.*

She composes herself though, good old Astrid, and delivers a great speech. Appropriate pauses. The audience laughs in all the right places. A success. Just like her.

And then, in the seashell silence between the fading applause and the next speaker, someone calls out, "Slut!"

Instantly, a ripple of sound, a low murmuring, expands to fill the space just before Paulie jumps out of his seat and charges into the middle aisle toward the place where the catcall originated. It was somewhere between him and the front, behind the faculty, and he's red-faced and bull-like and focused, scanning the crowd just as one of his football buddies points to a kid with flaming red hair sticking out from under his mortar board. Simultaneously, a few of the larger faculty members explode out of their seats to try to diffuse the situation, but it's too late because Paulie pulls the kid up by his collar and over three other graduates to throw him into the aisle, pin him with his knee, and pummel his face with big-knuckled fists while the kid pleads, "It wasn't me. Jesus, Paulie, it wasn't me." But Paulie isn't having any of it until four teachers pull off all two hundred and seventy-five pounds of Paulie and the kid manages, "It was B-b-bax."

Steve Baxter is, of course, the one who pointed to the now bloodied redhead. He's one of those guys whose downhill slide will begin immediately after graduation: a mediocre linebacker with thinning hair, crooked teeth, bad grades, and a pregnant girlfriend.

Paulie meets Baxter's eye and, when Baxter looks away, Paulie lunges out of the grip of the teachers, dives across a row of bodies, and goes for Baxter's neck. The dozen or so graduates immediately surrounding Baxter push back to circle the show Paulie's directing with fists to Baxter's head.

Astrid makes her way through the sea of red and black gowns, kneels beside Paulie, just outside of Paulie's range. She's never seen him like this. Never seen this kind of agony and rage. She can feel waves of it coming off of him with each blow to Baxter's face. She tries to be calm but her voice breaks, "Paulie, that's enough."

And that's it. That's all it takes. As soon as Paulie hears Astrid's voice, his bloodied fist hangs mid-air over Baxter's ground-meat mouth just long enough for the teachers to come back at him, but Astrid holds up an open palm and says, "It's okay," and they stop and Paulie looks up at Astrid with tears and snot smearing his face because he's crying, sobbing, really, this big, big baby of a man sobbing right in front of her, crawling over to her, burying his face in her sweet-smelling hair, and begging her, in that same mantra he's used since they met, not to leave him.

"Never."

And Astrid's cradling his head, cooing in his ear, telling him it's all right while she's trying to figure out how all of this will end. How she'll get away.

And when it will finally happen.

They'll Do as They Please

O f all the ladies Walter dated after mom left, he couldn't seem to shake "The Showgirl." After their first date, he leaned over my bed, kissed my sweaty forehead, and whispered, "This one's a showgirl, Brooks. D'ja hear that? A real live showgirl."

Which prompted the question, "Like a Rockette?"

Walter's bravado never lasted long. He paused, thoughtful for a moment, and answered, "Sort of, buddy. Sort of like a Rockette."

Eventually, he married The Showgirl and, shortly after that and much to her chagrin, he took a new job and we moved from Manhattan to New Canaan. In case you hadn't heard, there's nothing sadder than a couple of Manhattanites plunked in the belly of the Midwest. I'd become accustomed to riding the subway, translating my nanny's Spanish, choosing from hundreds of great places to eat. A chorus of sirens and traffic and jackhammers accompanied us to the park. Compared to that, New Canaan was like being exiled to Mars. Nothing seemed familiar—not the huge homes, long driveways, manicured lawns, or the nearly perfect silence of every street.

To get me out of the house, The Showgirl and I would walk her Pekingese, Barbra Streisand, around our suburban neighborhood. There I was, a ridiculously gangly teen with braces, glasses, and a mop of unruly hair, walking with my dad's wet-dream of a wife and her yappy little dog. Even then, her outfits threw me off: pumps, tight pants, and a blouse unbuttoned to show cleavage. As we passed, the neighbors would stop talking abruptly—the men elbowing each other, the women barely concealing their smirks.

The Showgirl didn't seem to notice. She'd walk up to a clutch of neighbors, her right hand extended, Barbra Streisand at her feet, and announce, "Hello, I'm Dovey." And, before those bastards could snap their jaws shut, Barbra Streisand would attach her little Pekingese teeth to a cuff or ankle, shaking her perfectly groomed head like a metronome. Dovey would toss her hair over her shoulder and coo, "Now, Barbra Streisand, stop that nonsense right this second."

At the time, I didn't think she noticed the neighbors' sidelong glances and eye rolls. But I think I was wrong. I think Dovey knew the score. And I think she played it perfectly.

•

When I turned fifteen, Walter bought me a piece of shit '76 Chevelle and, by my sixteenth birthday, I'd rebuilt the engine, replaced every spark plug, hose, and shock. It was boss. Every lunch period, my best friend Julie Mountain and I would hop in the Chevelle, grab lunch at Halo Burger drive-thru, and generally avoid New Canaan High. We were smarter than most of the Neanderthals and we knew it. That kind of attitude will get your high school ass kicked just about anywhere in the world, let alone New Canaan. One other thing: my name is Brooks Shield—S instead of E, no S at the end of Shield. Yeah. You can imagine. Whereas, the kids I grew up with in New York didn't make a big deal of it, as a new kid, my name became a major source of jokes. Long story short: I was always on the verge of getting my ass served up on a platter.

This particular day, the September sky seemed startlingly blue and shiny. It made me feel small and insignificant for some reason so I buried the speedometer in the triple digits. Van Halen blaring, the world became a blur—Ehrlich's Berry Farm, the gently sloping fields ready for harvest, the sad, divey bars plunked in the middle of nowhere, back into town, past the quaint brick stand-alone businesses, Holy Family, the mall, and New Canaan High.

On our way back out of town for the second time and right in the middle of a rant about how Mr. Orion gave her an A minus on her last presentation, Julie's head yanked back, "Was that The Showgirl's Caddy pulling into The Scenic?"

I adjusted my rearview to see Dovey's white Eldorado pull in front of a room at the end of the low-slung motel. The Scenic Inn was one of those places we passed every day but hardly noticed. Sitting high atop a hill, far off the road, it had once been a really cool Art Deco motor lodge, but the owners had let the façade crumble and the pool fill with trash.

I swung the Chevelle into the VFW Lodge parking lot in time to see one of Walter's coworkers, the lead Corvette engineer, Mr. Miracal, walking from the office with a key dangling between his fingers. Then the two of them disappeared into a room.

It kinda made me sick to see that, but I acted cool, the way I thought James Bond would act if he'd just seen his stepmom walk into a motel with some dude who wasn't his dad.

Julie started bouncing up and down, as much as she could, anyway, with the seatbelt tight around her lap as she pointed to Dovey's car again, "That's her, right? Your stepmom?"

I shrugged like it was no big deal, like I'd seen this kind of thing before, like I imagined Bond would act but, inside, I felt scared—the way I felt after mom left. I wanted to curl up in a little ball and sob. I realize, now, how blind I was about Dovey. But here's the thing: I'd grown to love her. And, although everyone made fun of her, she treated me really well. After she and Walter married, when I was a little kid, she'd read my favorite book, Hans Christian Andersen's folktales, and act out the parts. When I got older, she'd pick me up after chess club and bring all the guys Halo Burgers. She might have been the laughingstock of our stodgy little subdivision, but I loved her. What's more, I knew Walter'd be crushed if he knew about her and Mr. Miracal.

I figured Mr. Miracal's daughter, Astrid, would be upset if she knew, too. Astrid was one of the kids at New Canaan High who would tell the idiots to shut up when they teased me. She was quiet, but she wouldn't stand by and let stuff happen. And, since her quarterback boyfriend Paulie was always close by, no one messed with her.

Anyway, my hands started shaking and I bit my bottom lip the way I do before I cry, but I didn't want Julie to see so I pulled into the Bella Vista Mall parking lot, behind a thick hedge blocking us from the parade of cars on Saginaw, threw the Chevelle into PARK, and finished my Halo Burger in earnest. A pickle and some mustard landed on my white button down and I thought about the way Mom always said Walter and I should wear bibs because neither of us could eat without ruining our shirts.

Julie tore a tiny hole in a ketchup packet, painted a single fry with red, and popped it in her mouth, "Whatdya think The Showgirl was doing with that guy?"

Julie was super book smart, but disturbingly naive. With a mouthful of burger, I stared into the deep green hedge and rolled my eyes as if I considered it irrelevant, "She's probably interviewing for a job."

Just then, Father Silver's Caprice Classic pulled into the parking lot.

"Was that Father Silver?" Julie asked.

I nodded as the Caprice headed toward a Buick idling at the parking lot's far corner, by where the woods began. It was weird because Father Silver didn't seem like the kind of guy to go shopping in the middle of the day. He especially didn't seem like a guy who parked in the back of a parking lot.

In the rearview, I watched him pull into the spot between the Buick and a dumpster. And then nothing happened. After a few minutes, the Buick pulled out of the lot. Couldn't tell who drove. The sun visor was down, plus, black Buicks were a dime a dozen in New Canaan.

Julie swiveled to look out the rear window, "Why's he just sitting there?"

"Maybe he's taking a nap."

Julie rolled her eyes, "In the Bella Vista parking lot? He lives right down the street."

I shrugged, "Maybe he's carpooling."

"Maybe he had a heart attack."

That was unlikely, but I drove across the parking lot anyway and pulled into the spot the Buick had vacated. Julie poked her head out the open window to peer into the Caprice.

Father Silver wasn't there.

She plopped into her seat, "That's weird."

"You're weird."

"Shut up." She focused on a hair, raised it to eye level, and pulled a split end apart, "He must have gotten into the Buick. Let's go. We're gonna be late."

It *was* weird, but my mind was still locked on the image of Dovey and Mr. Miracal entering that hotel room. I couldn't un-imagine what they were doing in there and I couldn't shake the feeling that I might burst into tears at any moment. God, I was a pussy. But ever since Mom left, I would find my lip quivering and my tongue getting thick whenever a mother appeared in a commercial or while I watched *The Jeffersons* or *Happy Days*.

Tears blurred my vision.

Julie leaned over. "What's up, Brooks? You crying?"

I tried to deny it, but I was sobbing now, curled over, my head resting on the steering wheel, shaking.

"What is it? Why're you crying? Did I do something?"

I shook my head.

"Did something happen? Is it about The Showgirl? Was it because she went into—" Julie stopped and murmured, "Oh. Okay."

"NO!" I said it more forcefully than I'd intended and Julie shrunk into her seat. I'd grown nearly five inches since my sophomore year but still didn't see myself as the bruiser everyone else saw. I'd been such a scrawny runt most of my life that my newfound height took even me off guard. I immediately shook my head and lowered my voice, "Sorry. It's—"

Julie leaned forward, "What?"

"It's just that, sometimes, you know, I miss my mom."

Julie looked confused. She'd never known my mom and I'd never talked about her so I added, "Not Dovey. My real mom."

"She died?"

I didn't answer. In my mind, she *had* died. In my mind, it was easier to think of her as dead than to remember the day she left.

•

The rest of that week, we cruised by the Bella Vista parking lot and The Scenic Inn. Nothing. The next week, though, Monday at noon, Dovey's Eldorado appeared in the same spot at the end of the motel. I didn't acknowledge it. Julie saw it, too, but she didn't say a word.

•

The night before the homecoming parade, the weather turned blustery and cold. It was nearly eight o'clock, and we still had a lot of work to do on the senior float Julie had designed: a really sweet miniature Columbia Space Shuttle in anticipation of next spring's launch. About forty of us gathered in Rebecca Goynes's barn to lace tissue paper pompoms through the chicken wire frame. Even the fact that Astrid and Paulie were there couldn't distract me. I assumed Astrid didn't know about her dad and Dovey. And I had no plans to tell her.

The barn was brightly lit with bulbs we'd hung from the rafters. It smelled of clean hay and oil and machinery. Outside, yellow ribbons strangled every fence post and tree branch in anticipation of Rebecca's big brother, Marine Sergeant Will Goynes's return from Iran. No one mentioned it. It just *was*. He'd been gone so long that the ribbons had lost their color. Most had frayed to threads. Every time Mr. Goynes walked into the barn to see our progress, he would end up staring out into the night. I imagined that those ribbons, tied on by well-meaning Boy Scouts, once so cheery and bright, pricked at the hopelessness he felt.

Anyway, Julie's design took into account that the twenty-five-foot replica would have to clear the barn opening, so she incorporated hinges that allowed the shuttle to be hoisted up and down on its flatbed platform. That night, it rested on its belly, nose pointed west. In the morning, once I towed it to the parade route, we would hoist it up, and it would be ready for takeoff. She'd thought of every detail: the solid rocket boosters, the external tank, the shuttle's arrowhead design, payload bay doors, main engines.

An hour later, two guys who'd graduated a few years back, Lou Tremaine and Sammy Mansour, a couple of monumental assholes, showed up. They'd led the Bobcats basketball team to State Championships and, since then, couldn't quite shake their high school glory days. You know the type— dudes who buy high school kids alcohol and hit on the underage girls. Yeah. *Those* guys. When I was a freshman, they teased me mercilessly. "Hey, Brooke Shields. Your ass is fine in those Calvin Kleins." Or, "Look! It's Pretty Baby. How ya doing, Pretty Baby?"

They sauntered into the barn, reeking of beer and weed, slapping kids on the back, making inane small talk, barely able to focus. The mood in the barn shifted abruptly; it became so quiet that we could hear the Steve Miller Band playing on the little transistor radio and the crinkle of tissue paper. Everyone suddenly bent their heads to their tasks.

Lou walked with his shoulders back and his hands hanging behind his ass—as if he was sizing up everyone he passed. He wore a Members Only jacket, a cheesy silk shirt buttoned low so that his chest hair showed, a backward baseball cap, and PUMA sneakers. Sammy Mansour, on the other hand, could barely keep his eyes open. Dime slits, we called 'em. He'd pulled his hoodie over his head and the sleeves down over his hands. He leaned against a post, swigging from a bottle encased in a brown paper bag.

Julie and I worked on the American flag on the shuttle's side, knee deep in red, white, and blue pompoms. I kept my head down but Lou spotted me.

"Brooke Shields!" He weaved toward me, "Long time no see, buddy!"

I nodded and turned away but he caught my arm. He pressed his thumb into my bicep.

"You're all grown up, man." He spun me around to face him and used his free hand to measure the difference in our heights. He only had about an inch on me, but he'd gained weight and bulk.

He leaned over as if looking at my backside, "Still wearing those Calvin Kleins, huh?"

Julie turned to face Lou, "You need new material."

Lou squinted, unsure if he'd been insulted. After a pause, he brightened, "Whoa! Brooke Shields has a gal pal. Way to go, Brooke Shields."

He still gripped my arm, his thumb digging into my bicep until I winced. Jerking out of his grasp, Julie and I walked away.

He tailed us, singing, "*Not much of a girlfriend. Never seem to get a lot.*"

Sammy perked up, "Supertramp."

Lou stopped and pointed at Sammy, "Supertramp's bangin', man."

"No shit, Sherlock."

"Fuck you, Watson."

Sammy dropped his head forward, laughing. His thick black hair, usually swept back off his forehead, fell over his face and into his eyes. Lou tried to swipe the bottle from Sammy but fumbled it into his own chest. Beer leaked down Lou's shirt and onto the front of his jeans.

"Shit, now look what you've done, man. It looks like I pissed myself." Lou punched Sammy in the arm.

Julie and I walked to the other side of the float. Lou followed and cornered us between the float and a stack of leftover lumber and chicken wire.

Turning to gaze at the side of the shuttle as if he'd just now noticed it, Lou asked, "What the hell is this?"

Sammy stumbled behind Lou, stopped and tried to focus, "Looks like a gigantic dick, man."

"Yeah," Lou nodded, placing his hands on his hips and tilting his head to take in the length of the shuttle float, "it does look like big schwang."

"Shut up."

He was so quiet and there were so many people that I'd almost forgotten about Paulie. That's the way he was. He could blend in and then explode into your consciousness.

By the time Lou turned to the voice, all six-foot-five of Paulie, complete with biceps the size of Lou's waist, and hands that could crush his neck, appeared next to him.

Lou smiled, "Paulie Ehrlich." He turned to Sammy, "It's Charlie's little brother. How's your big bro, bro?" Lou extended his hand.

Paulie looked at Lou's hand but didn't extend his own, "Fine."

Lou tried to cover the insult by slapping Paulie's shoulder, "Good guy, that Charlie."

Paulie scratched his chin, "How about you let us get back to it. We've got a lot to do."

Lou raised his palms, "Who's stopping you? And *you*—" he poked Paulie in the chest with his index finger, "should rest up for the big game."

"I'm rested."

Lou and Paulie faced each other for an uncomfortably long moment. No one moved. Finally, Lou broke Paulie's stare, "Good luck tomorrow." He leaned forward, "I hear Beecher's defense has some real crushers."

"I'll be fine."

Lou stepped back but his gaze shifted to Astrid who had walked up to stand behind Paulie. Slowly, as if he'd just figured something out, he turned to me, "Hey, Brooke Shields, how's your *mom*?"

Sammy snickered.

Lou raised his eyebrows expectantly.

"Fine," I mumbled.

"You bet she's fine and," he tipped his head to Astrid, "look who's here—"

My stomach clenched.

"It's your mom's boyfriend's—"

Before he could finish, I stepped between him and Paulie, "Don't."

Lou grabbed my shirt and lifted me into his face, "Don't *what*, Brooke Shields? Don't *what*, you little pussy."

Lou shoved me into Paulie. Paulie caught me before I fell and whispered, "What the hell, Brooks? I can't get in trouble before the game."

Lou stared at me hard until he grabbed Sammy's sleeve and turned to leave. Over his shoulder, he yelled, "Your mom's a skank, Shields."

All eyes shifted to me and, in that moment, I saw my mom, my real mom, the night she left, standing in the entry hall of our apartment in New York. Her handbag rested in the crook of her arm, a suitcase sat next to her right leg. My parents' argument had woken me. Even at six, I knew that something was wrong between them. Mom was about to say something when she spotted me making my way down the hallway toward them. Dad kept pulling on his bottom lip with his thumb and forefinger the way he did when he got nervous. Shaking his head, he said, *Just go then*, before quietly disappearing into his study. When I took a step toward mom, she didn't smile or open her arms the way she usually did but raised her hand like a crossing guard telling me to stop. I did and, maybe for the first time in my life, looked at her face. Really looked at it. She seemed focused and granite hard. Terror swept over me and I asked her where she was going. *Away*, she said. And when I asked, *For how long?* she just shook her head as if she was already trying to forget.

Lou's verdict boomed through the barn one more time as he and Sammy walked out, "A skank!"

"She's not my mom," I said, quietly, wondering at the choices people made and the staggering blows unleashed in their wake.

•

I do realize that it was futile to try to dull the pain of my mom's absence or Dovey's betrayal with revenge. But then? Then I thought that inflicting pain would somehow ease my own.

So I'm not proud that, a few days after Homecoming, on a day when Julie was sick, I followed Father Silver to find that it was Mrs. Miracal who picked him up and took him to her home.

But, mostly, I'm ashamed of what I did after that: of pulling out Dovey's old typewriter (with the lowercase E that looked like it had been hacked in half) and writing that note,

I know about you and Leila Miracal.

III. EXAMINE

Striking Disclosure

Astrid just might love Paulie's mother more than she loves Paulie. She's not sure. What she does know is that Paulie's mom treats her the same way she did *before* as *after*. That's how Astrid divides her life these days: before and after. At school, she moves seamlessly between jocks, band geeks, honor society and debate team nerds, partiers, kids with no affiliation, kids no one notices. She's always been that way. Smart-band-geek-athlete. Hard to pin down. There's a sweetness about her that disguises what she's thinking. Nothing about her goes together. Even her beauty is mongrel: her mother's black curls, heart-shaped face, almond-shaped eyes; her father's severe cheekbones, milky pale complexion, green eyes. She's forever chewing her tightly bowed lips and getting cold sores. She wants to slice off the lesions with a razor but doesn't say it out loud any more. She said it to Nicky Giovanni, second trumpet to her first, who reported her to the band teacher, who sat her down and asked if everything was *okay*. The royal *okay*. She wanted to laugh at Ms. Aboujamra's earnest concern because Astrid is nothing like her mother. Don't they know this? Her happiness doesn't rely on the love of a man. In her way, she does love Paulie, but if they broke it off, she'd move on. She wants to explain that her mother was a fabulous cook but a terrible driver. She wants to tell them that, personally, she can't cut a carrot but drives like she's been doing it her whole life. Her mother's suicide was just one event. One insignificant blip in her mother's entire timeline. They know only the final plot point. She defines her mother by the elegant way she knelt to take Communion, the way she used a silk scarf to tame her hair, the sparkly blue broach she wore on her winter coat, how she carried a book in her purse, how her father had to drag her to cocktail parties.

Astrid wants to hand out a pamphlet stating all of this information and, at the bottom, in large, bold red letters, this:

I'M NOT GOING TO KILL MYSELF

She does love Paulie's mom. It's Saturday morning and they're standing side by side serving breakfast at the annual marching band pancake fundraiser. Mrs. Ehrlich tongs the hotcakes out of the aluminum trays and plops them on a plate for Astrid to distribute to bleary-eyed parents and kids. Mrs. Ehrlich is a sturdy plug of a woman with frizzy gray hair, bright blue eyes, and meaty, farm-weathered hands. Her cuticles are red and raw, nails chipped, the ring finger so swollen that the thin gold band makes it look like it's about to pop. Astrid thinks of a glacier: quiet, stoic, enduring. Astrid's hands are delicate and tapered (*musician's hands* is what Mrs. Ehrlich calls them) and with this observation, she's suddenly embarrassed by their lack of character and bracingly aware of the chasm that exists in this farm-town-turned-suburb. Mrs. Ehrlich with her farm hands and Astrid with her musician hands; the Ehrlichs working their family's strawberry farm, Astrid's dad in the cool, clean offices of GM.

Astrid's staring at her empty hand when Mrs. Ehrlich says, "What?"

"Nothing."

"There's a line a mile long. You gonna help or stand there staring?" She's gruff and terse but a smile curls the corners of her lips. This is the way she looks when Paulie rests his great quarterback arm over Astrid's shoulders. It's a smile that says *she knows what's going on between them and they'd better be careful—no babies, not yet—or there will be hell to pay.*

"I'd stop staring if you'd hand me the plate already." Astrid gives it back to Mrs. Ehrlich as best she can.

The two are in the cavernous gym with its black and red "BOBCAT PRIDE" banners and gigantic black paw prints and basketball hoops and too-bright lights and some dolt dancing around wearing an enormous bobcat mascot head. The line snakes past them, parents and kids alike talking about that week's assassination attempt on Reagan, when, suddenly, Mrs. Shield, the Cadillac-driving, tight-sweatered, platinum-blonde stepmom of a kid in Astrid's class, stops directly in front of Astrid. She has one of those unremarkable faces framed by "Farrah" hair. She's one of the other executive's wives, one Mama would have referred to as *inbred IQ, blonde, big chest.* Astrid holds the plate out to her but Mrs. Shield just stands there with her hands hanging like weights at her sides. Mrs. Ehrlich registers the slow down and is about to say something when she looks up at Mrs. Shield. Astrid pushes the plate forward, almost into Mrs. Shield's flat abdomen, and, just then, as Mrs. Shield's chin begins to quiver, Astrid *knows.* Mrs. Shield wasn't at the funeral. And, as Astrid remembers this fact, she is doubly certain. It's then that Mrs. Ehrlich takes the heavy cafeteria plate from Astrid and shoves it into Mrs. Shield's abdomen. Mrs. Shield coughs like the wind's been knocked out of her, turns, and runs out of the gymnasium.

Astrid seems to find herself suddenly hovering over the scene. Her head and hands are Macy's-Thanksgiving-Day-Parade huge. She's watching everyone's gazes follow Mrs. Shield out of the gym and, when she exits, the door's slam reverberates inside her skull.

Her mother wouldn't tell Astrid the names of the other women. But she knows there were at least five and that Mrs. Shield was one of them. She wishes she had the *I'M NOT GOING TO KILL MYSELF* pamphlet. She would run through the cafeteria, flinging the flyers into the air, push through the doors, run to Mrs. Shield's Eldorado, and shove one through her open window.

"Um hmm," is all Mrs. Ehrlich needs to say. She doesn't try to protect Astrid.

Astrid floats down from the ceiling and puts her hand out to receive the next plate. Mrs. Ehrlich doesn't wrap her arm around Astrid and pull her close. She doesn't ask if she's okay. She doesn't do anything but tong one too many pancakes, plop them on the scratched porcelain plate, and hand them to Astrid.

And, for that, Astrid is grateful.

Swarm Theory

Dovey Shield lived for dramatic exits and her most recent felt truly earned. The eyes of every dreary person in the pancake breakfast had followed her pumping ass and tight sweater out the door. Why did she storm out? Because that poor girl's expression simply *undid* her.

Later, on the phone, that's how she would describe it to her best friend Nora Peel. She would emphasize *undid* to make sure Nora understood.

"Honey, what's the big deal?" Nora lived in New York, Dovey's old stomping grounds and, at that very moment, gazed out the window of her third-floor walk-up, at her wet laundry and, beyond that, a bracingly blue sliver of New York Harbor.

"What's the big deal? You don't know what I have to deal with in this one-horse town."

Nora absentmindedly stirred cream into her coffee, "It's not like Manhattan, huh?"

"You don't live in Manhattan, Doll." Dovey liked to remind Nora of her recent relocation to Red Hook.

"Bitch."

Nora and Dovey had met as ensemble members to Mickey Rooney's and Ann Miller's leads in *Sugar Babies*. Two punch-drunk-fabulous years on Broadway until—with the show rumored to be closing—Dovey met a passably handsome widower exec, got knocked up, married, and then tragedy struck. Mr. Exec took a job with General Motors and they moved to this poor excuse of a Michigan town. Barely a town. There wasn't even a shopping district. What did it have? Cornfields and car plants, that's what. Who cared? Her husband, that's who. She could give a rat's ass about the automotive industry. Her life was in New York, under the bright lights, swathed in spandex behind Ann Miller, feeling Mickey Rooney's pudgy hand on her ass just a beat too long.

Dovey twirled the phone cord around her hand and watched a flock of Canadian geese wobble off her perfectly manicured lawn onto the velvet green golf course. "Don't be so cruel. But, seriously—"

"Don't get serious. It's Saturday. I can't take *serious* on Saturday."

Dovey ignored her, "She looked so devastated— like she'd just figured out who I was or …" Dovey gazed at her reflection in the window, "Maybe she wanted to connect. I don't know. It was like everyone *knew* and she came late to the party."

Nora poured herself another cup of coffee, "My money's on that."

"What?"

"That everyone knows."

Dovey considered this while gazing at the framed portrait of her family on the wall above the kitchen table. As Nora berated her for marrying Mr. Exec, Dovey wondered how anyone could have given birth to such a homely child. But there he was, her stepson, plopped uncomfortably between Dovey, Baby June, and Mr. Exec. His body language suggested disdain. Dovey's recommendation to *not smile* hadn't been heeded and, as a result, his orthodontia was on full display. The poor child's long oval face, egg-drop nose, thin lips, and frizzy brown hair didn't help matters. After receiving his graduation picture in the mail, Nora quipped, *Put a black wig on that kid and he's the spitting image of Ann Miller.*

Dovey had to agree.

Dovey, on the other hand, was a sought-after commodity among a certain group of husbands in her suburban neighborhood. She was curvaceous and usually blonde and could belt out a decent show tune, unprovoked, after a few cocktails.

"So ..." Nora asked, "What are you going to do?"

Dovey stretched the phone cord across the kitchen and into the living room so that she could sit at the baby grand. The house was empty except for Baby June napping upstairs. She lightly tapped the keys and fell into a reverie about taking piano lessons. "About what?"

Nora sighed. Dovey had the attention span of a beagle. "About what happened."

"Oh. I hadn't really thought about it."

"Well, you *ought* to think about it. You ought to do something. Write her a letter. I mean, her mother killed herself because you were fucking her father."

"Don't say that."

"Fucking, fucking, fucking."

Dovey bit the inside of her cheek. "It wasn't *my* fault. Luke said she was—"

What had he said? Boring? Difficult? Troubled? Oh, hell. At this point, what did it matter? Regardless, she finished, "You're right. She needs a steady hand."

"Don't get confused."

"About what?"

"The steady hand. There's nothing steady about you."

"I'm an actor, aren't I?"

"Not really."

•

"Where's Astrid working this summer?" Dovey lay on her side, breasts displayed like melons, the rest of her covered by a thin white sheet. She tried ignoring the stained carpeting, torn curtains, and fungal smell of the drab hotel room where they met every Monday at noon.

Luke Miracal tightened the knot of his tie and leaned into the mirror to remove a spot of lipstick on his jaw. "Ehrlich's Berry Farm." He paused. "Why? Dovey, what are you thinking?"

"I should talk to her, you know, woman to woman."

Luke shook his head in disbelief. "Absolutely not."

"Why?"

"Because you're the last person Astrid needs to talk to."

"Our kids are classmates."

"Your stepson and Astrid barely know each other."

Something about him drove her crazy. She wasn't sure if she was attracted to or completely repelled by him. At first, his square jaw and the dramatic precipices under his cheekbones turned her on but, later, like now, she would realize that she hated him for his complete and utter disregard for anything that came out of her mouth.

He turned around, walked to the bed, put both palms on the crumpled sheets and leaned in close, "By no means are you to talk to my daughter."

•

One morning, a few weeks after Luke had warned her, Dovey and Baby June were at the grocery store when she encountered a flock of six wife-pigeons in the produce section. She recognized them from her neighborhood but, for the life of her, couldn't remember their names. They all looked the same: preppy and sexless in their pastel polo shirts, plaid shorts, and Top-Siders. That's the kind of woman Dovey Shield was: she paid more attention to the boys than to the girls. Always had. The leader of this bland group, a square-faced woman with a Cleopatra helmet of black hair, called her over.

"Dov-ey! Dov-ey Shield!"

The women surrounded a freestanding display of melons, their carts pointing in all directions like spokes.

Dovey wanted friends. She wanted to sit with the other pigeons, no matter how dull their feathers, at the country club pool sipping cocktails while Baby June took swim lessons. She quite honestly didn't understand why the neighborhood wives shunned her or what she'd been doing wrong. Maybe she hadn't done anything wrong. Maybe there was simply a hazing period. Now that she'd proven herself a competent mother, perhaps they were ready to accept her into the fold.

Dovey was glad she'd spent extra time perfecting her feathered hair, and had chosen the skin-tight burgundy pants and tiny black tank for today's public foray. As she approached, the women's expressions morphed from amused to serious. A few of them crossed their arms and squared off as if readying for battle.

Cleopatra skirted the cantaloupe display to stand beside Dovey's cart. The pores on her cheeks erupted in volcano lesions and her nose needed powdering, "We're curious, Dovey. Did it ever occur to you that your behavior might have driven Leila Miracal to kill herself?"

Dovey stopped smiling. Baby June, facing her mother in the shopping cart, kicked her fat legs into Dovey's abdomen. When Dovey didn't respond, Baby June twisted her neck to see what her mother found so fascinating.

Dovey was speechless. The women glared at her. She hadn't felt this much negative energy since last summer's neighborhood gathering when she stood on the picnic table and slurred her way through "I Can't Give You Anything But Love, Baby."

"That's what we thought. Consider yourself informed." Cleopatra stepped into Dovey's face, "And stay *away* from our husbands. Do I make myself clear?"

Dovey nodded.

•

After the ugly scene at the supermarket, Dovey (with Baby June safely buckled in her car seat) barreled down Dixie Highway toward Ehrlich's Berry Farm. It was time she listened to her intuition. It told her to approach Astrid. Never one to dwell on ugliness, Dovey floored the Eldorado and thought about how much she loved this car. She loved its lean, long, thick front grill, towering taillights, burgundy leather seats, paneled dash, and steering wheel as big as a ship's helm. She loved it when one of her neighbors' husbands pulled her into the plush passenger seat after stopping on a dark country road. She loved how she could turn onto a flat, straight ribbon of road and floor it over a hundred in nothing flat.

The soundtrack to *Oklahoma!* blaring, she turned into the berry farm, flew through the parking lot, gravel spitting and dust swirling in her wake, past the stand where they sold all-things-strawberry, honey, and produce, down a narrow lane flanked by ground-hugging berry bushes and into an open, grassy area where she spotted Astrid's light blue Monte Carlo. The front fields were reserved for U-Pick. Astrid would be in one of the back fields picking berries.

Without the wind whipping past her, the heat felt stifling. Summers in New Canaan felt like Florida—without palm trees, of course—and the intensity of this Midwestern sun always surprised her. She got out of her car to scan the fields, open hand to forehead, eyes squinting down the long, straight rows of green and red. About a football field away, she spotted a group of pickers.

She put Baby June on her hip and thanked God for the umpteenth time that her daughter took after her side of the family: strawberry ringlets, cherub cheeks, button nose. True, Baby June had Dovey's hard little black eyes and, yes, Baby June wasn't petite. Dovey silently cursed this fact, straining to hold the child as she made her way between berry rows in her leather pumps.

Those dark pants and top sure were soaking up the heat. And the straw mulch was slippery and the berries she carelessly crushed showered her feet and ankles in a red, sticky mist. Dovey began to perspire. Thick drops of sweat streamed down her temples and, by the time she'd covered fifty feet, she felt her mascara melting and rings of sweat circling her underarms.

For her part, Astrid had been daydreaming all morning, breathing in the deep, sweet scent of ripening fruit. She was at the far end of the strawberry field, next to a wildflower meadow filled with clover, Queen Anne's lace, chicory, and buttercups. No one else would work this side of the field because of the honeybee hives—a dozen teetering stacks of weathered white boxes held off the ground by cinder blocks—just a few feet from the berries Astrid picked.

The honeybees hovered around her, buzzing elegantly from flower to flower busily collecting pollen. She loved this work. It was hot and dirty but she only had to think when Mrs. Ehrlich needed her to translate something into Spanish. Just pick. Out here, no one knew her. No one knew about her mother's suicide. The Mexican pickers treated her with a muted courtesy that Astrid welcomed.

Emelina, the picker a few acres west of Astrid, suddenly stood and waved her arm to get Astrid's attention. Astrid looked up to see that the others—a dozen women each dotting every few acres of land—had stopped and were all looking the same way. Following their gazes, Astrid spotted a woman in the distance with a baby on her hip. She figured it was a confused U-Picker who'd lost her way, but something about the determination in the woman's step unsettled her.

As the woman made her way toward her, Astrid removed her straw hat and wiped her forehead with a bandanna. There were no clouds and the sky's transparency nearly blinded her. On days like this, when the sun beat mercilessly and the sky pulsed a clear blue that hurt her eyes, she would look to the horizon where the color softened and wonder at the vastness of it all, how there might be billions and billions of galaxies bumping around out there. She always pictured them as stones tumbling in a rock polisher. Silly, she knew, since that would suggest they were enclosed somehow. But it helped her manage the uncertainty of it all, that there was no edge to it. That space went on forever.

"Yoo-hoo!" Astrid was easy to pick out from the others. Although they all wore wide-brimmed hats, Astrid's white, long-sleeve cotton shirt and khakis set her apart, as did the skin that did show—very, very pale like Luke's. The other women wore short-sleeve T-shirts and shorts.

"Astrid!"

The woman had stopped to wave the way a stranded person might flag down a rescue plane. Astrid finally recognized her as Mrs. Shield, that damn lady who'd stormed out of the pancake breakfast. A panic rose in her and she quickly knelt, attempting to hide behind the low-slung mounds, which, of course, was futile. The other pickers returned to their work but looked up nervously, shifting their gazes between this obviously crazy person and Astrid.

Astrid bit her lip. Mrs. Shield suddenly towered over her, an arm's length away, mopping her brow and shifting Baby June to her other hip. Her mascara formed two half-moon smudges below each eye. She looked like a well-dressed raccoon and smelled strongly of too sweet, cloying perfume.

"Whew. That was quite a walk!" Her voice, high-pitched and childish, immediately grated against Astrid's ears.

Astrid stiffly stood. She couldn't imagine what Mrs. Shield wanted. She felt nauseous and the muscles in her legs felt weak, yet she braced herself for the unknown.

"The U-Pick fields are over there." Astrid lifted her chin to the front fields and held the galvanized basket, its cardboard liner full of strawberries, in the crook of her arm. For every step Dovey took toward her, Astrid stepped back.

As soon as she spied the berries in Astrid's basket, Baby June, dressed in a crisp white jumper, clapped her hands, "Mama! Ba!"

"Silly. Those aren't for you!" Her voice sing-songed, tone unchanging when she addressed Astrid. "Astrid, I'm here to see you."

Astrid's instinct told her to flee. Instead, she asked, "Why?"

"Well, I wanted to apologize. Or, well, not really apologize but talk. I guess. Because of that little scene at the pancake breakfast and, well, you know——" Baby June squirmed, reaching for a berry. Dovey switched hips, "This kid is a sack of potatoes." She bunched her lips and cooed in her ear, "Aren't you? Aren't you just one big, adorable sack of potatoes?"

Dovey never imagined that Astrid might not want to grab this olive branch. In fact, she hadn't thought much beyond the fantasy of Astrid burying her face in Dovey's breast, sobbing and thanking her for being … What? Understanding? Oh, hell, she didn't know. But she had convinced herself that this would be one of those *moments:* the kind in after-school TV specials where one character suddenly realizes how much they need the other. Those pigeons in town were just jealous. And what did Luke know? There was no reason she and Astrid couldn't be friends. She would rub it in all their faces.

That was the tragic thing about Dovey: she didn't get it. She didn't get the fact that, in a small town, everyone knows your business, that since she'd moved here, wives kept close track of their husbands, that she was the favorite topic of *meet-for-coffee* conversations, that she was the train wreck from which the entire town simply couldn't tear their eyes away.

Baby June extended her pudgy hand, again, reaching for a berry. When Astrid didn't hand one over, she started making high-pitched *ba* sounds and breathing quickly.

"I just thought we could get to know each other. It's good to have a woman in your life. Hush now, Baby June." Dovey looked at the basket of berries, "Do you mind giving Baby June one of those?"

Astrid blinked. Everything about this woman annoyed her. Her voice. The way she dressed. The way she kept repeating, *Baby June*. This was a mirage. That was it. This wasn't happening. This was one of her dreams. Nevertheless, she answered, "A woman?"

"Well, yes. Since your mother's unfortunate passing. I mean, your dad said she was—" Dovey paused. Come to think about it, he never gave a reason for his wandering eye. Honestly, they barely spoke at all. So she made it up as she went along. She was, after all, an actor. *Troubled* popped into her head. It seemed fairly neutral. So she said it. "Troubled."

Baby June's fat hand slapped her mother's pouting lip, "What'dya say about a berry?"

"Troubled?" A blinding fury swept through Astrid. "Who are you to talk about my mother?"

Dovey started backpedaling, "No. No. I mean. I'm just repeating what your father told me."

Astrid's throat felt thick and she battled tears, "Please leave."

But Dovey didn't hear Astrid's request because, just then, Baby June's face turned crimson and a high-pitched howl exploded from her rosebud mouth. Her dimpled baby arms and legs wagged furiously, her mouth formed a perfect O of fury.

To Astrid, the baby's face became a fluttering flag. Dovey's words became needling, long-handled spears.

Dovey kept babbling and babbling, and walking toward Astrid. One step, two steps, three steps. Astrid matched Dovey's steps in retreat. It was like a weird Victorian dance during which Astrid could focus on nothing but the twisted, howling face of that baby. It infuriated her. She wanted to slap it and its mother for good measure. She blocked everything else out except that child's howling: she didn't hear Dovey's inane, illogical speech or Emelina's screams of, "Alto! La colmena!"

By the time she felt the stack with her left calf, she lost her balance and tripped backward. The galvanized basket soundly gonged the stack of hives to her left—right in the stack's heart. As she fell, Astrid's other elbow drove into the frames to her right and she and both boxes toppled to the ground. Against the impossibly blue sky, a few bees rose slowly. As she heard the angry buzzing of the warriors trying to get out of the toppled structures, Astrid righted herself and frantically tried to cap the stacks but only succeeded in upsetting the bees more.

"Run!"

But Dovey didn't run. For all she knew, the white boxes poised innocently at the end of the strawberry row might have been filing cabinets.

"Run, Mrs. Shield!"

Suddenly, the bees rose in a dark, Aladdin-out-of-the-bottle cloud. And since the bees identified Dovey as their dark-suited, sweet-smelling intruder—perhaps a bear or a freakishly large raccoon—the majority swarmed her. Dovey's eyes grew wide and her mouth opened to rival Baby June's. Within seconds, her face became a moving mass of angry bees. Baby June stopped crying and swatted at the bees on her mother's face, which only infuriated them more. Dovey jumped from foot to foot before unceremoniously dropping Baby June, running this way and that, crushing bushes in her wake. She kicked off her pumps and took off down one of the rows toward the Eldorado.

Astrid scooped up Baby June. *Jeezus*, she thought. The baby's heft slowed her. She needed to lose this kid. Looking back, the group of pickers stood at a safe distance. She ran as fast as she could toward them, flung the child into Emelina's arms, and took off after Dovey who was slapping and screaming and running in circles.

Astrid caught up to Dovey, "Stop smacking them and run to the shed!"

Mrs. Shield did not stop slapping. She tried to scream but, as soon as she opened her mouth, it filled with bees. Dozens took residence in her hair. They crawled in her ears, over her neck, beneath her shirt. She began spitting bees out of her mouth, sticking her fingers inside her cheek to scrape them out. Her dance became more frenzied: arms flailing, feet kicking, head whipping from side to side. Finally, she tripped and began rolling on the ground.

Astrid had a few angry bees on her and felt the stings on her neck and cheeks. Dovey's skin was barely visible beneath the swarming blanket. Astrid knelt, cleared as many as she could off Dovey's face, covered it with her bandana, lifted her beneath her arms, and dragged her toward the tool shed an acre away. The bees stung Astrid through her shirt until it felt like an electrical charge arcing between them. She tried not to imagine how much Dovey's skin was being pierced.

Once outside the tool shed, Astrid ripped apart a cardboard basket liner and used it to scrape as many bees as she could off Dovey before pushing her into the shed and closing the door tightly. The pickers used this shed to store lunch coolers and bags. She'd heard the ancient Ford's rumbling engine and knew Emelina would be on her way to the farmhouse for help. Astrid fumbled in her purse for something to scrape the stingers out of Dovey's skin. She quickly found her license and started working on the delicate stingers in Dovey's face. She took deep breaths to try to calm her shaking hands. She had to be careful to push each stinger in the right direction—like wheedling a splinter—so that it didn't simply snap and keep delivering more venom. Dovey's eyelids swelled shut. Her lips and cheeks ballooned to giant welts, the skin stretched so tightly that it shone like an overfilled water balloon.

The shed was ancient. It smelled of years of toil, dirt, and sweat. Dust-moted daggers of light fell through the window and Astrid positioned Dovey into that light. Dovey slumped, legs splayed, against a row of dirt-covered spades, pitchforks, and rakes while Dovey's chest heaved and her breathing became labored and difficult. Astrid concentrated on getting as many stingers out of her face as she could. Her skin felt taut enough to explode, and the bees ensnared in her hair buzzed angrily.

"Stay awake, Mrs. Shield. You awake?" Astrid shook her shoulders. Mrs. Shield nodded weakly.

Astrid concentrated on a clump of stingers in the middle of Dovey's long neck. She found it ironic that since finding out about her father's mistresses, she'd imagined elaborate ways to kill them. This could have been one most gruesome way.

Astrid used her thumbnail to dig out a particularly stubborn stinger just below Dovey's clavicle. As she worked, she whispered, "I wanted you to die."

Dovey pushed mangled bees out of her mouth with her tongue. They squirmed, belly up, on her chin.

Mrs. Ehrlich's truck rumbled toward the shed. The baking soda mixture she'd bring would surely be no match for the amount of venom pumped into Dovey. Mrs. Ehrlich would know that and would have already called an ambulance.

"I fantasized about kidnapping my dad and you— and those other women, too—and taking you to some abandoned barn, tying you up, explaining how badly you'd hurt Mama, and leaving you there to die.

I thought of everything: how I would give him just enough water so he would be alive to see you suffer."

Dovey pushed more dead bees out of her mouth with a swollen tongue.

Truck tires skidded to a stop and Mrs. Ehrlich, followed by Emelina, burst through the door. Mrs. Ehrlich's wiry gray hair looked electric. The shed felt too small for all of them. Astrid stood, found a Ball jar and, with Emelina, started coaxing the remaining bees tangled in Dovey's hair into it.

Mrs. Ehrlich knelt next to Dovey, "Called an ambulance. What in the hell was she doing in my fields?" It was an angry, rhetorical question. She abruptly motioned for Emelina to give her the baking soda mixture and, leaning over Dovey, started spreading it over the woman's face with a spatula as if frosting a cake.

Dovey tried to speak but her lips had swollen to the size of sausages. Since they couldn't make her out, Mrs. Ehrlich assumed it was about the baby.

"Hush, now. Just a few stings. She's safe at the house."

An ambulance whined in the distance.

Mrs. Ehrlich abandoned the spatula, dumped the paste onto Dovey, and used her hands to spread it. "Let's get her to the truck and meet the ambulance at the main road."

Emelina and Astrid positioned themselves on either side of Dovey, lifted her under each arm, and ungraciously deposited her in the rusted truck bed. They hopped up to sit on either side of her. She laid perfectly straight, one hand gripping Astrid's hand tightly and the other folded over her chest. In the distance, the ambulance's red flashing lights closed the gap. Mrs. Ehrlich fishtailed the truck, berries and plants spewing in her wake, and drove diagonally, right across her fields, to meet the ambulance at the main road. When she slammed the old farm truck to a stop, Dovey started to shake: first her head and then her shoulders and then her entire upper half. At first Astrid thought it was a seizure but then saw the tears sprouting from Dovey's swollen eyes. It was then, with Dovey hanging on for dear life, that Astrid peeled her fingers away, hopped out of the truck, and let the white-coated men whisk her away.

Cloaking Device

The first thing Marine Guard William Goynes, Jr. noticed when he stepped off the plane and onto American soil for the first time in four hundred and forty-four days was his wife's belly. It strained the buttons of her cream wool coat like she'd squirreled away an enormous nut for the winter. He wanted to ask, *Who knocked you up?* But how do you ask your wife such a delicate question with a flag-waving crowd of family and friends and hangers-on chanting "USA! USA! USA!" and cameras and mics and that hot brunette reporter from Channel 12 is inches from your face and Gwen throwing her arms around your neck to plant a wet kiss on your lips?

On the way home from Bishop Airport, the glow from the hero's welcome melting in the furnace blast of reality, snow falling outside like he'd become trapped on the wrong side of a snow globe, his dad driving, his kid sister in the passenger seat, he and Gwen both tucked in the back of the old Buick Roadmaster, she talked a blue streak. It was nervous talk and he knew, from the looks his dad shot him in the rearview, that she wouldn't stop until they got to Ponderosa. As Gwen's grackle-chatter continued, his sister turned to fix an insistent stare at Will and he noticed that, during his absence, she'd transformed from a slouching, angry teen into an elegant woman.

Breaking her stare, he buried his face in Gwen's hair, breathed in the powdery scent of it, felt its silkiness on his lips. Everything was coming at him too fast. He wanted to cry. He wanted to confess. He wanted to tell her what he'd done. He wanted to know what she'd done. He wanted to be forgiven and to forgive her.

His dad's gnarled farmer's knuckles, big as walnuts, gripped the steering wheel as he turned into Ponderosa. Throwing the Roadmaster into PARK, he turned to his son. "You two have a nice dinner. Talk. Pick you up in a few hours."

Alone, side by side at the salad bar, Will stared at his wife's pregnant profile and wondered who she was. Besides her body, he knew little about her. They'd met only two months before he left for basic training and, immediately after that, he became the youngest Marine assigned to the Iranian Embassy.

The night they met, he and his buddies used fake IDs to get into a popular yet skanky disco and, because he knew nothing of hard liquor, he pounded gin gimlets. With every drink, the floors glowed brighter. A huge disco ball reflected diamonds of light and Donna Summer's voice, like sex through speakers, became his personal soundtrack. He'd fallen into a fabulous, almost unbelievable dream where Gwen appeared suddenly, insistently, as if she'd been there forever. After he bought her a few drinks, she dragged him onto the dance floor where her tits bounced magnificently (when she wasn't rubbing against him) and, later in a dark corner of the bar, she let him pop one in his mouth.

The next day, his head delicate as an eggshell, he found her phone number in his jeans pocket. From the moment she picked up, she talked too fast—like a used car salesman trying to divert your attention from a busted frame. He kept asking, *What?* and only hung up after requesting a proper date the next night.

Everything with Gwen moved fast. Having sex with her felt like being tossed off a cliff; gravity evaporated until he hit the water hard, went deep, tumbled uncontrollably beneath the surface. He willingly lost himself in the tumult until, oxygen starved and weary, he clawed his way back to the surface. Sadly, he mistook this direct flight to sex heaven for love.

It wasn't until their third date that he noticed her eyes: bright, clear blue, and big with dark black lashes. The rest of her seemed relatively unremarkable: small lips, stringy hair, a high forehead, stooped shoulders, thick ankles. But those eyes and breasts were something else.

•

Today, at Ponderosa, Gwen wore a gold locket. The size of a silver dollar, it rested in the very pale indentation just above her sternum, between two perfectly curled tendrils of hair.

It looked new so he asked, "Who gave it to you?"

Gwen's head snapped to him, her eyes darkened, "What?"

"The locket?"

"Oh." She relaxed. "Got it for Christmas."

"Yeah? From who?"

"My sister. It's our wedding picture."

He smiled quickly. He didn't like his teeth. They were too small and closely set.

She opened the locket for him. His head had been sliced in half so that just the right side of his mouth smiled down at her. Her entire face looked not up at him but off to the side as if there were someone more important, someone who'd just walked by and taken her attention.

They made their way back to the table and sat across from each other. And then Gwen did something that Will did not expect: she bent her head to the pale mound of iceberg lettuce, motioned for Will's hand, and said, very quickly:

"Thank you for the world so sweet.

Thank you for the food we eat.

Thank you for the birds that sing.

Thank you, God, for everything. Amen."

Without lifting her head, she immediately began stuffing salad into her mouth. Will watched the perfectly straight part in her hair move up and down like a fishing line over the salad.

"So—" Will knew it wasn't the right question, that it was the coward's question, that it was too open-ended and wouldn't produce the desired results, but he asked anyway, "What's new?"

Gwen looked up, panicked, and stood too suddenly. "Excuse me! Everyone!" She tapped a knife against her water glass. "The man sitting across from me, here, is Marine Guard Will Goynes, Jr. just now returned from Eye-raq!"

A bald man, wedged tightly in the booth behind Will, asked, "Eye-raq?"

Will turned, "Iran."

Gwen continued, "Held four hundred-some days by the Iraqians. A real American hero!"

The customers, about thirty folks intent on choking down some U.S.-standard bovine, looked up from their plates. Within seconds, they'd pushed themselves away from their meals to give Will a standing ovation.

Soft-spoken and polite, Will raised his hand as if waiting to be called on in school. Gwen nodded, "Go ahead, Will."

Will stood. Everyone cheered. He wanted them to stop. He wanted to tell them what had really happened: that, as the youngest Marine at the Embassy, his captors targeted him to supply information. When he repeatedly gave his name, rank, service number, and date of birth, they handcuffed, blindfolded, and threw him in solitary. They told him they would gouge out his eyes, boil his feet in oil, chop off his thieving American hands. After a few months, they knew his sister's address at nursing school and promised to dismember her and send her body parts to his father's farm. After eighty days in a pitch-dark, freezing cell, he started hallucinating, crying, screaming to get out. After more than a hundred days, he stopped moving—just curled in a ball and tried to stay alive. They let him out after two hundred and fifty-one days on two conditions—that he rat out the hostages who spoke Farsi and promise to reveal the code the other hostages used to communicate.

Gwen tapped her glass with her knife to quiet the crowd, leaned over, and demanded, "Go ahead, Will. Say something."

Will stepped forward—all six-foot-three of him with a freshly-shaven head of dark stubble, round, sweet, freckled cheeks, and huge ears—and cleared his throat. He couldn't look up from the white and black tiled floor and realized he had nothing to say. Finally, after a prolonged period of licking his lips and swallowing hard, he managed, "It was Iran. Not Iraq."

The crowd waited expectantly and, when nothing more seemed forthcoming, the embarrassment folded them back in their seats. When Will sat down, Gwen clapped enthusiastically until everyone joined her. To his ears, the clapping sounded uninspired and slow, like the tapping he had been forced to decode. It triggered a dull, pulsing migraine he'd been fighting all day. Will looked at the bloody remains of his porterhouse—the too-white gristle, the curly, charred fat around the edges—hung his head, and began to cry.

•

His mother, who'd died when he was fifteen, always said, *Know thyself.*

When he left for his assignment in Iran, he'd thought he had. Now, he didn't know who he was. Or what he'd become. He kept seeing his interrogator, the one with the sleepy eye and corn kernel mole above his lip. He kept hearing himself telling that guy the secrets he knew about the people he was supposed to protect. He'd lost himself in those tellings. Didn't recognize himself at all. Now, he realized (and not for the first time) he didn't know Gwen. Couldn't tell you her favorite color or dessert, if she drank tea or coffee, if she smoked, if she was a side-sleeper, what she feared. He'd only known her body, and certainly not even that for very long. And after what he'd learned about himself, that didn't seem nearly enough.

He'd ratted out the CIA guys posing as diplomats. But how did his captors know about his family? Who'd ratted him out?

On the drive home, in the back seat of the old Roadmaster, with the snow falling more heavily now, the wind bullying it into commas that straddled the center line, Gwen shared the patriotic scene in Ponderosa. Every once in a while, Rebecca turned to look at Will. They were Irish twins born one year and one month apart. Shared the same smattering of freckles across their noses, the wide, doe-eyed stare some mistook for stupidity, the widow's peak of black hair neither could tame no matter how much of their father's Brylcreem they used.

The story kept going until Rebecca hooked her arm over the seat and looked from Gwen to her brother, "Now, who's the father of that baby? It can't be Will. Unless you froze his sperm and turkey basted."

Gwen gasped as if she'd been hooked in the cheek. "Yes. This. Well …"

Rebecca made a dramatic half-moon with an open palm and pointed to Gwen's stomach, "Yes. That."

There was no heat in Rebecca's voice. No righteous anger or indignation. She knew her brother hadn't asked. Wouldn't be able to.

They hit a slick patch and, for a split second, the Roadmaster pointed slightly off-course, became suspended, in motion but motionless, gliding, weightless.

Gwen dug her fingernails into Will's forearm and didn't let up, even when the tires firmly gripped the road. He knew how she felt. He'd been sliding, unanchored for what seemed like forever.

"Yes," Gwen kept her eyes glued to the back of Mr. Goynes's gray head, "Well, while you were gone, I found Jesus—"

"Jesus?" Rebecca rolled her eyes, "Well that explains it."

His Dad piped up, "You don't say?"

"Please," Will began, "let her finish."

"I met someone and I'd like a divorce." As soon as she said it, she adjusted herself away from Will as if he might pull her back into him. "I just didn't want to ruin your big homecoming. I didn't know how to do it. I didn't know. After all you've been through. I'm—"

Will held up his hand. He didn't need to hear it, didn't want an apology. Didn't know how to accept it. He wasn't angry or hurt or humiliated. He didn't hate her. He simply wanted Gwen and her worn overnight bag out of the Roadmaster. He wanted to crawl into his own bed and sleep until the pounding in his brain, the vice grip of revelation, the sidelong looks from his fellow Marines, the slaps on the back from his captors, the whispering of the diplomats, all of it, simply faded into the terrible, hazy mist of yesterday.

King of the Lakes

I hated these kids with their suped-up Novas and brown-bagged alcohol and weed and cigarettes and mohawks and hoodies and attitude and too-tight T-shirts and sex and pills and rock and punk and Chuck Taylors and malaise. Even through my ire their glittering youth nearly blinded me. Their young bodies pranced into adulthood, but first through New Canaan High, year after year, rosy cheeks and hormones and facial hair and developing bodies. They filed into my band class, every walking cliché making a goddamn statement. Flute-playing Amber with her flesh-hugging shirt and low-rise jeans. Just enough tawny, flawless abdomen, mind you, to catch your attention. Statement: slutty and proud of it. Trombone Jaz. One Z. Honestly. He wore a cigarette-burn bracelet on his wrist that would make an ER nurse flinch. Statement: self-mutilation is the last frontier, man. And, strolling in, late for the fifth time in as many days, was the if-you-flunk-senior-year-twice-let's-try-it-a-third-time Errol Flynn. He wore a baseball cap turned backward, a Technica tee, and chatted up Amber while beating out a rhythm on the bill of poor little Benjamin Jacob's baseball cap. Statement: I'm an idiot.

As for me, I'd been picked clean. A carcass curing in their light. Huge tufts of gray hair blotted out my natural black. I raised my music stand so I no longer looked down. Looking down revealed too many chins. My middle had turned thick and stiff. My right eyelid drooped. I hobbled. They whispered *Hobbit* behind my back. I knew. Someone etched it into the girls' bathroom stall door. Ms. Aboujamra = Hobbit. It was fitting, really. Since the accident, I did hobble. My right leg, now a whole two inches shorter, fitted with a thick-soled orthopedic shoe hidden under my long skirt, dragged over the gray-flecked hallways as I relived, in an unending loop, the moment seventeen years ago when I hastily fit my newborn's car seat into its base and got behind the wheel. I was in a hurry, doing fifty down Saginaw Street, looking back to pop in a pacifier, and didn't see a turning semi until I slammed on my brakes, far too late to do any good. Out of the corner of my right eye, just as my head hit the steering wheel and the dash came crushing toward me, I watched that car seat hurtle, unspeakably fast, through the funneled spider web of front window.

She would have been a junior this year. Maybe even would have sat in this very room with a saxophone, flute, or French horn resting on her thigh. But she wasn't. Every time I walked into that school with its heady aroma of deodorant and sweat and pine cleaner, and looked at those gorgeous children full of potential, I wondered at the simple fact that any of them had made it here alive.

All this, good lord, and it was only nine-thirty in the morning.

"Mr. Errol Flynn." I sighed every time I said his name, "Take your seat."

There was something dangerous about him. I knew this. He smirked, adjusted his jeans so that his wallet chain caught the light streaming through the room's eastern windows, walked to his stool, picked it up, and hauled out of the room.

As usual, snickers erupted from the trombone section.

I wrote him off and tapped my baton on my music stand. The cork slipped in my sweaty palm. Caroline Godrich, my first chair French horn, God bless her, adjusted her posture: Keds flat on the floor, shoulders down, chest out. As for the rest, they uniformly wore a look of blankness.

"Let's get started, shall we?" Skinny Kenny Franks, my third seat flutist, must have tangled with a bottle of his dad's cologne. I shifted my stool away from him and fluttered the sheet music over my head, "Take out Broege's *The Headless Horseman*." A chorus of moans erupted. I scoured the rectangular room with my gaze. The moans diminished and the sound of fluttering sheet music filled the room. I used to live for that sound.

Stevie Simpson, his rosebud face peeking behind thick red curls, raised his hand. Behind him, on the back wall, I had tacked note values, adorned with colorful flowers, to a corkboard running the length of the room. "Yes, Mr. Simpson?"

"I don't have the third tuba part."

"You don't have it at all or you left it at home?"

Well into a lifetime with no response, I swiveled on my stool, pulled open a drawer and rifled through the files to find the tuba sheet music. It traveled down the flute section, through the clarinets, past the horns perched at the end of the row nearest the percussionists (whose stools I moved as far away as possible), and back to the tuba section.

Lifting my arms, baton in my left hand, we began. Not twelve stanzas into the piece, Errol came tromping back in with his stool. Setting it down, he grabbed a pair of cymbals and promptly crashed them together.

I stopped. The band stopped. Everyone except clueless Stevie Simpson, of course, keeping the bassline on tuba, stopped. I rapped my baton angrily on the stand.

"Mr. Flynn. You are interrupting class and breaking your classmates' concentration. We are playing *The Headless Horseman*. Take out your music and get busy." Heart pounding, I continued. "Be aware of the music's dynamic and stylistic details."

I felt something inside me winding. Too tight, maybe. Yes, definitely too tight as I watched him adjust his ponytail and pull his wallet out of his back pocket. He snagged something that looked like a toothpick and stuck it in his mouth. Picking up his cymbals, he asked, "Why the hell's it called *Headless Horseman*? What's *that* got to do with anything?"

I ignored his intelligent, sensitive question. Again, I raised my arms, and readied the others to play when the usually quiet Caroline piped up, "It's from Washington Irving's *Legend of Sleepy Hollow*." And under her breath, but not quietly enough, she added, "—you Neanderthal."

Everyone laughed. Errol stood there for a moment, stunned, I supposed, that anyone, let alone a girl, would have the guts to call him out. "Wha'djew call me, Godrich?" He started for Caroline, cymbals in those big paws, chest puffed, head bobbing.

That winding, taut thing inside me suddenly snapped. I imagined Errol sandwiching Caroline's head between those cymbals. I wouldn't let it happen, so I stood, picked up my metal stool, and hurled it five feet into the open space between the two combatants. It hit the floor, bounced, and connected with the boy's chin to send him flying ass-backward into the bass drum.

Every last one of those kids tensed, anticipating my next move. Some even covered their heads with their instruments. After that, something inside me shattered. I slid down the wall, curled in a ball, and relived the accident all over again: everything moving slowly but swiftly, my bones breaking, sirens and flashing lights, the deep-down ache of sudden loss, and that sickening feeling that something wonderful had come to an abrupt and irreversible end.

•

Being asked to leave New Canaan High gave me time to think and investigate interests I'd never had time to pursue. At least, that's what I told myself. Since my daughter's death and, following that, the disintegration of my marriage, I'd worked nonstop, spending even summers directing high school bands at Wahbekaness Arts Academy. So, a few weeks later, I packed my car and drove north.

Wahbekaness occupied a wooded, sandy stretch of land between two inland lakes adjacent to the state park. The director's office overlooked frozen Lake Wahbekaness. Fifteen miles west, Lake Michigan's great blue belly bloomed into Wisconsin, Illinois, Indiana.

Her assistant hugged me a beat too long and eyed me with a mix of pity and concern. Bobby arrived balancing a travel mug of tea, books, and her brief-case. Her cheekbones were high and wide below deep-set eyes, touched by caramel skin, silver hair in a neat bun. She'd always moved easily, elegantly. I'd long admired her yet wouldn't admit that I'd always had a bit of a crush on her, one I would never act upon. Her authority was unquestioned. Faculty and students alike adored her. She was an accomplished dancer and taught at least a few classes every term. She squeezed my shoulder before settling behind her desk.

I opened my mouth to speak.

"I heard."

"News travels."

"That kind does."

Yes, well … I'd like to explain—"

She waved her hand. "Is it true you threw a stool at that kid?"

I nodded.

"Impressive." She tried hiding a conspiratorial smile. "Well, Elizabeth, I've known you far too long—what's it been, twenty years—to be concerned about an isolated incident." Her tone shifted, all playfulness aside, "It was isolated, right?

"Yes."

She leaned back in her chair. Behind her sat a credenza filled with framed photos of students, colleagues, headshots of Josephine Baker, Billie Holiday, Mikhail Baryshnikov.

"You need some time off. This is a perfect time to take a break before the summer campers arrive."

I had been determined to explain myself, to convince her that I could start teaching the academy kids—impressive kids who came from all over the country, all over the world, really, to study dance and music and writing and visual arts. And while her offer startled me, a break suddenly seemed like something I'd had coming for a very long time.

"A break," I nodded, "might do me some good."

•

My spartan instructor's cottage sat on the bank of the lake, framed by white pines. I quickly settled into a routine and, because the boarding school students didn't come to this part of the camp in the winter, spent hours every morning in one of the fieldstone and mortar practice cottages working on my technique, imagining the piano's notes winding through the forest, skating across the lake, curling up into the sky.

It was my habit to begin practicing at six-thirty every morning. I had been working on a particularly difficult passage of Janáček's *On an Overgrown Path in the Mists* when something passed the smudged window of the practice cottage. I walked to the wooden door and opened it. Two people, backlit by the morning light, stood in the lightly falling snow. Beneath puffy down coats, I could tell that one was tall and lanky, a teenage boy, perhaps, and the other slightly shorter. His mom?

"Sorry," the woman said, "it was just so beautiful." They turned abruptly and started down the path toward the state park.

"You're welcome to listen."

They stopped and, after a moment, the mother tugged her son's arm toward the practice cottage. As they approached, I noticed that she wore oversized sunglasses and that her lip bulged on one side.

I motioned to two folding chairs by the door, turned up the space heater, and made my way back to the piano. My arm had broken in the accident and, even after all this time, still ached in the cold. I tried to ignore it and started playing again. My unanticipated audience sat motionless as I began a particularly dreamy, dissonant passage. I had the fingering down but I was trying to capture Janáček's intent, the music's texture and finely-honed nuances, its grief-stricken mood.

I'm not sure how long I'd been playing when the pain in my arm became unbearable. I stopped and the two stood abruptly. I walked around the piano to get a better look at them. They were definitely mother and son. Their round faces, sandy blonde hair, and nervous movements were nearly identical.

I extended my hand, "Elizabeth."

The woman removed her glove and took my hand. "Audrey. And this is my son, Jason." Now that I was close to her, I could see an angry welt beneath her sunglasses. She also had a vertical cut on her lip. Both injuries looked fresh and painful. She noticed me looking and brought her fingertips to the welt. I remembered using that same technique to cool my injuries.

She slowly removed the glasses. The welt extended in varying purple-red hues from her temple to the bridge of her nose, halfway down her cheek and above her eyebrow. The white of her eye nearest the temple was startlingly red.

"Would you like some tea?" I asked a little too quickly.

"That would be nice. Thank you."

We made our way through a light snow that made the path slippery and coated my eyelashes. I settled them at the kitchen table and pulled out a bag of frozen peas. "Try this," I said, handing the bag to Audrey who sat rod-straight and alert as if awaiting a call to battle. When she pressed the bag to her eye, her entire body relaxed. The boy kept glancing at the door as if he expected someone to appear suddenly.

"Cold for camping. You must have the whole place to yourself." I motioned to the state park.

She smiled. "It's been very peaceful."

She knew that I knew why they were there, why she'd pulled her son out of whatever life they had to be here, secluded, and alone.

I made a big production of offering them sugar or cream, some scones I'd made, and settled myself across the table. Behind me, through a picture window, the lake sat frozen and motionless, pressed flat by a heavy sky.

I guessed that Jason was sixteen or seventeen. His long bangs covered gray eyes that were at once wary and innocent. Baby fat still clung to his cheeks but his body was lanky and lean. Audrey had the hungry look of a woman who'd had her choice of men, married too young and too hastily, and was just figuring it all out.

•

In the months immediately following my baby's death, I saw Jesus four times: in the dairy aisle of Mitchell's Finer Foods buying cheese, at the post office waiting to mail a stack of Christmas cards, shopping for a pickup at Tremaine Chevrolet, and eating a Coney dog at Angelo's. At first he startled me, but then I got used to his hippie clothes and long hair.

He'd abandoned me, though, and I hadn't seen him in years. So when I walked out of my cottage that February morning to find him in the middle of the lake, I stopped abruptly. The cold had transformed the lake into a giant luminescent skull, stretching from shore to shore, jagged in places where it had thawed and refrozen. He'd always been busy with his errands, unaware of me staring at him, but this time he gazed directly at me. He wore a one-piece, bright orange snowmobile suit and held a fishing line that disappeared into a hole in the ice.

There'd been so much talk of him at my baby's funeral. Complete strangers approached to say Jesus would ease my suffering. Jesus would lift me up. Jesus this. Jesus that. As if he would rush in with thick gauze to cauterize my anguish. Why hadn't he saved Charlotte? Why not a preemptive strike? How about that, Jesus? Huh? Why did he think I would need him now after such utter neglect?

I suddenly felt furious, balled my fists, stomped my foot. I screamed, "How dare you! Showing up after all this time! Who do you think you are?"

He didn't answer.

"Elizabeth?"

I turned to see Audrey and Jason standing in the practice cottage entrance waiting for me.

When I approached, Audrey leaned in, "You see him, too, huh?"

But when I stopped to look at her, she had settled herself on the folding chair, face blank, hands still on her lap, waiting for me to begin.

•

One afternoon, I walked to the park entrance with the sole purpose of seeing Audrey and Jason's campsite. Only three were occupied. Two hosted fancy RVs owned by retired couples who cooked on propane grills. The third held a dented pickup with DEVINE LANDSCAPING stenciled on both doors, an ancient Play-Mor camper, and a clothesline strung between two trees.

•

Audrey and Jason joined me every morning, promptly at seven, in the practice cottage, followed by my invitation to tea. After a week of small talk, I learned that they'd come from Fenton, where Audrey and her husband owned a landscaping business and Jason had been a junior. After the second week, I started letting them use my kitchen and shower.

The third week, I told Bobby about Audrey's predicament and asked, since the camp would soon be full for the summer, if she might offer her a job. After an interview and reference check, she hired Audrey as a maintenance worker—one of a team responsible for landscaping, emptying trash cans, painting cottages, repairing torn screens, and generally keeping the facilities looking good and running smoothly.

Bobby set up Audrey and Jason in the camp staff apartment at the edge of the campground, hidden from students and campers by distance and a thicket of pines. Nearly every day after work, they came to my cottage to have dinner, play *Risk*, and drink tea.

One evening, Audrey poked Jason in the ribs (which she was always doing because, she said, it made him laugh and he was entirely too serious) and encouraged him to tell me about his science project. He'd enrolled in the local public high school and won a statewide essay contest. The award was to work with scientists from Michigan Tech's Geological Engineering Department on a weather balloon project. His usually cool demeanor changed as he excitedly detailed how he would be interning with the scientists most of the summer. They would teach him the physics behind the launch, how to attach the payload lines and parachutes, calculate lift, fill balloons with helium, launch them, tracking the lofty rigs with ham radios. He invited me to the first launch scheduled when the weather warmed.

Audrey sat across the table listening intently to her son. She'd changed in just the few weeks I'd known her. The tension that kept her alert and on edge had eased somewhat, she laughed and smiled. She was very lovely in a rough-hewn way with her hair pulled away from her face, her arched dark eyebrows framing gray eyes, her fingernails bitten down to the quick. She moved athletically, surely, like a pretty woman who'd constantly had to prove herself.

I felt a strange possessiveness over her. I couldn't explain it but I know now that I wanted to, at the very least, protect her. I wasn't sure how I would do that. She was only five years younger than I was. It was intense, though strange, this feeling.

When she noticed my gaze, she tilted her head, smiled, and looked away.

•

The summer campers always arrived like a cacophonous flock of birds. Spring's dramatic thaw, so breathtakingly lovely in this part of the state, accompanied their descent. The instrumentalists lugged heavy black cases, dancers flitted by light as air, theater students spoke loudly and dramatically, writers and visual artists brooded.

Something about having Jason in my life, and being part of his, softened me towards these kids. I'd hated them for so long that this emotional thaw took me completely off guard.

On Move-In Saturday, Audrey, Jason, and I stood at the entrance of one of the lodges. We directed parents, answered questions. Just as the last campers said goodbye to their folks, I felt a tap on my shoulder. I turned to see Caroline Godrich with a French horn case in one hand and a large duffle slung over her shoulder.

"Hello, Ms. Aboujamra."

"Caroline! How nice!" I turned to Audrey and Jason. "Caroline was a student of mine—"

Caroline finished my sentence, "At New Canaan High."

"I thought you usually went to Blue Lake?"

"I got a scholarship. Plus, I knew you taught here summers."

My breath caught. I wanted to gather her in my arms. "Well, isn't that nice. Is Astrid here, too?"

"No, she decided to stay in New Canaan. But we'll be ushering at Whiting together this summer."

She so reminded me of her mother—that classic beauty of thick hair and dark-lashed eyes and intelligent expressiveness. Katherine Godrich and I had been classmates at New Canaan, friends even, until she started running around with a fast crowd, so unlike her in every way, and got wrapped up in drugs. She tried, after giving birth to Caroline, to clean up her act but failed. Eventually, she moved out of New Canaan altogether and left Caroline to be raised by the child's grandparents. I doubted that Caroline even knew her.

The girl's gaze suddenly shifted to Jason who hadn't taken his eyes off her since we'd turned to find her standing there.

•

One night, when Jason stayed home to do summer school homework, Audrey and I sat at my kitchen table drinking tea.

"Jason's been meeting Caroline after practice."

I nodded. I'd seen them. Tall, lanky Jason waiting patiently for Caroline to pack up her French horn and join him.

"She's a good kid. She was in band until I left—" I stopped to recall the rumors of what those animals did to Caroline beneath the bleachers. I'd never asked Billy Vance, the custodian who found her, if the rumors were true. Why hadn't I? I guess I was still too wrapped up in my own tragedy to clearly see the implications of hers. Why hadn't I demanded that the administration look into the allegations? I suddenly felt complicit. "I—"

Audrey poured herself more tea. "What?"

"Nothing."

"You left your job right after the first of the year?"

I eyed her. "I threw a stool at a kid who was about to attack … another student."

Audrey nodded. "And that was wrong?"

I laughed and considered telling her that I was protecting Caroline, how Errol had been coming after her, how I'd felt, even then, that my part in the collective silence of her rape was a crime.

"At least you're not hiding."

"I've got that going for me then."

After a while, she started talking about her husband Nick and how he got mean when he drank. How she'd filed for divorce but he wouldn't let them alone. How she'd tried sticking it out, hiding the abuse, for Jason's sake.

She shook her head. "Yeah, well, he's found us twice before. It's just a matter of time before he finds us again."

"What'll you do then?"

"Whatever I have to."

•

The next morning in the practice cottage, Jesus appeared while I worked on Ravel's *Gaspard de la Nuit*. I'd been practicing this particular piece so fervently and knew it so well that I lost myself in the music. When I stopped, Jesus leaned in the doorway. He wore the exact same outfit as Errol did the day I kicked him out: a baseball cap turned backward, jeans, a Technica tee, and silver wallet chain hooked to his right belt loop. He'd even pulled his hair into a ponytail. Producing a leather-bound journal, he read Aloysius Bertrand's poem in a soft, lilting voice:

"Her song murmured, she beseeched me to accept her ring on my finger, to be the husband of an Ondine, and to visit her in her palace and be king of the lakes.

"And as I was replying to her that I loved a mortal, sullen and spiteful, she wept some tears, uttered a burst of laughter, and vanished in a shower that streamed white down the length of my blue stained glass windows."

I stood. "What do you want?"

Jesus stuck his finger in his ear, scratched vigorously. And then he was gone.

●

The second week of camp, warm breezes and clear skies replaced spring's chill. As I walked out of the open-air theater after band practice, I spotted Jason and Caroline near the log gazebo at the center of camp talking to a tall, powerfully-built man I didn't recognize. From the opposite direction, I saw Audrey moving quickly toward them. Even fifty yards away, I could see the resemblance between the man and Jason— the slope of their shoulders, the shape of their heads. Audrey took Jason's and Caroline's arms to lead them away. The man lifted his hands, palms forward, as if in surrender, walked to a green truck and drove away.

●

Since I knew Mr. Godrich, I called to arrange for Caroline to stay a few days with me, between sessions, to join us at Jason's weather balloon launch. It was all Jason could talk about.

The weather was clear and still the morning of the launch. The plan was for us to leave at daybreak to meet the scientists from Michigan Tech about thirty minutes away in Empire. They'd been spending the spring researching weather patterns at Sleeping Bear Dunes. We were on US 31 when I noticed a green pickup following us. I didn't say anything, figured they didn't need to know, and hoped that my imagination was getting the best of me.

Of course, it wasn't my imagination. The truck stayed a good ways behind Audrey's truck the entire journey. Audrey seemed carefree and happy until, when we got onto M-22, she glanced in the rearview and spotted the truck closing in.

"It's Nick," she mumbled under her breath.

At the intersection of M-22 and M-72, Nick pulled up close and honked his horn. Jason and Caroline flipped around. Then Jason leaned forward, panicked, "Mom—"

"I see him."

I looked at Audrey. "What should we do?"

"Let's get Jason there. Then I'll talk to Nick."

Nick tailed us through the little town of Empire, down the drive leading to the deserted stretch of Empire Beach. To our west, Lake Michigan's wide beach would serve as the perfect launching pad. To our east, fish-shaped South Bar Lake stretched parallel to Lake Michigan. A parking lot, playground, and outhouse occupied a two-hundred-foot land bridge between South Bar Lake and Lake Michigan. When we pulled in, two young, scruffy-bearded men were already unloading helium canisters from a van. As soon as she parked, Audrey jumped out of the car but Nick was already walking toward us. She met him halfway and Jason kept close behind. Caroline and I introduced ourselves to the scientists and got to work unloading the van, but I kept an ear and an eye on what was going on. Nick slapped Jason on the back and asked him, jovially, what was up. Jason stood next to his mother, hands in his short pockets, shoulders curved inward.

I couldn't hear much of what followed. Audrey stood a few feet away from Nick, out of his fist's range, I imagined, and from her gestures it looked like she was trying to reason with him. Jason kept scratching the back of his neck with his knuckle. Finally, Nick turned around, walked to his truck, pulled out a beat-up aluminum lawn chaise and big red cooler and pulled both onto the beach.

As Audrey and Jason walked toward us, I watched Nick flip open the red cooler, dig around, produce a beer, and crack it open.

Audrey pulled me aside. "He's reasonable when he's not drunk. Drove all night to get here and just happened to see us pulling out of camp. But that cooler is full of beer. It's only a matter of time."

"Should I drive back to town? Get a cop?"

"No. That would ruin Jason's day."

"Won't he ruin it anyway?"

"Fifty-fifty chance."

•

Since the scientists didn't know about the situation with Nick, it was full steam ahead. Their enthusiasm took Jason's mind off of his father's presence. Jason helped one scientist lay out big blue tarps, unroll weather balloons, and begin filling them. The other scientist put Caroline to work untangling lines and parachutes.

Thin, high clouds etched the sky and a gentle offshore breeze polished Lake Michigan's azure surface. Audrey and I pulled out our own folding chairs and dug our toes in the sand. It felt so good to do that—bare feet digging into cool sand. Bumpy, white scars patterned my right leg, so busted up from the accident, and I tried to bend my left knee so that my right didn't appear so much shorter. Audrey's long legs and muscular arms were already tan from landscaping the camp's entrance and public areas.

To our left, past Nick, Sleeping Bear Dunes' cliffs rose like earthbound waves about to crash into the lake. Even from fifty yards away, I could hear Nick cracking open can after can. When he finished one, he'd crush it and drop it to the sand.

By eleven, all thirty of the enormous weather balloons had been filled and placed under gigantic nets to keep them secure. They undulated beneath the nets, rising and falling with the slightest breeze.

Jason walked up. "Ma, Dr. Martin forgot the ham radio trackers back at their campsite. Or—" he looked back to where the two scientists seemed to be arguing as they hopped in the van and pulled away, "they can't remember if they even brought them from Houghton. It's gonna take them about twenty minutes … at least. Dr. Barrow is pissed because the balloons only have so much loft and if they left the trackers in Houghton, all this will be a waste."

We decided to eat lunch until they returned. I opened a blanket, settled down cross-legged, and unpacked the sandwiches and drinks I'd brought. As I distributed the food, Nick wove toward us dragging his lawn chaise and cooler. He managed to pull both between us and the netted balloons before stumbling over to stand beside Audrey.

He pointed to me, "Who's this?"

Audrey looked at me and shook her head just barely to tell me to keep quiet.

"My teacher," Jason lied.

Nick's eyes were swollen and bloodshot. He pointed to Caroline, "And you?"

Jason answered again, "Her daughter."

"They have names?"

"Ms. Aboujamra and Caroline."

"Mzzzzz Abuhum-wha? What kinda name is that?" He poked his bare toe into Audrey's lower back.

Audrey bit her lip and looked ready to cry. "Let's take a walk, Nick."

"Don' wanna."

"Let the kids eat."

"Who's stoppin' 'em?"

Audrey didn't answer.

He kicked Audrey so that she pitched sideways, "I said, who's stoppin' 'em?"

He leaned down, grabbed Audrey's arm and, with surprising strength, yanked her up. Jason scrambled to his feet to hold Audrey's other arm. Just then, I looked at Caroline. Her eyes were wide in terror. I got up, took her hand and stepped out of Nick's range.

Nick leaned into Audrey. "I asked you a question."

"Let her go, Dad."

"Shut up, Jace."

Jason's face hardened and he put one palm on his father's shoulder.

"Back off, Jace. It's between us."

Audrey's voice shook. "It's okay, Jason. Let me handle this."

Jason shook his head. "Let her go."

Nick's arm snapped up and his open hand caught Audrey's cheek. Her head snapped toward Jason but she didn't fall.

Jason started crying, "Dad—"

"Big baby, Jace. Blubbering like a little kid. Jesus."

Just then, a pristine VW van—red on the bottom and white on top—screamed into the parking lot. Jesus, long-haired, painfully thin, wearing yellow surf shorts, jumped out, pulled a windsurfer board from the van's back hatch, and carried it to where we stood.

Nick shook his head as if he didn't trust his eyes.

Jesus didn't move or shift his gaze from Nick who finally asked, "What's it to ya?"

Jesus crooked his finger at Nick. "Come here."

Nick stepped within inches of Jesus. He towered over him, brought his face into his, breathed fire.

"You've got to chill, man."

"What?"

"Chill." And with that, Jesus dropped the board, brought his index finger just over Nick's heart and, as if his finger had become a magnet and Nick a piece of steel, he pivoted and lowered Nick into the aluminum chaise. Then he put his index and middle fingers on Nick's eyes and brought them down. Nick laid perfectly still, eyes closed, apparently in a deep sleep.

Jesus turned to us and threw his thumb over his shoulder. "You want to help me with the balloons?" He made his way under the netting and took out one enormous bunch of balloons. They nearly took him off his feet until Jason grabbed them, too, and they walked the bubbled mass toward Nick. "Well," Jesus motioned to us, "tie them on."

We did, of course, until we'd tied all thirty balloons around the chaise's aluminum tubing. Caroline and Jason held one side while Audrey and I held the other. The balloons bobbed above us, the lines jockeying back and forth.

Jesus rested both hands on the aluminum tubing above Nick's head. "Of course, I'm no scientist, but based upon my calculations, he should reach peak altitude in about ninety minutes. Once the balloons start bursting, it will take another thirty minutes to parachute back to earth. You ready?"

We nodded.

Jesus stepped back and, on the count of three, we let go.

Undesirable Interruptions

The blaze of yellow ribbons outside Will's bedroom window, ghostly in the twilight, served as a constant reminder of his disgrace. In his absence, scout troops had tied the ribbons to every stationary object on the Goynes's farm—on pines, beeches, the old oak, the fence posts surrounding what would be a summer kitchen garden. How strange, he thought, that while he sat alone and naked in solitary, a near-hysterical, patriotic fervor had strangled the country in the form of yellow ribbons. They fluttered off gas station signs, on shopping carts, car antennas, strollers, three-ring binders, flagpoles.

Will's dad told him that when it first happened, when he first heard of his son's capture, he'd tried to distract himself by humming an old Andrews Sisters song about a woman who wore a yellow ribbon for her missing soldier. It had been one of his favorites and reminded him of his jubilant return from World War II. He didn't know the current song by Tony Orlando and Dawn. But

Will, Jr. did. And he knew it was about a convict coming home from prison, waiting to see if his girl still wanted him. Well, his girl didn't want him. And neither did the U.S. Army.

•

On a bitterly cold day in February, Will grabbed the freight's steel handle and hopped the engine's steps. He'd been doing it since he was a kid: ride to the edge of their fields and hop Harry Keck's freight just as it slowed at the bend of Thread Creek.

Harry's orange, white-man afro nearly hit the engine's ceiling while his long legs stuck out at odd angles when they weren't engaged in running the freight. With his deep voice, perfectly defined jaw, a head so square it sat like granite on his thick shoulders, his cheeks red and full, Will imagined him the red-headed Dudley Do-Right. Shave his head, take away his weed, and he'd be the picture perfect image of a Marine—except he'd had no interest in war. He'd been drafted in 1970 and, ever since he held the draft notice in his hand, had damned-to-hell Representative Alexander Pirnie every night in his prayers.

A plume of pungent smoke escaped as Will entered the cab and, almost simultaneously, Harry wrapped him in a bone-crushing hug that lifted him off his feet. "Lemme look at you." Harry stepped back, shifted his gaze to the tracks ahead, turned back to Will. "Bastards let you keep your fingers and toes, huh?" He offered Will the blunt. "Great stuff."

Will tried to smile but only managed a sullen nod.

"Hit that thing!" Keck pulled a lighter out of his overalls and relit a cigar that had gone cold.

Will didn't feel like smoking but took a small, reluctant hit. The cab smelled skunky, sweaty, of engine grease and something indefinable that wasn't unlike the smell of the room in which he'd been held—that distinct odor of a human trapped in a small space.

Harry settled back into his worn seat and kept the train slow as Will stamped his feet, took off his gloves, and pulled up a milk crate. Will looked out the spattered windshield to the track stretching in front of him like a long, dull promise.

Harry killed the blunt and, since Will had never been much of a conversationalist, filled the space with his encyclopedic knowledge of current events. He devoured every paper he could get his hands on and had rigged a simple wooden frame with clothespins to hold newspapers so he could read while he kept an eye on the track.

"Let's see, man, what have you missed?"

Without waiting for Will's reply, he explained how the FBI had entrapped a few greedy bastard congressmen in Abscam, President Carter's missteps, and Thatcher and Reagan and Castro and El Salvador and Qaddafi and on and on until Will just heard the timber of his voice, the rise and fall and rhythm of it, and let it wash over him. How did Harry store it all? Why was it even important? But, as Harry talked, he started to sense a connection between himself and all of these events. A connection he couldn't trace from point A to point B but a connection he felt, now, more than ever, pulling at the seams of him. When he'd been in solitary, he'd become convinced he was suspended in a spider's web. It wasn't fine and invisible like the ones he'd walked through at home but instead moist, sticky, and ominously dark. In the murky cold, starving, his clothes conspired against him, to become part of the web and, in a fit, he'd ripped them to shreds with his teeth and nails. After that, the cold nearly killed him. It took his captors a week to bring new trousers and a thin, cotton shirt.

Harry's talk about gunrunning and underhanded government deals and his theory that Reagan sold arms to Iran in exchange for the hostages helped Will piece things together. Hearing about the calculated dealings of politicians and officials somewhat softened his humiliation.

He'd always wondered at a person's ability to withstand public humiliation and, now, it was him they'd be talking about in hushed tones in diners and on street corners. He wondered how long it would take for the rumors to begin.

And then he thought about Caroline Godrich. Back in elementary, Caroline and Astrid Miracal had pulled a bulky and punching Ricky Hatterfield off him during recess. Ever since then, the three had stuck together. Caroline and Astrid were both away at college now, though, and although he'd called them, he hadn't seen them since his return. For some reason, he kept thinking about how, when Caroline was a freshman, he'd heard rumors that three seniors raped her under the bleachers during a football game. What quiet, shy Caroline was doing under those bleachers with those boys, Will didn't know. Regardless, they'd gotten her drunk. She'd passed out. They saw an opportunity. That next week, at school, with everyone hissing, *Caroline got fingered* as she slid silently against the lockers, he'd marveled at her grit and wondered about the toll it took on her. What did the focus of so much mean speculation and gossip do to a person—aside from the very crime itself?

Harry's voice buzzed over Will's internal chatter. The night before, a freezing rain covered everything in a slick, glossy coat. Branches bent and cracked like crystal candlesticks. A thick crust armored the snow. The tracks glistened and Will imagined the ice shattering, spraying, crushing beneath the train's heft.

Will couldn't tell you what the hell Harry'd been talking about. It was like white noise or listening to Ernie Harwell call a Tigers' game. But as they passed a farm, its silos ice-coated and glistening, fields silent under the crust of ice, Harry asked, "Well, have you?"

Smoke haloed Harry's head and red blotches patterned his cheeks.

"Have I *what?*"

"Heard of the Bath School bombing?"

Will nodded. He'd found his grandmother's scrapbook complete with newspaper clippings from 1927. In it, his grandmother detailed the gruesome crime committed by a farmer who had wired a schoolhouse with explosives and detonated it one morning as kids settled into their classes. Thirty-eight kids, two teachers, and four others died that day.

"That was my great-uncle. The guy who blew up that school. Fucking nutcase, that guy. Killed his wife, tied up his animals, and blew up his own farm, then drove his car to the school where he'd wired explosives in the basement. First explosion knocked the building four feet in the air."

The train picked up speed. "Didn't know until I was in high school. My history teacher mentioned it in class. As if I knew. As if I'd had anything to do with it. And then, I realized, that guy's DNA is inside *me*. All tangled up in me. What if, someday …" He puffed on his stogie, "I mean, what was I supposed to do with that information? Goddamn. I mean, really? What the hell?"

Ahead, a huddled mass appeared on the tracks. By the time Will recognized it as a big, white dog feasting on a deer carcass, it started running ahead of the train.

Harry pulled the air horn, which only panicked the dog. It slipped, righted itself, but couldn't get footing on the icy ties. Harry blasted the horn one last time and the dog leapt in the air just before the train hit. The impact threw the dog ten feet up and out until it landed on the snow and tumbled the rest of the way down the embankment to slide, blood etching its journey, across the frozen ground.

Harry shook his head, "Shame. Good looking dog, too."

"Up here, Harry." Will nodded to the sharp bend, just before the train got into Flint, where he usually got off.

"All right, man. Take 'er easy." Harry slapped Will on the back and opened the door, "Cuddy'll let you hobo it back. I'll radio him a head's up."

•

Will slogged through the deep snow until the train passed and then ran up onto the tracks toward where the dog had been hit. It was at least a mile and slowgoing because of the ice. By the time he saw the blood trail, he feared that the dog was dead. He slid down the embankment and found the dog alive, its white coat matted with deep purple frozen blood and fresh, bright red patches. Its back left leg had been nearly severed below the joint and hung by a tendon. Shedding his coat, Will ripped his undershirt and used it as a tourniquet. The cold, so brutal that it hurt to breathe, had stopped the dog from bleeding to death.

Removing his puffy down jacket to make a hammock, he cradled the dog, as best he could, and started toward Saginaw Street in hopes of finding a pay phone or a ride. But this part of town, especially in the cold, looked deserted and mean. Bungalow shutters hung askance, paint peeled, corner stores hid behind iron gates, garbage cans tipped by strays or raccoons. It was only a mile or so from the heart of Flint, from St. Paul's where he'd been confirmed, from all the memories of going *downtown* to Smith Bridgman's, the Capital Theater, Whiting Auditorium, the museums, but ever since General Motors started pulling out of town, the streets felt narrow and unwelcoming.

The dog's breath was shallow but its eyes never left Will's face. It had one brown eye, one half-brown, half-blue on the bottom, split horizontally like the top rested in a milky pool. Its coat looked Husky (scrappier and rougher, though, not as fluffy) but its body was long and lean like a shepherd.

"You part Husky, girl? Not sure what you are, huh?"

He found a pay phone and called his dad who had, luckily, just walked in from church. He picked up Will, drove him to Dr. Rupert's office and, sitting in the car as Will gathered up the dog, said, "Call me when you're done, son. And good luck with Rupert."

•

Dr. Rupert's specialty was farm animals but, since farmers were selling their land to developers, he'd converted a pole barn behind his house into a clinic.

Holding the dog like a baby, Will rang the doorbell with his elbow. Dr. Rupert appeared instantly, as if he'd been expecting him to show up on a Sunday with a half-dead dog.

Without missing a beat, he opened the door to let Will in, "Who picks up a dog in this weather? On a Sunday, to boot?" Ruperts's black-framed glasses rested in what looked like a painful red divot on the bridge of his nose. His avian features—beakish nose and long, curved back—reminded Will of a vulture. Even disheveled and cantankerous, he always looked elegant in his black trousers and starched white shirts.

He kept grumbling as they made their way out the back door, across the lawn, into the clinic. Entering the clinic, a series of sounds erupted from the back: bleating, whining, meowing, barking.

"I was watching *Steel Magnolias*. You rang the doorbell right when Olivia Dukakis says to Dolly Parton, 'If you can't say anything nice about anybody, come sit by me.' You think I wanted to tear myself away from *that* to see your mug at the door?"

As long as he'd known him, and he'd known him all his life, Rupert had greeted him with rhetorical questions and, unless he was talking about an animal, mostly spoke to himself. He pointed to the stainless steel table, "Put that bag of bones there." He turned to wash his hands, "You probably think it's hysterical that I watch old-lady shows."

If Will had bothered to answer, Rupert would've ignored him. Once he leaned over the dog, though, his face softened. He started cooing, talking like a lover. He lifted the dog gently and motioned for Will to pull his coat out from under her as he whistled low and mournfully, "What happened?"

Will could barely talk through chattering teeth, "Train."

"Ah. What were you thinking tangling with a train? Huh, girl?" He checked her thoroughly, gently prodded and poked, "I'll have to do X-rays, of course. She's not bleeding from the mouth. Good sign. But she could be all busted up inside and, well, this leg." He lifted the severed paw, "If she lives at all, that leg'll have to come off at the hip."

"Will she be able to walk?"

"They get along fine—adapt much better than humans. But like I said, she could be all busted up inside. Things we can't see."

The dog kept her quiet, pleading eyes on Will until the tranquilizer kicked in, "Whatever it takes. I don't care how much it costs."

"I'll do what I can. On the house." He added, sarcastically, "You being a true American hero and all."

Will leaned against the doorframe. He wished everyone would just give it a break.

Dr. Rupert motioned for Will to help him slide the dog onto a board, "That bubble-headed Scout leader must have asked me a half-dozen times to tie a yellow ribbon on my sign, for Chee-rist sake. Babies had ribbons tied around their wrists. I contemplated self-medication with a solid dose of ketamine after seeing that."

They pushed through a swinging door and entered the back room where Rupert performed surgeries and X-rays. It smelled of antiseptic and something else, yeast, maybe? A goat with an eye patch tried wrapping its agile lips around the bars of its cage. A tabby extended a paw to Will. Two retrievers sat at attention, anticipating freedom.

While Dr. Rupert got to work, Will gazed at the abnormalities Rupert had preserved in murky jars of formaldehyde. Grotesque, spaghetti-like heart-worms twisted through damaged hearts. Tapeworms, diseased livers, a baby pig born without a heart, kittens with five legs, puppies with two noses, you name it, Rupert preserved it. Ever since they were kids,

Will and his sister Rebecca had wandered around the clinic to gaze at the labeled jars set neatly on wooden bookshelves: FETAL PIG DEFORMED SNOUT (circa 1963), EQUIDAE TAPEWORM (circa 1970), BOVINAE DISEASED LIVER (circa 1979).

"Why all the abnormal organs?"

"More specific?"

"I mean, why not healthy specimens?"

Rupert studied an X-ray and answered distractedly, "Pathology is always more interesting."

Will lifted a large jar labeled OVIS ARIES MAMMARY TUMOR (circa 1974). A pink, gelatinous blob floated inside and he contemplated its grotesque, alien form. His entire life had been *normal*. Everything he'd done had taught him that there is only one standard: grades, sports, the Marines. Being a farmer's kid had taught him to fear too-dry summers, snowless winters, swarms, disease, ectopic omens. But, here and now, as with the rest of the world, what shouldn't *be* seemed normal. Or, at the very least, not surprising.

Will kept his eyes on the tumor, "I'm not a hero."

Dr. Rupert hesitated only a moment before administering an IV into the dog's shaved forearm, "You don't say."

"I broke in solitary."

There was a long pause before Will turned to find Rupert's black eyes fixed on him. His voice remained eerily unemotional, "People break every day. Think you're something special?"

Will stammered, "I meant that you didn't have to do it for free."

Rupert began shaving the dog's hip, "Oh, false advertising, huh?"

"I just meant—"

Will walked back to the dog and gently stroked her soft ear. "I'm ashamed—"

Rupert handed Will a huge magnifying glass and told him to hold it right over the severed leg, "Ashamed? Damnit," he unwrapped the blood-soaked rag from the dog's upper leg, "this is the sloppiest tourniquet I've ever seen. That's what you should be ashamed about—"

"It's cold as hell out there in case you hadn't noticed."

"I noticed while I sat comfortably on my couch watching TV on a Sunday afternoon."

"*Steel Magnolias*."

"Makes me cry. Every time. Every single time." He examined the dog's hip, "So let me get this straight: you blubbered to those bastards, gave away national secrets, undermined the security of the good ol' USA, and you're ashamed."

"No. I mean—Yes. Not national secrets."

"It's a real, crying shame that you're ashamed. I got it. Now shut up and let's concentrate on this poor animal."

Rupert steadied his hand just above the dog's hip and began. Blood bloomed onto the dog's white coat. Will's knees buckled and he dropped the magnifying glass.

"Pick that up," Rupert snapped, "and go sit over there. I don't need you distracting me."

The ancient smell of fresh blood filled Will's head. Working in silence, Dr. Rupert removed the leg. Will stared at the floor. He couldn't bear to watch.

"This much blood is never good."

"You see it all the time, though. You must get used to it." Will looked up to see the upper half of the dog's leg on the table.

Dr. Rupert's voice softened, "You never get used to it. I grew up on a farm, like you, but a pig farm. So I saw a lot of blood. Always had dinner at four-thirty p.m. Sharp." He began to clean the joint where the hip used to be. His voice became very quiet. "I was ten when my sister's boyfriend walked into the kitchen and leveled a shotgun at her chest. Right over my shoulder." He pointed one bloody, gloved hand over his right shoulder. "I saw the barrel out of the corner of my eye, but before I could register what was going on, he pulled the trigger. Killed her right in front of my folks."

Dr. Rupert pushed his face into his shoulder to reposition his glasses, "If I'd been clever or quick, I'd have knocked the gun and given my dad time to stop him."

Will recalled his mother telling him about the Ruperts' tragedy. He must have been in fourth or fifth grade when she'd read him the *Journal* article about the murderer's early release from prison. It had always seemed like a fable, though, because Will couldn't imagine Dr. Rupert as a child. Couldn't imagine him in anything but a white shirt and black pants with glasses perched on that enormous beak.

"It's been fifty years. I try like hell to forget, but the only relief I get is when I dream. I see her, alive, and I have this wonderful feeling—I can't even describe it. It's not so much that she's alive. I mean that's part of it. But the real reason I'm happy, I guess, is the weight of all that shame—"

Will watched as Dr. Rupert's bloody palms fanned out like a magician's while he searched for the right words. "It just disappears."

IV. RESULT

Proving Grounds

It was times like this when Luke wished he knew more about people and less about cars. He could gut an engine and put it back together in his sleep. Years ago, he'd singlehandedly transformed the Corvette to compete with the Europeans. In the corridors of GM, his engineering prowess was legend; he was revered and exalted. But all this—his wife's suicide and his very much alive daughter—couldn't be resolved. Why couldn't life work like a simple equation? Say, nine x + three = thirty. The variable, x should be three, right? But the damn variable kept changing every time a woman passed him on the street, or he met a coworker's wife, or took a message from a secretary.

Luke floored it out of the turn and down the straightaway so effortlessly that he might have been flying. The late summer foliage and slate blue of the lake to the west of the track blurred like watercolors as the speedometer climbed. Even on the test course, he held the steering wheel with the pad of his right palm, just so, like he was on his way to church. But for some goddamn reason he couldn't focus. Probably because he hadn't stopped since Leila's death, hadn't spent more than a few minutes with his daughter. God knew he felt guilty. Bringing Astrid out with him was the first step in making up for it.

He tried to concentrate on the Corvette's acceleration, but his thoughts drifted to Leila and how things could have been different, perhaps, if he'd been different. Could have. Yeah. If he hadn't been such a prick, would Leila have killed herself? But if he hadn't been that man, would Leila have given him the time of day? He couldn't resolve it. Had she loved him at all or had he simply happened into her life at the right moment? Of course she'd loved him! She'd nearly gone crazy with grief over his affairs. But, by the end, she'd seemed completely disinterested in him and his other women. She'd actually seemed happy. She'd been buoyant and carefree and radiant. Like she'd been when they'd first met. Like she'd been when they were in love. Jesus. Was that it? Had she been in love? As he neared the hairpin turn, this thought startled him and, instead of easing up on the gas, he tapped it. The back end kicked out dramatically so that the Vette slid perpendicular to the track, the rear tires kissed the shoulder, gravel popped, and all sense of control evaporated. He wanted it to last forever, that feeling of not caring, of letting gravity take over, of forgetting. But his reflexes kicked in and he maneuvered her out of it, the way he knew he could—just so—to send her screaming, once again, down the straightaway.

He could have easily lost control. But he hadn't. He rarely did. And, what's more, he knew his daughter, sitting next to him in the passenger seat, would be elated.

He downshifted onto the road that led to the Gate House, brought the Stingray to an abrupt stop under the old oak and turned to look at Astrid. Her profile, so like Leila's, wore an expression of complete joy. He hadn't seen that look since her mother's death.

She turned to him, "My turn?"

"It'll cost you next month's allowance and then some. Johnny'll demand a box of Cubans to look the other way."

"I haven't gotten an allowance since ninth grade." Astrid popped open the door, swung her long legs out of the Vette, rounded the hood, and waited for her father to get out. When he finally did, a glowing cigarette already dangling between his lips, she nodded to the guard tower, "And Johnny's probably asleep up there." Luke inhaled dramatically, nodding. He smoked with such regularity that, when Astrid was a child, she thought that the white stick between his index and middle fingers was simply an extension of his body—the same as his hands or ears.

Even now, in his early sixties, nothing could diminish his elegance; not his white hair or the milky scar running along his jaw. When she was very young, Astrid realized, and had come to accept with a certain resignation, that women were drawn to him. She'd known for a long time that he'd been the source of her mother's sadness, but how could she stop loving him herself? He adored his only daughter.

Showed her his designs, made sure she understood roll center and axis location, aerodynamic design, and resistance. She couldn't resolve her affection for him. And now, with her mother gone, the guilt she felt at the thorough and complete joy of spending a few hours with him nearly buckled her with grief.

They leaned against the driver's door, both staring at the curving road leading to the track. It was a still day and, without the engine's roar, the quiet tugged at them.

In the oak's shade, a mosquito landed on Astrid and she raised her forearm to watch it gorge itself. For some reason, mosquito bites never left itchy welts for Astrid or her mother. It was freakish—something in their blood, an antibody only they shared. His welts blossomed to the size of golf balls and it bothered him that he'd been excluded from their little club. After all, he'd been the World War II hero, racecar driver, epic Corvette engineer. He should be the one immune to irritating pests.

The oak's leaves shivered in a light breeze. It had been protected behind the high barbed-wire fence surrounding the Proving Grounds, from kids with hammers and nails trying to conquer her height and breadth with tire swings and tree houses and all matter of other nonsense. When Astrid was younger, Luke had propped a ladder against its trunk so she could reach the first branch. Once there, she would climb dangerously high until she found a bird's-eye perch to watch her dad on the track.

The mosquito's abdomen swelled with blood, big as a ball bearing, gorging itself, completely oblivious to danger. Astrid lifted her forearm higher to get a better look and, as she did, Luke, in one swift movement, pinched the mosquito's wings and pressed its abdomen against the glowing end of his cigarette. The smell of it sickened Astrid. When there was nothing left, he blew the delicate wings off his fingertips.

"Dad!"

"What? You would have just let it take advantage of you? It wouldn't even been able to fly. No forethought. Stupid pest."

Her father's offhand cruelty had always repulsed her and, without warning, her voice rose. "Speaking of stupid … Mrs. Shield visited me the other day."

He took a deep drag and tipped his head back to stare at the canopy of green. Astrid tried to steady her voice. "Dad—"

"Um hmm."

"You … know her. Right?"

"Knew."

"Whatever."

He lit another cigarette. "I heard."

"Nice choice in women. Jeez."

He couldn't help but suppress a smile even as he felt murderous towards Dovey's poor judgment. "How did she knock over the hives?"

Astrid launched into the story; told him how Mrs. Shield brought the baby through the field, about how Astrid had tripped into the hives, the swarm, getting Mrs. Shield into the shack, and then, "I told her I'd wanted to kill her. And you."

Luke snagged a bit of tobacco off his tongue. He took his time lighting another. "Really?"

Astrid nodded.

"Just curious. How would you have done it?"

Astrid detailed her plan.

"Okay, Squeaky Fromme. Terrible plan. It would fail. You're capable of much better."

"Why?"

"Too many holes. And——" Luke pointed to Astrid's forearm where another mosquito feasted, "too soft-hearted."

He was right, of course. She never would have done it. She wanted, so badly, though, to ask him, *Why?* Why did he have to be the way he was? Why hadn't his family been enough? Why was he so quick to throw it all away for someone new? It couldn't be that he admired those women's intellects. Dovey'd seemed like the dullest knife in the drawer.

So, what was the point?

She wanted to ask him all of this, but the questions piled up and stuck somewhere between indecision and speech. What came out was, "Auntie blames you."

"Yes, well …"

"Calls you a self-centered shit of a dog. Only in Arabic. She doesn't think I know that expression."

"Dog shit can't be self-centered, can it?" Her father's face transformed completely when he smiled. He usually looked gruff and critical. But when he smiled, the lines in his forehead and between his eyes smoothed and the creases spoking off his eyes became very deep.

"You are a self-centered prick, though." Something about seeing her father smile chipped away at the dam barring her emotions.

Luke cleared his throat. He'd long ago given up reprimanding Astrid. After all, she was right, "Maybe so. But do you blame me for your mother's death?"

"Not now."

"But then?"

"I felt so helpless for so long. I couldn't help her. Or fix her. And you were always gone. I couldn't resolve any of it."

His voice softened, "So you don't blame me?"

"Does it matter?"

In the distance, a plane climbed out of Metro. Luke followed its frilly contrail for a moment before contemplating his response. "I—" He stopped. He wanted to explain himself but how? Say he was a dog? That he couldn't be faithful? Confirm that he just might be the most selfish person he knew? That, had he known it would end like this, he would have changed? Bullshit. Nothing would have changed. Through it all, he had never stopped loving Leila. Good Lord, even *now* he couldn't resolve his feelings for her. How could he explain all of this to his daughter?

Instead, he said, "It's so much more than I can explain."

"You need to try." Her lip quivered, "I'm not okay. I miss her. I mean, I'm not—" She hated to sound weak, especially in front of him. But she couldn't help it. Her dreams, since she'd found her mother on the bathroom floor, surged with razors plunging like guillotines and swimming pools brimming with orange and red capsules. They waited like traps. And Leila would appear, happy at first, and then frantic—pulling out her hair in great chunks—about something Leila couldn't see in the distance. And, lately, Astrid couldn't bear Paulie's touch. It caused a visceral reaction of withdrawal. She didn't know what any of it meant. She didn't know if Paulie's love should or even could be tossed aside. Was Paulie right? Would no one love her the way he did?

All of this flashed through her mind, but what she said was, "I'm afraid that I'll turn out like you. The way you treat people. The way you treat women. That I'll be that way—"

Luke dropped his cigarette, stubbed it out with the toe of his loafer, laced his arm over her back, and squeezed her shoulder. She felt so solid. She'd always been so grounded that he'd thought she didn't need him. He'd been so driven and focused that he'd left all the parenting to Leila. And now Leila was gone.

"I married your mother in my mid-forties. I'd been a bachelor for a long time … I guess I had a hell of a time adjusting. But I always loved her. I know that may be hard to believe." With his free hand, he fished out another cigarette, "My behavior had nothing to do with the way I felt about her. Or you. That's not an excuse. It's just fact."

"I just can't stop thinking about things. I can't figure it out. She'd been so unhappy. And, then, my sophomore year … after you moved out, she, I don't know, rebounded."

There it was again. Even Astrid had noticed her mother's joy. He stared down the long concrete slab that curved into the test course. She *had* been happy. Why? How? He'd become so accustomed to her resentment that, after he left, her happiness nearly drove him crazy. He recalled the day not long before she died when he'd tried to patch things up with his suddenly desirable wife (he simply couldn't bear losing) but she'd only laughed and pushed him out the door. He thought about all of this, but what he said was, "You're not thinking of hurting yourself because—"

Astrid swiped at her wet cheeks, "No. Not like that. Not like her. I would never. I'm just sad. It's so … it's like, I'm just full of, I don't know, everything aches. I don't know what to do with it."

Although he rarely spoke of it, he'd lost his parents at a young age. He had made his way on his own and didn't have much respect for those who, under perfect circumstances, were unable to. He certainly didn't want his daughter to fall into the latter category. "You have to figure out what to do with it. Like I did. No one can help you do that."

"But you had the war. All I have is school."

"You have the rest of your life. And what about the goon?"

"His name is *Paulie*. What about him?"

"I don't know … he's your boyfriend, isn't he?"

"I'm breaking up with him."

"Ah."

"Yeah. You can't imagine. He's kind of crazy about me."

"Been knocked in the head too many times."

"Because he loves me?"

"You know what I mean."

"He's not as stupid as you think."

"Well, that's *something*."

"I mean, he's very focused."

"A good bird dog is *focused*. It's not an advisable trait in a boyfriend."

Astrid laughed.

"And you want to get rid of him but you don't know how?"

Astrid nodded.

Quick as a flash, Luke pinched an imaginary mosquito between his thumb and forefinger and positioned his fingers at the glowing end of his cigarette, "You snuff him out like that mosquito. Quick and painless. From what I've observed, he can't possibly function at a much higher level than a pest."

Astrid shook her head. What did she expect? That he would suddenly become a perfect TV dad? That he would say just the right thing? He had always been a self-centered prick. He was still a self-centered prick. And she didn't expect things to change.

The fact that she still adored him made something buzz in her brain. To drown it out, she opened the door and slid into the driver's seat.

Luke settled into the passenger seat and turned to Astrid, "You noticed it, too, eh?"

"What?"

"She seemed happy."

"She *was* happy."

"You know why?"

"How would I?" Astrid didn't *know* but had a far-fetched idea bumping around her brain. It had something to do with Father Silver but she hadn't figured out what.

There was the curious fact that, at Mama's funeral, Father Silver had appeared completely disheveled or, she wondered now, completely awed by grief. And the day Mama died, the priest had left a message asking her to return his call. Was that just coincidence? He had always been so solid—at fundraisers, barbecues, in his sermons—that his transformation after her mother's death, to tipsy if not downright drunk, seemed odd. Or the timing seemed odd.

She wasn't sure.

It was ridiculous. She knew it. He was their religious guide, after all. Even so, she felt that this knowledge wedged a feather's width of mistrust between her father and her. Long ago, in her grief over Luke's infidelities, Leila once mistook Astrid's genuine ignorance of Luke's affairs as loyalty to him. After that, Astrid realized the delicate balancing act with which she'd been saddled and she resented both parents for it.

Luke looked up through the aperture of leafy green to a very blue sky. He then lowered his gaze to the slab of concrete leading to the test track, "You driving?"

She wanted to talk but she knew her father's limits. Turning the key, the Corvette roared to life. She could shed everything when she was behind the wheel. Nothing mattered. Nothing weighed her down. Not her father's mistakes. Or her mother's death. Not Paulie's smothering love. Nothing.

•

By the time they turned into their subdivision with its perfectly kept lawns, trimmed hedges, and sprawling homes, a glowing crimson sun sent horizontal ribbons of pink and gold across the western sky. But what took their attention was the new Cadillac Eldorado sitting in their yew-lined drive. They knew, immediately, that it was Walter Shield's car. For years, Luke had arrogantly scoffed at what Walter's team had done to the Eldorado, complained that they'd compromised its elegance, that they'd down-rated the horsepower, that they'd made it into a glorified Seville.

All this in addition to screwing Walter's wife.

Luke didn't hesitate as he pulled up beside the classic sedan, threw the car into PARK, and got out.

"Walter?" Luke palmed the Eldorado's hood.

Astrid walked into the garage and stood next to her father's parked '67 Corvette. Mr. Shield swung out of his car and, from her vantage point, Astrid noticed that he was a good head taller than her father, with thick, solid shoulders. He'd always struck Astrid as a kind, quiet man with sad eyes that never seemed to mesh with his intimidating stature.

Mr. Shield walked to his trunk, opened it and took out a nine iron.

"Hold on, now, Walter. What's—"

Mr. Shield rested the club on his shoulder and walked straight at Luke. Luke took a step forward and Mr. Shield swung the club at him—not with great force—more like he was trying to shoo an irritating fly. Luke stepped out of the club's trajectory, backed up, and stood between Mr. Shield and Astrid.

"Go inside, Astrid," her father warned over his shoulder.

Astrid couldn't move. She felt rooted, as if tendrils sprung out of her feet, burst through the cement, burrowed through the hard clay. She stood in the garage next to the Corvette. Everyone knew when he fired her up because the big Holley carburetor practically sucked all the air out of the subdivision before emitting a low, rumbling growl. She was the first car he'd designed and Mama'd said it was his one great love.

"Let's be reasonable about this——"

Mr. Shield stopped, briefly, looked into the pale evening sky as if contemplating Luke's request, and said, "That would have been *before* you screwed my wife."

Luke pressed his hand against Astrid's shoulder, ordered her into the house. The nudge took her off guard—she stumbled and landed on her ass, legs stretched in front of her. Luke then went for Mr. Shield who simply pointed the club at Luke's groin and jabbed hard like a bullfighter burying the blade.

Luke doubled over, fell to his knees, brought his head to the ground, and wretched. In one swift movement, Mr. Shield buried the club's head in the Vette's curved back windshield. The next door neighbor's beagle brayed to accompany the repeated thunks of the nine iron against glass, and of the club pulling away from the splintered fiberglass.

When he'd finished, Mr. Shield turned toward Astrid. The club hung in his right hand. She didn't feel the pieces of glass digging into her palms as she pushed herself across the cement, away from him. Luke pushed himself up and lunged for the club. Mr. Shield looked at him, confused, and released his grip. Luke flipped the club around to squeeze the leather grip with both fists. His voice planed eerily, "Don't touch her."

Mr. Shield looked confused as he knelt just in front of Astrid. Tears ran down his cheeks. His eyes looked hollow, like he'd been shattered from the inside.

He bit his bottom lip and took a deep, ragged breath.

"I'm so sorry about all of this, Astrid. Please forgive me."

And, with that, Mr. Shield stood, steadied himself on the busted carcass of the beauty formerly known as the '67 Vette, walked to his Eldorado, and pulled away.

Kinetic Friction

It's just past two in the morning, an hour or so before the farmers wake. Ten minutes before she meets the guys. Thirty minutes before the first race begins.

Astrid only sneaks out to race when her father is away because Luke would wake to the Corvette's throaty growl like a mother to her newborn's coo. Their driveway slopes toward the street and their house is at the top of the hill. These two facts make it easy for her to coast until she's nearly out of the subdivision, out of her well-intentioned but nosy neighbors' range. This night, she doesn't turn on the headlights or start the engine until she passes the Morgan house.

The '67 Stingray is, hands down, the fastest car around. Its racing engine guarantees that. Out there, though, on the country roads, with their S-curves and dips, sandy shoulders and potholes, it's not just about the fastest car but how you drive it.

Dixie Highway feathers off Saginaw at the edge of town. The asphalt is wet from a light rain, illuminated by a gibbous moon—a flaring ring around it, brighter than she ever remembers—between towering clouds. This stretch of road is straight and deserted, lined with elderly black walnut trees, their limbs arcing to meet high above the yellow line. It's the only place where Astrid lets herself think about her mother's death and, simultaneously, she opens it up and the world flashes by, slightly off the way a Super 8 movie doesn't quite capture reality. She's trained herself to look far, far ahead because, right now, nothing close matters. At this speed, nothing would survive impact. It's the stuff in the distance she might be able to avoid.

It's just a few minutes at this speed, so fast that no one—not her father, Paulie, Caroline—would believe it. So fast that the most insignificant mistake would kill her. It's the time, the only time, when she feels the weight of her loneliness lift, when she feels invincible and solid and undamaged. It's the only time when her brain shuts off and her life boils down to a series of reflexes and she feels the way she felt when she was a little kid, before her mother's depression became something Astrid tried to hide. As she downshifts, getting ready to turn onto the stretch of road where the boys wait, her anger at her mother comes rushing in, and she knows that the pressure valve inside her brain has snapped closed and nothing will escape until she's moving fast once again.

She eases off the gas and turns onto a road canopied by trees, broken fences lining the shoulder like busted teeth. The Stingray is a shark skimming the dark road, gills sucking air into the big Holley carburetor, nose devouring the night.

Tonight, there will be all the usual suspects. Jimmy Nichols will appear in his silver '70 454 Chevelle with its sloping grill and flowing roofline. Little Alex Tartoni drives that cherry red Dodge Charger like he's got a big, fat chip on his shoulder. And TJ McClean's put a new engine in his black '68 Plymouth GTX and has been bragging about how he'll finally leave them all behind.

They're already there, leaning against their cars. But they're not cool—at least not Jimmy or Alex. Jimmy continually pulls his Grand Funk T-shirt over the gap between his jeans and belly. Alex shifts nervously from foot to foot. Alex and Jimmy spent their entire high school careers avoiding guys who wanted to slam them into lockers.

TJ, built solid and compact, wrestled his way to number one in the state. He didn't need to avoid anyone but keeps a low profile. You'd never know how smart he actually is. His goal is to be an astronaut. Ever since he watched Apollo 11 land on the moon when he was seven, the image of Buzz Aldrin and Neil Armstrong bouncing over the opalescent surface has been seared into memory. He's on an athletic scholarship to U of M, first in his family to go to college. He wrestles the same way he performs in class—like he's got something to prove.

The boys have been tight since grade school. In high school, they and Astrid set the curve in honors courses. They play Galaga and Asteroids instead of partying. Their dads work on the line. During summers, they flip burgers and mow lawns and bag groceries and save every penny for college. And for their cars.

Astrid's been racing them since she got her license and, since Luke is General Motors royalty, she's their princess. She's feeling cocky. Invincible. Like she just might own tonight.

They race during the week because the farmers are still asleep, not puttering in their pickups or crossing the road in their tractors. No one's out this way, at this time, unless they're up to something they'd rather keep quiet.

They meet in a field and, after Astrid's arrival, their cars form a disjointed square. The rain holds off for now but the damp weeds soak their sneakers. The air feels electric with an impending storm. They stand in the middle of the square and draw numbers out of TJ's worn baseball cap. The first race will be between Jimmy and Alex. Astrid gets out her stopwatch and the Chevelle and Dodge line up behind TJ's outstretched arm. The course would take an everyday driver twenty-five minutes start to finish. Alex's record is eight minutes twenty-six seconds. It runs long and straight along a county line bordered by cornfields and turns off to follow Thread Creek. There, the road twists and curves through hills and ponds. That's where they lose the most time, where their reflexes take over, where their timing must be precise and their concentration complete.

TJ stands a few inches taller than Astrid, a towhead with blue eyes, lashes so light and the skin just inside the eyelash pale pink. Something about his quick movements used to remind Astrid of a rabbit. But not any more. He's grown into himself. Astrid can't put her finger on it but ever since he's returned from college there's something very different about him that she likes. He's standing on the other side of the road, flag raised, swooping down as Astrid thumbs the stopwatch and the cars disappear. The cars have modified mufflers that sound like rockets. Astrid always resists the urge to cover her ears.

Astrid knows that TJ has a crush on her. He's so sweet and talks so quietly that she has to lean in to hear him. He's next to her Vette, now, palming a flashlight, running his hand over the side of the car.

"Nice job," he's kneeling, looking at the passenger side door.

Astrid nods. She doesn't like to think about Mr. Shield's face the night he pummeled the Stingray with his nine iron. She told the guys that she'd left the garage door open, that someone vandalized it while they slept. "Had to replace both windshields. Taillights. New body."

TJ whistles, "Musta cost a fortune. Your dad musta been pissed."

Funny thing was, Luke didn't seem pissed. After Mr. Shield left, he went inside, made himself a Scotch, turned on the Tigers' game, and called his guy at the body shop. Like the husband of the woman you're screwing coming over to crack the crap out of your car was to be expected; like collateral damage or something inevitable he'd expected for a very long time.

"How long'd it take?"

"Just got it back last week. I thought my dad was going to sleep in the garage with it."

"I would," he laughs.

Astrid can see, even in the moonlight, how his ear has gotten worse since high school. It's as if someone hooked a tire pump to it, now shaped like a conical seashell with a pale, swollen top and small lobe. "Why don't you wear a helmet when you wrestle?"

"Why?" But he knows the answer. His mom's been all over him about it, too.

"You know why."

"It intimidates my opponents."

"Still."

"It's a sign of toughness."

She's following him as he shines the flashlight over the car. She studies his profile. His forehead and eyebrows form a precipice so that his eyes rest in shadow. This is part of why he always looks so intimidating. He uses it to unnerve his opponents. But it all changes when he smiles and the muscles pull back to break the smooth planes of his cheeks and temples.

It's been a little over seven minutes and Astrid hears Jimmy and Alex approaching.

TJ trains the flashlight on a chrome taillight, "Look here."

Astrid's pulling her black curls into a ponytail, pale skin reflecting the moonlight. She's wearing jean shorts, her lucky Coppertone tee, Keds.

"Missed a spot." Astrid kneels to look at the place where TJ runs his forefinger over the chrome.

She's very close to him and can smell Irish Spring on his skin. He's licking his lips and staring at the tiny dent, "How's Paulie?"

Astrid hesitates, "We're going to—"

"Break up" is about to fall off her tongue and the anticipation of this, of being free from Paulie's overbearing love, opens a door of possibility she's been wanting to walk through for a very long time. TJ turns to her, leans in and kisses her very gently. Nothing but their lips touch and he tastes like Teaberry gum, sweet like clove and cinnamon. Just as he's about to raise his hand to cup it beneath her ponytail, Astrid stands to look into the distance, past the cornfield, to the intersection where Jimmy and Alex come screaming toward them.

TJ's hand hovers in front of his face, momentarily frozen in the moonlight.

Astrid turns quickly, walks through the wet grass to the road's shoulder. "Come on," she yells over her shoulder, "what are you waiting for?"

He snaps out of it and pushes himself up to follow her. They have fewer than thirty seconds to get to their places on either side of the road where they've drawn lines in the shoulder. TJ stands across from Astrid attentive as a puppy. He's got the rest of the summer to get up his nerve and ask her out, after all, why rush it? Right now, he and Astrid have a job to do and he slices the flag down precisely as the chrome of Alex's bumper breaks the imaginary line between them.

Alex is forty-two seconds over his best time. Blames it on the damp pavement. Jimmy says a deer darted in front of him.

"Excuses," TJ laughs. "This engine's gonna *eat* damp pavement."

"Can't eat a deer."

"Just watch."

The guys give TJ shit as he and Astrid pull their cars up to the line. TJ blasts Aerosmith but Astrid likes to listen to the road. They're idling when TJ looks over at Astrid and, just before Alex waves the flag, TJ smiles so wide that she gets that feeling in her stomach, that sweeping feeling, like she's filled with helium, like she's about to fly.

On the straightaway, her speedometer hovers at one-forty but TJ was right about his new engine because he's tucked behind her. He's being patient, planning on overtaking her before the S-curve, just before the lip of the hill. Last month, Astrid lost her nerve and tapped the brakes a little too hard. He took advantage of her mistake, easily slid in front, and kept the lead until the finish.

They've chosen their route carefully but the corn must have grown half a foot since last week, just high enough so that when they blow through stop signs, they tell themselves they'd see headlights approaching the intersection. But that's a lie. Last week they could. This week they can't. And Astrid hopes that if there is another car out here tonight, it doesn't wander into their path.

They've left behind the course's straightaways and cornfields to arc around a pond so still that the moon reflects off it like a spotlight. The road's lined with trees, thick trunks immovable, the road is shiny and wet. Astrid knows, instinctively because her dad has drilled it into her, that a dry road's static friction is greater than this wet road's kinetic friction, and she feels the car slide away from center, slightly to the right, as she makes the turn. Pulling out of it, onto another straightaway before an S-curve, she sees TJ's headlights sliding around her. He's making his move. They're side by side, now, the hum of the engines filling her, leaving no room for error. TJ's probably smiling as he tries to overtake her. She doesn't let up, though, so he has to floor it and, just before the S-curve, Astrid knows he's going too fast, knows she should have let up because the road seems shinier here and, in that split second as he pulls in front of her to bank it, with the road curving left, TJ's car keeps pointing straight, as if he's hit a patch of ice, his headlights momentarily illuminating a thick clump of trees. Astrid doesn't hear a thing, not a screeching of brakes or skidding of tires, before TJ's car launches off the embankment, rocket-like. There is no sound, only a thick vacuum of no-sound before the sickening whoomp of the Plymouth hitting something big. And, almost simultaneously, Astrid's slamming on her brakes, the sound a condensed crescendo filling the night with urgency, and jerks the steering wheel around to head back.

The Plymouth is tangled in the trees like a black parachute, not something made of steel and chrome and rubber but a memory of steel and chrome and rubber now woven into the forest's fabric and Astrid knows, the way she knew about her mother, that knowing without knowing, that TJ's gone, and if not dead, broken beyond repair, because the young trees just off the shoulder have been sheered off like someone took a machete to them and the car's entire front has come to rest around a tree half the width of its grill.

Astrid slams on the brakes and runs down the embankment. Her feet sink in muck, thorns snag her skin. One back tire still rotates and the radiator hisses. Above it all, she hears the roar of Alex's and Jimmy's motors; they would've heard the crash because the ones not racing listen very carefully, whispering or not talking at all, knowing the danger, tamping images of cars tangled in trains, or around each other, or hugging utility poles. When Jimmy and Alex arrive, they park so that their lights illuminate the scene and look down at Astrid, her face whiter than the moon, with her right foot on the car, the other on the ground and both hands pulling on a crowbar she's wedged into what used to be the driver's side door. They know it's futile because there's no front seat; the engine's been displaced into the back cabin and TJ's bleeding head presses unnaturally against the rear windshield.

Standing on the top of the embankment, they know that the crowbar is useless, that it'll take cutting the car in half to get TJ out. Jimmy slides down the embankment and Alex hops in his car to drive to the nearest phone. They know the risks, but they also know the flip side of it. Even that pales in comparison to the feeling of bending time, of outsmarting physics, of being invincible once more.

Other than Honorable Intentions

The three-legged dog curled at his feet, Will sat on a milk crate within the aperture of the barn's wide doors, oiling and cleaning his rifle. It had been his grandfather's, and Will kept the stock gleaming, the mechanisms lubed, and the barrel polished. Clouds blotted the sky as the sun lumbered into the west, shooting bolts of light into the distance. When the rifle gleamed, he loaded it, walked to his truck with Riley at his heels, laid it gently behind the driver's seat, and covered it with a canvas tarp. He'd already stashed a few other things he would need: the Sony Beta movie recorder, fully charged and stocked with tape, and a few coils of nylon rope.

He knelt to pat Riley's head, digging his fingers into the thick white fur under her collar. She lifted her brown nose up to gaze at him lovingly. He took a deep breath to calm his nerves and went over his plan once again. Everything seemed to be falling into place. Rebecca and his father had left earlier that day to visit family in Grayling for the weekend.

The weather was perfect for a bonfire with a light breeze to keep the mosquitoes at bay.

Their fields bolted out in all directions for nearly ten thousand acres in varying shades of green, even as subdivisions Pac-Man'ed adjacent acreage. Past the Goynes's land, in town, just a dozen miles away, those boys who raped Caroline, those boys who were now men, those spoiled, arrogant SOBs were loosening their ties, getting off work, heading home, driving like robots over the curving asphalt, to change, grab their weed, and drive out to weird Will Goynes's farm to party.

Those boys would be easy targets.

•

Riley sat at attention and followed Will's line of sight down the gravel drive. Trying to relax, Will adjusted his Tigers' cap and leaned against his pickup parked in the lane separating the Goynes's modest clapboard farmhouse, barns, and fields. He wished he smoked. His fidgety hands needed something to do. Instead, he forced himself to take his eyes off the main road and shifted his gaze out over the fields. Summer had ambushed him the usual way—like a curtain being jerked up to reveal the scene he knew by heart. He loved this land and couldn't remember, now that he'd been discharged, why he'd ever wanted to leave.

Next to his dad and sister, he played his role flawlessly: tilled, planted, prayed for rain, watched the crops, assessed storm damage, oiled and maintained the machinery, mended fences. If you'd looked at just his face, at his now shaggy, dark hair tucked under his cap, his bowling ball head, freckles, and big ears, you might mistake him for an oversized kid. Since returning from captivity, he'd gained back the weight he'd lost, and hardened overall. His neck, thick and muscled, tapered into solid shoulders and chest, narrow waist and legs that strained the seams of his jeans. His eyes, too, had hardened. Beneath the cliff of forehead, his eyes were oil-slick black, surrounded by long lashes, punctuated by purple sickles beneath his eyes.

He finally spotted Tremaine's Camaro turning off the main road. As it approached, Will reviewed his plan—right until the doors swung open and Lou Tremaine, Sammy Mansour, and Johnny Henderson longlegged themselves out of the car. Back in high school, they'd been a triple threat for the Bobcat basketball team, leading them to multiple state championships. Lou and Sammy, dressed almost identically in khaki shorts and striped polo shirts with the collars turned up, had added a few pounds since school. Johnny still looked very much the same with his curly blond hair pulled into a ponytail, his easy gait, and slow, blue eyes.

"Willkenstein, man, how you been?" Lou pulled out a pack of cigarettes and packed it against the heel of his hand.

Johnny extended his hand, "Long time no see, GG."

Will hadn't heard those nicknames since New Canaan High. In ninth grade, everyone started calling him Frankenstein because of the awkward way he moved his lanky legs and big feet. He simply didn't know what to do with the growth spurt that ambushed him that year. At some point, some clever bastard changed it to Willkenstein and the name stuck. But the next year, Willkenstein transformed into track and field star *The Great Goynes*. He broke all kinds of state records, those long legs pistoning him into the air as if his bones had hollowed. With just the slightest lift of his chin, he could hover, magically, like a god.

Johnny motioned for a cigarette from Lou and squinted at Will, "This the party?"

"Some guys from the track team are stopping by later. I thought we'd get drinking. You wanna wait?"

Johnny shook his head but eyed Will suspiciously. "Why'd you invite us out here after all this time?"

Will had anticipated the question, "Just thought I'd get the guys together who were still around, who haven't moved away." He pulled off his cap and replaced it more firmly on his head, "Plus, I saved up some cash and invited some *ladies* to join us."

"Ladies, huh?" Lou raised his eyebrows, "What kind of ladies?"

"Nice ladies?" Will suddenly felt foolish.

Johnny took a drag, hinged back his head and blew a few smoke rings. They traveled into the cloudless sky like ghosts. "Will, man, since you've been gone I've settled down. I'm a married man. I have kids—twins."

"Speak for yourself, faggot. I like nice ladies," Lou cracked his neck with the heel of his hand and smirked. "Suppose you didn't get much action while you were locked in that cell, huh?"

Will eyed him until Lou kicked his toe into the dirt.

Johnny pulled out a worn leather wallet and flipped it open to reveal a thick stack of plastic-sleeved photos.

Lou rolled his eyes at Sammy, "Here we go."

Johnny took a step toward Will to show him photos of his girls—all grins and missing teeth—and began the excruciating narration of, "This is them at Christmas, this is them on the first day of school …"

Sammy interrupted Johnny. "Did they torture you?" His eyes were set too close together and bulged. It gave him the look of being perpetually excited.

Johnny's head snapped up, "What kind of idiot are you?"

"What?"

"Will doesn't want to talk about that stuff tonight, man. He's trying to relax." He shook his head, "Anyway, those are my kids. Funny how you change when you have kids."

Will nodded but didn't want to think about Johnny's kids tonight. "Well, what do you say we get going? I built a bonfire back by the tree line."

Johnny looked like he wanted to say something else, but Sammy pointed to the three-wheeler, "I've always wanted to drive one of those."

Will tossed him the keys. Sammy stepped forward to pet Riley who had remained motionless next to Will. As soon as his hand came within a foot of the dog's face, she growled and backed away. Sammy snatched his hand away, "What the—? That mutt's got three legs."

"You think he doesn't know that his dog has three legs, asshole?" Lou shook his head and opened the passenger side door.

"Will's freak show, huh? What else you got around here? A cow with two heads?" Sammy mounted the three-wheeler.

"We don't raise cattle," Will replied as he hoisted Riley into the flatbed.

Lou and Johnny hopped into Will's truck and followed Sammy who, on the three-wheeler, kicked up dirt and looped around the Ford, crushing rows of high corn. Will tried not to let him divert his attention, tried not to let his anger flare, so he turned his attention to Johnny who was laughing and pointing at Sammy, and Lou's long, delicate fingers fiddling with the radio's ancient knobs. Lou's nails were clean, pale, and wide. Will's own hands were gouged with scars and stained deep brown from motor oil.

The AM signal filled the cab with static.

"Will, man, we've got to get you into a new truck. This Ford's a piece of shit. We're gonna get you in a new Chevy." Lou reached into his jeans pocket to produce a baggie of weed.

"Gets the job done," was Will's response.

Lou was surprisingly adept at rolling a joint while the Ford lurched over bumpy terrain. When he leaned forward to lick the rolling paper, Will noted his profile. He had one of those faces that would look good on a billboard—angular and equine with full lips. Hell, his dad's face was plastered everywhere you looked in New Canaan. "I CANNOT TELL A LIE! TRE-MAINE-DOUS CHEVY DEALS!" the ads proclaimed with Ed Tremaine wearing a white wig, chopping down a tree labeled "HIGH PRICES."

In the distance, field rocks surrounded a huge pile of wood. Between the fire pit and the tree, Will had placed a few tree stumps in a half-moon around the bonfire and, a ways off, a pony keg chilled in a metal barrel filled with ice. After they piled out of the Ford, Will made his way over to the keg and started filling plastic cups with Budweiser.

"Aren't you quite the little hostess?" Lou took a swig from the plastic cup Will handed him.

Sammy jumped off the three-wheeler, "Damn, Will, that's a lot of wood. They'll be able to see us from outer space."

"TGIF," Lou raised his cup and drank. The three men settled onto the stumps and passed a joint while Will started the fire.

The breeze had settled and the smoke traveled straight up to curl around the oak's branches. Riley sat bolt upright next to Will and followed his every move with just a twitch of her head. As Sammy, Lou, and Johnny downed beer after beer, Will stole glances at one particular tree branch above their heads. It extended at least thirty feet from the oak's massive trunk and, because of its girth, Will had chosen it to secure the fixed pulleys. He'd attached two more into the tree's trunk and, even though he'd been climbing this one since he was a kid, shimmying out on that branch with the coil of rope, pulleys, and tools had definitely tested his nerve.

Sammy stood, swaying slightly, looking at Will over the flames, "You've got the creepiest eyes, man. Doesn't he have creepy eyes?"

Lou took off his shoes and dug his toes into the dirt, "At least he doesn't have froggy eyes."

Sammy had always been the butt of their jokes. But the gap yawned wider now and Sammy seemed edgy. A nervous tic—pulling his left shoulder up to his ear—seemed more pronounced and frequent.

A train's horn moaned in the distance. Will refilled their beers.

"You were a total freak in high school, man. But look at you now." Lou rolled another joint.

"Army hero," Sammy added.

"Marine."

Johnny knelt close to the fire and poked the logs with a stick, "Funny how things turn out, huh?"

Will sipped his beer and stared into the flames.

"I mean," Johnny continued, trying to catch Will's eye, "high school seems like such a long time ago. What a bunch of assholes we were, huh?"

Will glanced at his watch, "The girls should be here soon."

"Wait," Sammy's shoulder twitched, "not those two girls you hung with in high school?"

"Astrid and Caroline? No." Will walked to his truck to grab the ropes.

Sammy's expression became serious, "Yeah, Caroline the punk chick. Remember her?"

Lou shot Sammy a glance. Johnny stared into the flames.

"These girls aren't from New Canaan." Will stood in front of them with figure eights of rope. He raised his eyebrows, "BJs ten bucks a pop."

Lou stood to slap Will on the shoulder.

Will smiled, brought his hands in front of his face and wiggled his fingers, "But no hands."

"The fuck?"

"Hey, not my rules. Said we can't touch the girls." Will threw the rope from hand to hand, "So I thought it would be weird to tie our hands behind our backs."

Lou nodded, "Like in pornos. Kinky shit."

Will raised his eyebrows. "What do ya say?"

"Hell yeah, man," Lou downed the rest of his beer and put his hands behind his back, "You learn this shit in the Marines?"

Johnny shook his head, "No thanks, man. Not for me."

Lou turned to Johnny. "You're such a pussy lately." Lou looked at Will, "He's gotten all church-y on us."

Johnny shook his head but kept his eyes on Will as if he wanted to ask him a question or confess something. It made Will angry.

Sammy whined about the rope, but Lou told him to shut up.

As the sun dropped behind the trees' lush canopy, dusk swallowed every detail outside the fire's reach.

Riley sat perfectly still while Will finished tying Lou's wrists. He then connected Sammy and Lou's hands with a length of rope just long enough to trip them up if they tried to run. As he finished tying the knots, he debated on what to do with Johnny. He could just scrap the entire plan, act surprised that the girls didn't show, have a few beers, and call it a night. But then the memory of Caroline slinking down the hallways, head bowed, shoulders slumped, ambushed him. He decided that he'd have to take

Johnny down. It would be easy. Johnny was stoned and drunk. He could have probably taken them all down if he'd wanted.

"They coming soon, man? These ropes are a little tight."

"Yeah," Will threw his thumb over his shoulder, "I think I hear 'em now."

Will stood in front of Johnny, tossing the last rope from hand to hand. "You sure?"

Johnny shook his head.

"Well, I guess you can tie me up, then." Will stepped toward Johnny and, in one swift movement, kicked him in the chest. The kick knocked him off the tree stump, his back hit the ground hard and he tried righting himself but, when he rolled to his stomach, Will dug his knee into his back, grabbed his hands, and bound them with the rope. His feet proved more difficult and he caught Will in the stomach with his bare heel.

The kick nearly launched Will on his ass, but he caught himself with both hands.

By this time, Sammy and Lou had panicked, tried to run, but didn't count on the rope connecting them. Since they ran in slightly different directions, the rope yanked them back, threw them off balance and sent them to the ground. By the time Will reached them, they were covered in dirt and weeds and brush. Will bound their feet.

"What the fuck, Goynes?" Lou's voice cracked, he inched away from the fire pit.

"Shut up."

Snot and tears cut rivulets in the dirt on Sammy's face. "He's gonna kill us. Everyone's said—"

"Everyone said what?"

Johnny tried to even out the panic rising in his voice. "The fuck is this all about, Goynes?"

Will stood over Sammy. "What is everyone saying?"

"Shit, man, let us go." Sammy tried rolling onto his side. "Please, Will."

"What are they saying?"

"Shut up, Sammy." Johnny tried to mask the fear in his voice. "Nothing. Nothing, Will. No one said anything."

Will walked behind them, to the oak's trunk, to retrieve the lengths of rope he'd run through the pulleys. He didn't say a word as he tightened the ropes around the men's ankles and wrists. When he was done, accompanied by an escalating chorus of curses and threats and, eventually, panicked begging, he walked back to the tree and started hoisting them up one at a time.

When each swung a few feet above ground, Will secured the ropes, went back to his truck, grabbed the Beta recorder, adjusted the tripod, fired it up, and tried to steady the men in his frame.

They looked like possums with their feet and hands bound together, backs rounded, asses drooping. It surely was damn uncomfortable. Sammy was nearly bawling.

"Shut up, Sammy. When we get down, we're going to waste him."

Riley sat at attention as Will rested his index finger on the red RECORD button, "Now, who wants to start?"

Lou's lips curled and he reminded Will of a raccoon he'd once cornered in the barn. "Start what, you psycho maniac? Is this because we used to tease you in gym about your skinny legs?"

"Or because we knocked off your hat in the hall-ways?" Sammy's voice caught in his throat. "Because everyone did that, man, it wasn't just us—"

"No, you idiots," Johnny cut them off, "It's because of what we did to Caroline Godrich."

Will nearly thought about cutting him loose but said, "Confess you got her drunk and raped her."

"You're fuckin' psycho, Goynes." Spit edged Lou's lips, "Rape? We were just goofing around. My dad will have you thrown in jail for—"

"You spread the rumor that you'd done her while she was passed out. That's rape."

Lou spit at Will's feet, "We're not confessing nothin'. After all, someone told Principal Bunch and he didn't seem to think it was such a big deal. We were just having a little fun."

"Bunch just wanted to win games." Will pushed Lou's head with his hand and sent him spinning, "You're not gonna want to swing for very long. Eventually your shoulders will pull right out of the sockets. You think it hurts now—"

"Fuck you, man."

"I'll leave you all night. Let the coyotes get ya."

Sammy's face glistened with tears and snot ran into his mouth. He started blubbering, "I always felt bad about it. I didn't—"

"Shut up, Sammy." A vein in Lou's forehead bulged. "We—"

Will pressed RECORD.

"I said, shut up, Mansour."

Will steadied Sammy so he wouldn't swing out of the frame, "What did you feel bad about?"

"We—"

Lou shouted over Sammy, "You know what I heard about you, Goynes?"

As far as Will knew, no one, besides his family, knew that he had been discharged from the Marines.

"Yeah, Goynes, my dad's got a buddy in the Marines who told him stuff."

Will pressed STOP.

"He said you're a rat."

"Shut up."

"You get a service medal, Goynes?"

Sammy and Johnny kept quiet. Will licked his lips.

"I bet you didn't. I bet you didn't 'cause you're a rat."

"Shut up."

"You told those camel jockeys who the intelligence officers were. You're not a hero, Goynes. Those officers were tortured because you're a rat."

Will got up, walked to his truck and grabbed his rifle.

"What you gonna do? Shoot me while I'm tied up? So you're a rat and a coward?"

Will held the butt of the rifle close to Lou's face, "Shut up."

"You're a fucking traitor, Goynes."

Will popped Lou in the face with the butt of the rifle and heard the bridge of his perfect nose snap. Blood poured down Lou's chin. He spat it out as best he could. His voice leveled, "Traitor."

Will popped him in the jaw. "I told you to shut up."

Lou made a sound like an injured animal. Riley sat with her ears pricked, her eyes glued to Will.

"You think you were going to get us to confess to something we didn't even do?"

"Yes, we did, Lou." Sammy could barely speak.

"Listen to you crying like a little girl. Shut up, Mansour."

Will sent Lou spinning with one shove of his foot.

"I always felt bad about it."

Will pressed START. "What'd you feel bad about?"

"We did. We did get her drunk and then Lou and Johnny—"

"Shut up, Mansour," Johnny warned.

"Think about it, Mansour," Lou's face looked very pale against the blood now running down his neck and soaking his T-shirt. "He's not going to kill us. He'd rot in jail. I told everyone at work I was going to weird Will Goynes's place tonight."

Sammy shook his head, "It's just—"

"Shut up, goddamnit!"

"Johnny and Lou did it. I was there but I—"

"What'd they do?"

"You know. They *did* Caroline Godrich that night under the bleachers."

•

There was more to the confession. Over Johnny's and Lou's protests, Sammy gave details. After cutting them down, Will removed the ropes from their feet, ordered them into the flatbed and drove them back to Lou's car where he loosened Sammy's wrists and told him to remove Lou's and Johnny's while he stood by with his rifle aimed at them.

Lou shoved Sammy. "Get in the trunk, pussy."

Lou popped the trunk and Sammy sat, crying softly now, with his legs hanging out the open trunk.

Before they pulled away, Lou rolled down the passenger window, "Everyone knew you were a freak, Goynes, but I'll make sure everyone knows you're a traitor and a nutjob, too."

The Camaro's headlights illuminated the space between the house and the barn. Lou gunned it, fishtailing gravel all over the yard, and tore down the lane.

•

When their taillights disappeared, Will went inside, fed Riley, made copies of the tape, and put them in his dad's gun safe.

Then he sat on his front porch and waited. With Riley at his side, Will watched bats dive and bugs swirl around the porch light. The wheezy screech of a barn owl accompanied the gravel-crunch of a squad car rolling up his drive.

The officers, a lean, nervous kid with a big Adam's apple and an older cop named Spitz who Will recognized, got out of their squad car and walked slowly toward Will.

"Put that dog inside."

Will did.

When he walked back onto the cement steps, Spitz asked, "You know why we're here?"

"Yes, sir."

"I know your dad. Known him for years."

Will nodded.

Spitz stood a few feet from Will. The younger cop hung back shifting from foot to foot and keeping his hand close to his holster.

"Lou came into the station with a busted nose and a story about you kidnapping him and Johnny Henderson." Spitz hoisted up his pants, rested a foot on the bottom step, and leaned toward Will, "Said you tied 'em up and held 'em at gunpoint?"

"Yes, sir. Except it wasn't just Lou and Johnny. Sammy Mansour, too."

Spitz squinted. "You want to tell me why?"

"They raped a friend of mine."

Spitz didn't look surprised. He nodded slowly and scratched the stubble on his chin, "So you wanted revenge?"

"A confession." Will handed him a copy of the tape.

Spitz took the tape, turned it over and tapped it on his thigh. Quietly, he asked, "You made a copy of this?"

Will nodded.

"Your dad home?"

"No, sir. He and my sister are in Grayling for the weekend."

"Well, you probably know I'll have to take you in."

"Yes, sir." Will stepped off the porch, turned, and put his hands together behind his back.

"No need for that. Just get in the car."

As they turned onto the main road, Will gazed into the night to watch the lightless fields transform into glowing subdivisions, sidewalks, gas stations, grocery stores. He knew he was in for a fight. And that he'd probably lose. But he didn't care.

The tapes were safe. He'd learned how to wait. And, this time, he'd do it right.

Angle of Entry

Derek stood behind me on the cliff's edge, middle fingers pressing my hipbones, thumbs dug into the top of my ass. My desire to dive felt like an itch. The incongruous rocky island erupted out of the water like a black beak topped by wildflowers and windswept bushes. Two willows clung to the top, their exposed roots witch-fingering the island's sides. Caroline and I had always gone alone. Never taken anyone. Not even Paulie.

Thirty feet below, the late afternoon sun transformed the water into dark glitter. I lived for the moment I could climb the rocks, drop, let my hands slice a path through the frigid lake until the cold squeezed the breath out of me. Caroline taught me. Said it felt like flying. For me, it wasn't so much about flying as it was about clawing my way back up.

Caroline and I ushered at New Canaan's summer stock theater, the red velvet-seated Whiting Auditorium. When *Seven Brides for Seven Brothers* rolled into town, we tried desperately to calm our thoughts, but during rehearsals, two of the brothers—Derek and Tony—would wink at us, blow us kisses and, even though we knew they probably weren't interested in girls, let ourselves fall into desperate schoolgirl crushes. They were wild stallions with their long hair and sideburns and chiseled bodies, and they milked our adoration for all it was worth. They were part of what the rest of the company called "The Three Musketeers." But the third Musketeer, Eric, had been sick with something that, in the towns where they'd been performing, doctors couldn't quite pin down.

After Sunday's matinee, Caroline and I challenged Derek and Tony to a game of euchre. In the theater's common area, the other company members looked simultaneously bored and sophisticated, lounging in layers of leotards and leg warmers, watching TV, reading books.

Derek sighed. "God, what do you do for fun around here?"

"They wait around for summer so they can beat the traveling minstrels at cards." Tony threw a ten of spades. "This hand's just awful, honey. Deal me some real cards."

Eric lay on the carpet with his head on a pillow. His eyes looked sunken, as did his cheeks. His skin sallow and waxy. An angry rash ran up one ankle.

Derek studied his cards. "What's spade again?"

We'd already beaten them four times and Tony was exasperated. "Jesus, Derek, you have the concentration of a tittie fly."

"Tsetse," Eric offered.

"It's this town. It's killing my brain cells," Derek moaned.

Eric added, "It's the Nagasaki of mind-numbing."

"The Hiroshima of tedium," Tony sighed.

We'd already taken them to Angelo's for Coney Islands, gone ice skating at the IMA, to the bowling alley and roller rink. Farrell's for ice cream. What else was there?

"We dive," Caroline offered. I was surprised. Caroline was shy to a fault in front of them and barely spoke. She looked at me imploringly.

"Yeah," I nodded, "We dive."

"What, like, off a diving board?" Derek had perfected his eye roll during their run in New Canaan. "Daring."

"No, silly," I added, "Off a cliff."

This stopped them. They perked up and stared at us. Even Eric opened his eyes.

"Into the water." Caroline threw the left bower. "We just euchred you."

Derek and Tony leaned forward. "Take us."

So we did.

•

Derek reminded me of a crow: impulsive, slick, dark, hovering over everything, ready to pounce. Tony was reptilian with his easy moves and steady eyes. Eric played the tow-headed, blue-eyed innocent and was 100% human. Vulnerable. Soft. In just the two weeks Eric had been in town, he'd noticeably lost weight. Now, leaning against Tony as we prepared to climb down the boat's ladder, with the light slanting the way it does late in the afternoon, he looked frighteningly gaunt.

There was something terrifyingly over-the-top about Derek and Tony. They were constantly outmanning each other, strutting, primping and, just generally, doing things that didn't seem at all reasonable. *If I do this, you do something ten times more daring and completely amazing. If you kick this redneck's ass, I'll kick two redneck asses.* The makeup artists used more concealer on their black eyes, cuts, scratches, busted lips than anyone else in the company. They were gorgeous to a fault: Derek with his flawless skin and black curls, olive complexion, expressive lips, and eyes that showed disapproval with nearly everything. Tony was as tall as Derek—well over six feet—with dirty blond hair and a chest so wide it nearly toppled off his narrow waist.

•

Ever since senior year, ever since Astrid had Mr. Jones for science, a chill had slipped between us. And, then, when her mother killed herself, things got worse. It was like something huge and unstoppable was splitting us down the middle, unraveling everything we'd shared.

That summer, through excellent detective work, I figured out that Caroline and Astrid took Mr. Godrich's Chris-Craft to the island. I would park on the other side of the lake, behind a pine copse, and hike to an outcropping of rock to observe her through a pair of totally righteous binoculars. All of my honey profits went to buy those bad mothers. I'm totally serious. These things could bore through the friggin' walls.

I guess it was spying, but I chose to think of it as watching Astrid—more like something Columbo might do to gather evidence. I'd watched every episode and rerun of *Columbo*, knew everything there was to know about Peter Falk. Falk might have seemed like an unlikely hero for me, but I *got* him. We were a lot alike. People always underestimated him. Always thought they were smarter than him. But he was a different kind of smart. He was the kind of smart that took you off guard. The kind of smart that nailed you when you least expected it.

I took those lessons to the football field. Made the opponent think I was off my game, let them feel cocky, and then blast a thirty-yard bullet to win the game.

It was weird though. Even though I couldn't concentrate for shit in class, I could concentrate on certain things all friggin' day. Like, when I was on the field, I could hang in the pocket until the last moment and, even though it drove Coach Haney crazy, calmly assess the entire field from left to right in the time it took most people to blink. I could figure out where a receiver would be in half a second. Where he'd be in two seconds, how much time defenders had to sack me (which they rarely did). I could rifle that ball off my front foot if I wanted to.

This worked for me on the farm, too. Where my brothers were smart with numbers and ideas, I could stand at the edge of a field and tell you where the plants were wanting for water or showed signs of purple spot or blight or bearing exceptionally or not at all.

Clutch player. Hero. Best arm since Joe Namath.

I didn't need to read what they wrote about me. I knew who I was. I made big plays and the crowd cheer. I won.

•

Out of all of them, Eric had been the most excited to dive. But the climb to the top, which the rest of us barely noticed, wore him out. His understudy had been filling in for him until he got over whatever it was that was making him so exhausted. At some point, he'd been diagnosed with mono and told to rest. Tony and Derek constantly needled him about it—said he smoked too much weed and called him a pussy for not keeping up.

As soon as we got to the top, Eric rallied, dug out some freakish superhuman strength, and insisted we let him dive first. As Caroline told him how far out he needed to jump and where to aim, I wrapped one arm around his waist to steady him. I could feel his spine against my palm, his ribs needling my side and questioned if he could leap far enough out, away from the cliff's face. But when we let him go, he raised both arms above his head, dropped them like wings, and propelled himself so high that he did a pike—his fingertips grazing his ankles—before extending his body into a perfect arrow. He barely made a splash when he hit the water.

Tony and Derek fished him out of the water and helped him up the rocks where he collapsed. He looked elated but exhausted as Caroline and I wrapped him in towels.

Derek plopped down next to me reeking of the skunky weed they'd smoked on the way there. He leaned into my ear, "Help me make Tony jealous. He's been fooling around with an understudy. Thinks I'm too stupid to figure it out."

I shook my head and looked at Caroline sitting between Eric and Tony. She'd wrapped herself in a towel and her wet hair clung to her neck and shoulders. When she laughed at something Eric said, Tony turned away from Caroline, saw Derek leaning into my ear, and glared at me.

"Come on, Astrid," Derek begged, grabbing my arm, pulling me to my feet and over to the cliff, "let's dive together."

In my experience, guys always wanted to do idiotic things. It seemed my job to talk them out of it. And, yet, I didn't like the way Tony had looked at me. So I suddenly faced Derek, slid my arms around his waist and kissed him, hard, on the mouth. When he pulled away, he shot a glance at Tony.

I stood on the edge of the cliff with him pressed behind me, "There are rocks on either side," I said. "The deep part isn't wide enough for us both."

"I'll be fine."

"It's not you I'm worried about."

"Don't be such a girl." His breath scorched the back of my neck. He pulled me into his groin and wrapped his arms around my belly. He felt like a snake—all muscle and intent coiling around me—but he wasn't hard, even with our wet bodies pressed together.

"You go first. I'll follow."

"Come on."

"No."

"Girl," he hissed before stepping around me to balance on the ledge. Raising his arms, he jumped high enough to do a somersault before hitting the water at a slant and producing a huge splash. When he surfaced, he blew a water spout, his hair slick as a seal, and yelled, "Beat that!"

The setting sun turned the usually clear water into an opaque, glittering sheet. I knew where to dive. At the beginning of the summer, Caroline showed me how far to jump away from the rocks and where to aim—at the tallest pine on the opposite shore. All the same, it still gave me that skitchy feeling in my stomach. I preferred to dive when the sun was high and I could see the underwater opening—like a great, wide, toothless mouth—between the submerged rocks.

•

Even this far away, I could see everything: Astrid's gestures, the lift of her chin, the curl of her lip, the way her brow knit at something he whispered in her ear. He was close enough to stick his god-damned tongue into that little hollow behind her ear, that secret place I found when I stood behind her, hugged her, reminding her how much I needed her. *God, Astrid. Please don't do this to me. Please, Astrid. Please. I love you. I love you. I love you.* I willed my thoughts across the calm expanse of water but I don't think they reached her. The binoculars made everything seem painfully detached and, at the same time, incredibly close. I pressed them so hard against my face that they left red rings around my eyes.

I held my breath when that asshole got up slowly and walked behind Astrid. Caroline had turned her back to them. She'd been fussing over the other guy, tucking him in a blanket, and just turned in time to see that fuck shove Astrid from behind.

I kept my sights on her as she fell and, in that split second, a feeling of complete and total agony nearly sunk me. It was like watching her die. She panicked. Flapping her arms as if she wanted to grab something, anything. Trying, desperately, to get in a position to hit the water. I'd never seen her like that. Not even after her mom died. Not even after that.

•

I fell too close to the rocks—I knew, could feel it— and too horizontal. Just before hitting the water, a sharp rock sliced my foot and calf. The water, like a solid wall, stunned me. Knocked the breath out of me. I sunk quickly. My body felt boulder-heavy, as if I no longer had arms or legs but had become a solid, sinking mass. I watched myself sink—an observer of a short film on drowning. I panicked, my heart pounding, but I still couldn't move. Opening my eyes felt like a battle but, when I finally did, the shafts of sunlight I usually used to trace my way to the surface weren't there. The water swallowed and deposited me deep in the lake's belly. As I continued to sink, my panic subsided and, without warning, the water peeled away to be replaced by burgundy roses. They surrounded me. Pressed close. Who knew roses flourished at the bottom of the lake? For as long as I'd been diving with Caroline, I'd never seen them. Never. But there they were, huge blossoms, open fully, pressing close to my face, their velvet petals soft against my cheeks. I kept sinking, my arms and legs useless, the roses tickling my skin. It suddenly felt so good to be sinking. Nothing mattered. Not the constant ache of no longer having Mama. Not Paulie's overbearing love. Not my dad's reserve. Not my grades and achievements. Nothing.

Something belly-white passed close to my face. Five tentacles fluttered in front of my eyes but I didn't recognize them as fingers. They pawed my face, found my hair, and yanked.

I momentarily mistook the stinging pain of my hair being pulled with the roses' thorns burrowing into my scalp. The pain reminded me of something but I couldn't decide if I should embrace it or flee.

My hand found the thing on my hair and grabbed hold.

I erupted from the water coughing and gasping with Caroline's arm hooked under my armpits. She and Derek helped me out of the water but I imme-diately started retching. It felt like I'd swallowed the entire lake. When I'd recovered, leaning on Caroline for support, I heard Tony say, "Jesus, it was just a little shove." I felt murderous. Out of my head with rage.

My anger was unnaturally fierce, as if he ignited all the emotion of the past year.

Before I could get up, Caroline lunged at Tony and pinned him against the rock face. He brought one knee to cover his groin and crossed his arms over his face. She pummeled him with kicks and slaps and punches and screamed about how he could have killed me. Her voice pitched like a wounded animal.

Something about Caroline's rage sobered me. I'm not sure why, exactly, but I found my arms circling her instead of joining in. I pulled her away and we slid down the rock face in each other's arms. Her entire body shook and she buried her face in my chest. She smelled of green lakeweed and dark water, her hair satin against my cheek.

Eric looked from Derek to Tony, his blue eyes sunken, dark-ringed. He shook his head and started down the path toward the boat.

•

Astrid stood next to Caroline, leaning on the windshield, her long arms dangling over the glass, as I ran like a maniac toward the dock. It only took Astrid a split second to figure out what I'd been doing. In that moment, a look traveled over her face that said, *This is it.* I can't explain it. It all happened so fast. But even as I barreled down the dock, toward that fucker who'd pushed her off the cliff, I knew she was done with me. That I no longer had the right.

They were still about a hundred feet from the end of the dock, Caroline at the helm, gliding in slow, when I launched off the dock and swam to the boat. I couldn't help myself. The guys probably wondered who the crazy dude was but I couldn't hear them or Astrid's screams for all my thrashing about. When I heard the motor cut, I grabbed the stern and, in one fluid movement, leaped into the boat. That fuck who pushed Astrid stood but, before he knew what hit him, I grabbed the towel wrapped around his shoulders and drove my forehead into his nose.

It was then that Astrid wrapped her arms around my neck. Here's the thing: I would never hurt a girl but I would die if I hurt Astrid. She squeezed so tight that I couldn't breathe. I tried to dig my fingers under her arm but she held tight with her other hand gripping the wrist of the arm that choked me. My fingers were wet and kept slipping off her arm. I could have driven the back of my head into her face, I could have flipped her, I could have done a few things but I couldn't hurt her so I dropped to my knees and simply let her choke me while that fucker covered his bleeding nose with his hands. Caroline stepped in front of me with this look that kept switching between fear and pity and Astrid kept hissing into my ear, "Stop it! Stop it! Stop it!" with the hard bone of her forearm pressed firmly against my Adam's apple and even though I couldn't breathe, I felt her pressed close to me, nearly naked in that bathing suit, warm and wet, draped over the back of me. For a moment, it felt like before, when she'd jump on my back and I'd swing her until we both fell to the ground laughing and lay on our backs with the world spinning around us. It had been a long time since I'd been alone with her. Practically all summer. But I remembered. When I dropped to my knees she didn't let go, didn't ease up, and I started seeing spots, these one-dimensional spots that turned into fat, glowing jellyfish with long, fringy tentacles. I figured that we'd gone underwater because my head throbbed and these spots kept multiplying and pressing close to my eyes and then they were in my eyes because they stung like sharp electric jolts and I figured that this would be a good time to die so my head dropped to one side and my body went slack with this weird resignation, something I'd never felt before, even in sleep.

As I fell, I heard Caroline's voice, very far away but close, booming but hushed, begging Astrid to let go.

Initial Encounters

"Bless me, Father, for I have sinned."

Father Maurice Silver is very hungover. Since Leila's death, this is not uncommon. But it does result in two things: his sense of smell becomes beagle-sharp and anything above a whisper strikes his eardrums like a tympani. This young man's voice is so low and solid that Maurice wants to cry. The smell of sweat and something undefined (composting leaves or chemicals, he can't decide which) fills the confessional.

Maurice whispers his response, "Lord, you know all things; you know that I love you."

"My last confession was … I don't even remember."

Maurice doesn't particularly care. It's Friday, a hot-as-hell-dog-day-of-summer Friday, and it feels like a blast furnace inside that confessional. He just wants Father Simms to get back from his dental appointment and take over.

After twenty-some years, he's heard every sin. The mortal ones: adultery, fraud, murder. The venial sins of impure acts with oneself, impure acts with oneself, and more impure acts with oneself (you'd think it was all young people did these days), violation of copyright law, bestiality, forgery, excessive sex, fraud, embezzlement, cheating, stealing, transvestitism, wife swapping, cohabitation, bribes, anal sex, gambling, oral sex before marriage, excessive waste, impure sexual fantasies, fetishes, abortion, promotion of prostitution, and on and on. It's a helluva long list and rolls like a timeline against his career. At one time, he could name the first congregant who confessed each of these sins. Now they have become a congealed mass. He can't untangle one from the other. Did Mrs. Hicks have sex with her mailman, or was that Mrs. Anderson? Did the Johnsons and Roarks wife-swap? Or was it the Jacobs and Smiths? It didn't matter. It was all the same. They sinned. He sinned. God forgave. Amen.

The young man begins sobbing and the words catch in his throat, "I think——"

"Yes, son?"

"I think I'm dying."

This is not what Maurice expects. This was to be the last confession of his morning. He'd planned on dispensing a few terse *Hail Marys*, be done with it, drive to Angelo's for a Coney and fries. He looks through the fleur de lis screen and edits his first impression: this isn't a boy but a gaunt young man with a sharply-defined, delicate profile and shoulder-length hair.

Maurice still isn't too concerned when he responds, "You *think*?"

"A friend of mine back in New York died in January. And I have what he had."

Maurice wonders if this boy is a hypochondriac. He leans forward, "Dying is not a sin."

He swipes at his eyes, "It is if you're gay."

Maurice pauses, "I see."

Quickly he adds, "She said you wouldn't turn me away."

"She?"

"Astrid Miracal. She brought me. She's waiting outside."

A sigh escapes before he can check it.

His words come quickly, "Because I really need to talk to someone. My family—they won't—my dad calls me a faggot—I'm sorry, Father—"

"It's okay—"

"He won't let my mom or brothers speak to me and I need to figure some stuff out, so if you won't talk to me—"

"You're welcome here." Just that name—Astrid Miracal—pulls him apart. It's been a year since Leila's death and, besides the cliché words of consolation that spilled from his lips at the funeral, he's never spoken to the girl. He doesn't know how much, if anything, she knows. He doubts that Leila would have told her only daughter about their affair. That wasn't her style. All the same, he's had the impression that Astrid knows *something*. At the funeral, which he'd officiated, there'd been something about Astrid, something beyond grief—a question, was that it?—that kept snagging his conscience.

Even though he sees how much pain this kid is in, Maurice badly wants a drink. He hears an exterior door slam and Father Simm's pigeon-toed gait plodding down the hallway. He tells the young man to exit the confessional and, even though Maurice had seen the worst of two wars, he gasps. The young man's hipbones barely keep up his jeans, his wrists and hands are skeletal. Maurice guides him to his office by cupping a palm around the young man's elbow. His fragility throws Maurice off, makes him feel lightheaded, so he asks him his name, which is Eric, and silently repeats it all the way down the parish school's long, shiny hallway, their shadows ushering them past posters of Jesus and crosses and cotton-ball lambs, leading to his office.

After settling himself behind his desk, Maurice's hand instinctively reaches for the desk drawer handle behind which resides a bottle of bourbon. He'd always had a drink or two to steady his nerves but, lately, he drinks with the destructive ferocity to forget. He forces himself to look at Eric. Even though it's hot, Eric shivers. Before wrapping him in a blanket he keeps for the winter (the radiators in this part of the building are notoriously faulty) Maurice notices a savage, blistered rash running in perpendicular lines down the boy's neck.

He sits back down, his hand instinctively pulling the drawer's smooth wooden handle. He stops, pushes the drawer back in, deliberately folds his hands over one another, and lays them on his desk where he can keep a close eye on them.

After a while, he's getting a better idea of what's going on. Eric's originally from Nebraska, youngest of four boys, where the father's a small-town politician. One day, after school, his mom walked in on him and a guy, an afternoon when she wasn't supposed to be home, an afternoon when he shouldn't have been making out with some guy in his bedroom and, after that, his dad made it pretty clear that he wasn't welcome in the family home any longer. So he made his way to New York, worked odd jobs, took dance lessons and, eventually, started landing jobs in musical theater. Been there ten years. His partner died last winter and, feeling like he had to get away for a while, he took a summer stock gig. But the first week on the road, he'd started feeling ill. He'd toughed it out, kept performing but, by the end of the run in New Canaan, the company moved on without him.

Eric insists that his symptoms are the same as his partner's who, it turned out, had been ill for a while before finally being diagnosed with a rare cancer called Kaposi's sarcoma. He became progressively sicker; no drugs seemed to help and, unable to fight off infection, a particularly vicious strain of pneumonia killed him.

"Where are you staying?"

Eric's hands are long and delicate and he moves them like wings when he talks, "With Astrid. She's an usher at the theater. I was going to fly to New York this week but I don't think I can. These last two weeks … I feel … it's as if everything's shutting down. I have no appetite. I'm feverish. I know it's the same thing as Max … but you can't catch cancer. Can you?"

Maurice isn't sure. But he has seen his share of dying people and only has to look at Eric's sunken eyes, the skin inside the eyelashes swollen and milky-pink, the whites very dull, the waxy pallor of his cheeks, to know that whatever he has is indeed taking the life force out of him.

Eric talks slowly, as if each word exhausts him, about something else, the rumor of some disease striking gay men, junkies, and prostitutes. Maurice is listening, taking notes now because his head pounds so fiercely that he has to take drastic measures to pay attention. But it's more than the hangover. Against his will, his memory has tumbled back to the feeling of Leila in his arms, of her body pressed against his, and he's wondering at the unlikely parallels between this young man's life and his own: the person they loved most in the world dead, this young man dying, and Maurice pretty much killing himself with every bottle he tosses in the trash.

•

Maurice makes a call to a friend who also happens to be the head of Oncology at University Hospital. A few minutes later, they're in Astrid's Monte Carlo barreling south down US-23. In the back seat, Eric's wrapped in blankets, his head resting on Maurice's lap. Maurice barely feels him. It's as if a hollow-boned bird has landed on him. Maurice feels as helpless as Eric, as helpless as the moment he learned of Leila's death. In lieu of bourbon, he's been drink-ing Coca-Cola. Now, his hands shake, he's nauseous, clammy, and sweating—high on caffeine and withdrawing from alcohol. Perfect.

Cornfields line the highway. The midday sun casts no shadows and makes the road shimmer. It's been a good summer, though, plenty of rain, and the corn is at least four feet high, tasseled, its deep green fading under the sun's blast. He holds a cool washcloth to Eric's forehead and tries to avoid looking at Astrid. She has pulled her curls back into a ponytail and Maurice can't help but notice that everything—the shape of her ears, the curve of her jaw, the length of her neck—resembles her mother. Ever since Leila's death, he's thought of Astrid as his daughter. As if she is his and Leila's. He knows this is ridiculous. He barely knows her but wants desperately to love her like a daughter. But a mountain of absolute nothing separates them.

"I'm so scared." Eric's eyes are closed and his lips barely move.

Maurice refolds the washcloth and presses the cool side against Eric's forehead, "Give your burdens to the Lord, and he will take care of you." He pulls another washcloth out of a cooler Astrid has packed and adds, "He will not permit the godly to slip and fall."

"What if I haven't been godly?"

Maurice wants to ask, *Who has?* but lowers his voice as if telling a secret, "I'll tell you something." Astrid's eyes flick into the rearview mirror. "Everyone sins. Even the Pope."

"The Pope ..." Eric's lips curl into a smile.

"Yeah. The Pope. And even St. Astrid."

"St. Astrid," Eric says with such devotion that it nearly brings Maurice to tears.

Eric adds, "Before Max ... I was with a few guys."

"Yes. Well, it's in the past."

"And I'm gay. Doesn't that mean I'm going to hell?"

"It's the teachings of man, of the church, that distinguishes homosexuality as a sin. Not Christ's teaching."

Eric opens his eyes, "How can you say that? You represent the church."

"Yes. Well ... it's not the first time I've said it." And adds, almost without thinking, "They'll get me for it, eventually."

Astrid's eyes appear, again, in the rearview and Eric's brow wrinkles, "You're still a real priest, though, right?"

Maurice nods and closes his eyes, "For now."

•

It's just a hunch but Maurice feels like Astrid is willing him to broach the subject of her mother. As he's contemplating this, an enormous fact weighs him down: if he hadn't fallen in love with her, Leila would still be alive. There's no way to deny it. Every day, he wishes he'd been stronger or, at the very least, never told Leila about the defrocking inquiry. It's been dragging on for over a year. If he'd said nothing, she might have seen how problems work themselves out or, at the very least, that things weren't so dire.

He's sitting across from Astrid in the pastel waiting room with its molded chairs, magazines, and pamphlets. He's already exhausted his repertoire of *safe* questions about her first year of college: about pre-med, what she'd studied, her roommates, the food. Now they sit quietly across from each other. Maurice still feels like hell. Like his head's been snagged in a vice. He pops aspirin at the water cooler.

"It was nice of you to help." Astrid looks up from her magazine. "Last night, I helped him get undressed. He has this rash, like big spider bites, all over his back. He cried pretty much all night. I laid next to him in Mama's bed and held his hand. I didn't know what else to do."

Maurice absently flips through a *Ladies' Home Journal*. "I was in New York for a conference this past winter. A few priests, city priests, were talking about something like this. They called it *wasting disease*."

"What is it?"

He shakes his head, "Hard to say. It's a puzzle for sure."

Astrid's long, tan legs, punctuated by white Keds, stick awkwardly into the space between them. She's looking at her purple shoelaces. "Now we see things imperfectly, like puzzling reflections in a mirror …"

That verse was Leila's favorite. Maurice acts like he's reading some inane article about stain removal, but the words hit him and he's gone, again, thinking of Leila, wanting to say her name out loud.

"That's an interesting article, huh?" Leila leans over to tap the title, "On stain removal. You don't seem like a *Ladies' Home Journal* kind of guy."

When he realizes what he's been staring at, he closes the magazine and shrugs.

Astrid studies his craggy nose and full lips (so different from her father's delicate features), his large hands, chest, and shoulders straining the seams of his suit coat, the scuffs on his black leather wingtips. Behind him, there's a row of windows overlooking a garden. The sun is just about to set and shadows fill the waiting room. A ray of dwindling light illuminates the silver at his temple.

"You left a message for her that afternoon," she says simply.

The magazine slips between his knees and falls to the floor. He looks down as if the space between it and his hands is insurmountable.

She wishes that getting the truth out of people were as simple as dissecting monkeys and rats. There's the heart and lungs and liver. If only she could slice through this quickly. Slice him open and find a file folder with all the answers. Her mother had debilitating bouts of depression but had never threatened suicide. It just didn't add up. It's been nagging at her. She's tried to extinguish it, explain it away. But, like her father asking, *How did the blood get on the knob? What the hell did she do? Cut her wrists and go watch TV?*, she's unable to resolve it.

She knows the answer will be messy. Muddied by emotion. Hurtful. It will be all of those things and then some. It occurs to her that she already knows the answer because, at the funeral, she saw his chin quiver and, during a prayer, she opened her eyes to see him wipe his sleeve across his face and, during the homily, he took extra care to steer clear of every delicate, telltale link that might suggest intimacy.

He leans over, picks up the magazine, rolls it into a tube, and taps his knee. He's nodding now, trying to decide how to respond. What's the point of protecting Leila? After all, *she* left them.

"There were so many messages that day. Everyone kept calling—Auntie, Edie—that's her best friend—you. The next week, I kept playing them. I couldn't stop listening. Mama was never able to figure out how to work that machine ... so most of her conversations were recorded. I kept those. Just to hear her voice. She didn't really say anything important. At first I was just looking for clues. Anything. But now I just listen because it's her voice, you know?"

During the silence that follows, Astrid doesn't back off or apologize. She could have panicked, said, *Never mind, sorry I asked.* Or, *It's not important.* But she isn't sorry. And it is important. She just keeps looking at him, leaning into the space between them. Somehow he knows that she's determined, tenacious, fierce. She'll peel back his skin, yank at the muscle to get to the bone.

"I—" he begins but falters. Until this moment, he'd felt like he had no right to mourn or like he had no one with whom to share his grief. The bourbon helped. It was the only thing that smoothed the rough patches. It couldn't erase it but kept it in check.

Astrid has drawn aside the curtain. Might as well walk in.

He's still looking at her sneakers like a naughty brat. "Your folks—" the words taste stale on his tongue, "were having problems and your mother came to me." He stopped again. This isn't what she wants to know. What is he going to do? Detail their affair?

He pulls both hands over his face and through his hair, "I would have left the church for her. There wasn't even a question in my mind."

They're looking at each other now. The aperture between them, which once seemed incredibly wide, closed.

"I'm sorry, Astrid. I'm just so sorry."

Astrid is nodding. Biting her lip and nodding as if he'd just confirmed a reservation she'd made a very long time ago. "But why kill herself?"

He tells her about the move to defrock him, emphasizing the fact that it was his conflicting stance on certain issues that made him vulnerable. He doubts his decision to tell her this but pushes on, "And there was something else. Someone—I still don't know who—threatened to tell the congregation about us."

"But—"

"I think that she was protecting me. The way she saw it, the only way for it to go away was for her to go away." He tries covering his face with those big swollen hands.

"She meant everything to me."

Astrid wants to lean in and tell him it'll be okay, that he'll be okay, that she's going to be okay, but if she's learned one thing it's that you can't intrude on someone's grief. All you can do is sit close and let them feel it.

Tell Me Something I Don't Know

"What do you mean by *sting,* dear?"

Louise's mother kept her eyes on the *Flint Journal* entertainment section. She was only *half-listening,* which was what Louise called Mae's ability to capture key phrases so that she could lob back a question and not be accused of ignoring her daughter.

Louise rubbed her eyes. "A sting. Like *The Sting.*"

Mae ruffled the paper. "You mean that movie with Robert Redford?"

From their corner booth at Big Boy, Louise gazed past her mother's expensive dye-job and carefully applied makeup, out the window, at Big Boy's checkerboard backside, his pumpkin head, and perfectly coifed hair.

"Sort of," Louise continued. "The police had been getting complaints of guys, lots of guys, visiting that rest stop. Spending time in the stalls. Someone reported three pairs of feet in one stall. "

"Heavens," Mae closed the *Journal,* sipped her steaming coffee and, for the first time since they'd sat down, registered her daughter's distress. She watched Louise twirl her hair around her index finger. It's what she did when backed into a corner. Mae focused on her daughter not only because of the story that was unfolding but because Louise hadn't kept up with plucking that niggling uni-brow or coloring the gray sneaking in at her temples. She blotted her mouth with a paper napkin, "You haven't been to see Trenton, have you? You need him to take care of that gray."

Louise was so used to her mother's constant appraisal that the slam barely registered. She squeezed her eyes shut. She couldn't shake the image of her husband, in one of those dirty stalls with those dirty men doing dirty things. He wouldn't even eat a strawberry if she accidentally dropped it on the floor. He folded his socks. He *ironed* his boxers. "Are you listening? Brian was one of them."

"Brian?" Mae laughed, thinking Brian helped execute the sting, "Why in heaven's name would Brian help the police?"

"No. Brian wasn't *helping*. He was *caught*. In the sting. He was one of the guys in the stalls."

Mae gasped. Their waitress, too young and too anxious to please, approached her regular customers with a smile. "What can I get you, Mrs. Shaheen?" Mae held up her hand and told her to scoot.

Louise opened her eyes to see the waitress backing up. "It's all right. I'll take a piece of banana cream pie." At forty, Louise had perfected the good cop to her mother's bad. She did it as naturally as breathing. But, right now, she needed serious doses of cream and butter and sugar—all the things Brian had berated her for eating during their fifteen-year marriage. "In fact, bring a slice of lemon meringue, too."

"One of the men in the stalls. You mean?"

Louise looked at the brown Formica table separating them and nodded, "Yeah. I bailed him out last night."

"But he's married. To you."

"Yes."

"He's a homosexual? I don't understand."

"I don't understand, either."

"He's a homosexual football coach? Is that even possible? How could this be? Are you sure he just wasn't at the wrong place at the wrong time?"

"The wrong place at the right time."

Mae looked out the window, annoyed.

Louise rested her head in her hands and massaged her temples. "I don't know. It certainly explains a lot, though."

The waitress gingerly set the slices of pie in front of Louise.

Mae watched as Louise dug into the pie. "What about the kids?"

"They were asleep when I got the call. Jackie came over while I went to the police station. And Brian left before they woke up."

"God bless Jackie."

"Yeah. God bless Jackie."

"So, what's going to happen? Will he go to jail? Will there be a trial? What would they try him on?"

Louise's face, that lovely face, nearly identical to her mother's only younger, angrier, and smarter, somehow, creased into a grimace. "They said something about sodomy laws. About public sexual acts."

"You'll get frown lines."

Louise tried to keep her voice down. "My husband was just caught *fucking* men—plural—in bathroom stalls. Frown lines are the least of my worries."

Mae spoke into her coffee. "You'll want to look your best—"

Louise stuffed meringue into her mouth. "Really?" Her mother was of the generation that believed a new purse and the right lipstick could fix just about anything.

Louise dug into her purse and rummaged until she found a pack of cigarettes.

"When did you start smoking?"

"This morning." She struggled to find the little tab to open the pack but her hands were slick and shaky. She tried ripping it open with her teeth.

"Never use your teeth. And you're not smoking at the table. I raised you better than that. You will not fall apart like some—"

"Woman whose husband prefers men at rest stops to his wife?" She broke two cigarettes trying to extract them from the pack. "I'm going out."

Outside, in the thawing spring, she leaned on her LeSabre—the baby-blue sedan Brian surprised her with on her fortieth—managed to get a cigarette to her lips and lit it. She watched the parade of cars passing on Saginaw. She wondered how many of them knew what happened last night to the cocky but most successful football coach the town had ever seen. The football coach who, it was rumored, but never confirmed, bribed a rival school's quarterback into transferring to New Canaan. The kid showed up on the first day of school driving a late-model Corvette. How blind had she been? How had he paid for those gifts on his teacher's salary? What else hadn't she seen? Certainly she didn't make enough to justify such gifts. She'd bent to his every demand which included, but was not limited to, moving back to New Canaan, raising a family, giving up her writing and, not insignificantly, eating anything made with cream, white flour, or sugar.

She felt completely lost but it seemed familiar, as if she had been carrying it for a very long time, as if it'd been packed tightly into a place that only expanded to prick her conscience when she was particularly vulnerable.

Mae joined her at the car, fanning smoke dramatically. "You smoke like a teenager."

Louise ignored her.

"Didn't you ever learn to smoke?"

Louise's jaw tightened. "Obviously not."

Mae motioned for a cigarette. She took it between her long, tapered fingers, motioned for Louise to light it, dropped her head back, and took a deep, long drag. Mae's skin was flawless, even in her late sixties, olive-toned and wrinkle-free. They shared the same wide-set dark eyes and curvaceous figure. Sucking on the cigarette caused the hair-width lines above Mae's lip to crease. She knew this instinctively and, after a few demonstrations, smothered the cigarette with her sensible pump. "The chip's still there."

"What?"

"The chip." Mae pointed to a chalky-white inden-tation the size of a baseball in Big Boy's sizable backside. "From when you kids dropped him. Right there."

When Louise was in high school, she and a group of kids stole Big Boy. Huge scandal. They'd hidden him in some bushes behind a potting shed in Louise's backyard, wrote silly ransom notes, and mailed them to the restaurant. The next weekend, when her father found Big Boy, Louise thought she would be grounded for the rest of her life. He'd firmly explained, as he always did, that the owners could press charges that could put her and her class-mates behind bars. Scared the shit out of her coming from her district attorney father. He never raised his voice. But when that vein on his temple throbbed, the one just above the gray sideburn, Louise knew she'd messed up. She also knew, without a doubt, he'd take care of it.

"I thought Dad would kill me."

Mae laughed, "Actually, he found it funny. Everyone at work teased him about his delinquent daughter. About kidnapping charges. They razzed him for months. He loved it."

"Really?"

"Really."

"I never knew."

"There's a lot you didn't know. About your father."

Louise figured that was true. But today, of all days, fielding new (albeit, most probably, fascinating) infor-mation about her father was at the bottom of her list. She had to get herself and her kids through this. And she had no idea what might come next.

·

"Get dressed. I'm taking you to the Renaissance Faire. We'll eat turkey legs and pretend we're having fun." Jackie pulled a book off Louise's face and read the cover, "*Crime and Punishment?*"

Louise rolled onto her other side, pulled her pillow over her head and said, "Go away."

"Come on, Louise. It's past noon." Jackie firmly shook Louise's shoulder, "I want my best friend back. We haven't had fun in ages. Mae took the kids to the pool. We'll dance like wenches, drink gløgg, and listen to lute solos."

"I've scheduled this as a sleeping-slash-moping day."

They'd met in fourth grade when Jackie's mom moved their family from Virginia to marry the Shaheen's widowed neighbor. Since the *incident*, as they referred to it, Jackie had been Louise's rock. She'd gotten the charges against Brian dropped and helped her sell and pack her and Brian's house. Brian moved in with a friend, and Louise and the kids moved in with her mother.

"Come on, Lou, it's been over a year. The worst is over. Stop feeling sorry for yourself. There are wars, plagues, massacres, people starving in—"

"Don't say China. They eat just fine. They're healthier than we are. Militarily and economically. Mark my words."

"Whatever."

"Ethiopia." She rolled over to face Jackie. Her hair pooled on the pillow and stuck to her face. "Now there's a country I could get behind. A few million people worse off than me."

"Get up. I'm tired of this." Jackie yanked the covers back. Louise curled into a ball. "I'm taking you to the Faire and you'll like it."

•

Louise did not like the Renaissance Faire. But then she spotted the sign ALL WEAPONS MUST BE SHEATHED and read the error-ridden fine print beneath:

Longbows are allowed as long as they are not strung, arrows with tips are not allowid unless you are completing in the longbow competition that day. Swords, knives, dirks and daggers must be completly sheathed and peace-tied. Axes, claymores, maces, antique firearms, pikes and halberds are NOT allowed on the Festivel site. No drawing of any weapon at any time. Must be 18 or older to carry a weapon.

"What's a *dirk*?"

Jackie bit into a fried piece of dough. "Wasn't he that guy who lied about fingering Maria Kasseo in eleventh grade? Dirk the Jerk?"

"Now you're talking my language. Jerks."

"Okay." Jackie cut her off and grabbed Louise's arm. She was at least five inches taller and built like a blonde Amazonian. "Here's the deal. No talking about Brian or anything to do with Brian."

"Can I talk about weapons I might use to kill Brian?"

"Not if you directly reference him."

"Can I talk about unstrung longbows and tip-less arrows?"

"Yes."

"This should be fun."

•

After the Queen's Tea and a few oversized mugs of mulled wine, Louise started enjoying the oppressive July heat, the gritty dust between her toes, the jugglers, the awkward teens, the disquieting adults dressed in tights, a completely inane play entitled *Washing Well Wenches*, and off-key fife solos. Maybe *enjoy* wasn't quite the word, but she was having some fun after such a long time of not having any.

They had just passed what seemed like a spontaneous reenactment of Robin Hood meeting Lady Marian when she heard, "Professor Shaheen! Hey! Professor!"

Louise turned to see a boy in black tights, a royal blue doublet, plumed hat, and sheathed dagger (sheathed!) running toward her. When he stopped in front of her, breathless, she couldn't quite place him. He dropped his hands to his knees and gazed up. "I've been looking all over for you. Saw you in the audience. Did you enjoy the performance?"

Performance? Louise couldn't place him.

The boy, regaining his breath, stood and raised his eyebrows. He was tall with blond curls touching his shoulders, a dimpled chin and still-gangly, adolescent body, "I was the Italian nobleman in *Washing Well Wenches*."

"Gavin," Louise drawled unenthusiastically, recognizing him as a student in her summer class, "From Creative Writing I, right?"

He threw his hands out as if anticipating a hug. Louise did the same but leaned back.

She introduced Gavin to Jackie.

Without taking his eyes off Louise, he chimed, "She's the best teacher I've ever had."

"Really?" Jackie raised her eyebrows.

"Yeah. She's really helped my writing."

Jackie seemed genuinely interested. "Oh, and what are you writing about?"

Louise jumped in. "That play was something else."

"I wrote it. My folks are the executive directors of the Faire."

"Huh."

"Yeah, well, gotta run, M'lady." He looked at his digital wristwatch, "*London Broil* starts in five." Before twirling and disappearing into the crowd, he added, "It was really great to see you, Professor."

They ducked into the Just Joust Tavern tent and sat at the corner of a roughly hewn bar. From their stools, they watched the sun wither over acres of fake medieval tents.

Jackie wobbled her head and looked adoringly at Louise, "It was *really* great to see you, Professor."

"Stop. Now."

"Come on. Aren't you ever attracted to your students?"

"Gavin?"

"Well, not Gavin, but others?"

"They're so young … and uninteresting. And, never forget: there's a fine line between Mrs. Robinson and Mrs. Cleaver. Of course, it's perfectly fine for 99% of the fully-tenured male faculty."

"Please."

Louise sipped her beer. "Wine before beer beware?"

"Beer before wine yer fine."

"Well, then, we're screwed."

Even though it wasn't funny, they laughed. They hadn't laughed together in ages and so, the realization that they were actually doing so, and uncontrollably, made them laugh even harder. Regaining their composure, Jackie looked at her adoringly. "You're the best teacher I've ever had."

"God." Louise shook her head. "That kid has sabotaged my class. The other students think he's genius. They're all writing about homeless people. Twenty white middle-class kids writing about living on the mean streets. It's brutal."

"Ouch."

"And, last week, he elbowed his buddies and smirked during an oral reading of *Rape Fantasies*."

"What's *Rape Fantasies*?"

"It's a short story by that Canadian writer I love. Remember I told you about her?"

"I block out nonessential information."

"You do?"

Jackie nodded. "Sorry."

"So what qualifies as nonessential?"

"Well, in the past year, anything other than the *incident*."

Louise knew Jackie had stuck her neck way out for her regarding Brian's case. As the district attorney, she'd steered her office away from going after the guys and let them off with misdemeanors and monetary fines.

Jackie looked around. "I don't recognize a single person here."

"It's nice."

"No one knows who I am."

"No one knows my husband screwed men in restrooms."

"Something we should all try before we die." Jackie threw back another beer. Louise hadn't seen Jackie drink like this in years. "They would hang and quarter him."

"Stock and whip him."

"Duck him upon a cucking stool."

They laughed again and Louise lost count of how many beers they drank.

"Isn't it weird," Louise began as the barkeep brought two more, "how things turn out?"

Jackie rested her head on her hand. "Don't get morbid. I was just enjoying myself."

"No. Not about *that*. I'm totally over *that*."

Jackie rolled her eyes.

"I mean, remember, when I was living in Chicago, going to grad school, and you visited and were so jealous of me, and then I met Brian that summer when I came home at the Buick Open and ended up marrying him ... and having children—not-that-I-regret-the-kids-for-a-moment—and throwing away my dreams ... and now you're successful and powerful and I'm just a non-tenured professor at the satellite branch of U of M-Flint."

"You're right. That's not morbid at all."

"I'm proud of you, Jacks."

Jackie adjusted her off-the-shoulder top, removed her hat, and let her hair fall. She had always been an awkward, too-tall adolescent but she'd become close to pure gorgeous in her forties. "It hasn't been easy. I see the worst of humanity every single fucking day. And it's such an old boy's club down there. You can't believe the shit I put up with now that your dad's gone."

Mr. Shaheen had hired Jackie out of law school and became her mentor. Jackie had been, after all, like a daughter. She'd accompanied the Shaheens on family trips to Mackinac Island and Florida and Mount Rushmore. Louise had always been mature for her age and Jackie liked getting away from the Brady Bunch situation she'd been thrown into when her mother married *Mr. Morrison* (who they teased mercilessly—behind his back, of course—for his imprecise overuse of *consequentially* and his sincere delight in new pocket protectors).

Louise dropped her head to her shoulder and turned to Jackie so that their knees touched. "I miss my dad so much."

Jackie finished another beer, rested her head on the bar, and closed her eyes dreamily. "Me, too."

Louise felt the alcohol spinning her brain off balance. "I can't believe it's been five years since he died."

Jackie closed her eyes. "Four years, ten months, one-two-three-four-five days."

Louise's reasoning felt sloppy and misguided like she'd tripped into an alternate universe. She stared at Jackie. "I really loved him."

Eyes still closed, Jackie's lips curled into a smile. "Me, too."

A curious thought fluttered mercilessly into Louise's consciousness. Jackie had always insisted she'd been too busy to get involved in a relationship and had stopped dating a few years after she started working for her dad.

Louise knew she shouldn't but couldn't stop herself. "How was the sex?"

"Amazing."

The barkeep bellowed, "Last call!" and Jackie's head sprung up. She blinked, shook her head as if she'd awakened from a dream, but when she looked into Louise's eyes, she knew, immediately and with a ferocity that somewhat sobered her, that she'd revealed the thing she most wished to keep hidden.

•

Louise didn't look up when Gavin walked into her office. "You're thirty minutes late."

He smelled of stale cigars, beer, and a certain kind of sex that took hours to achieve. Louise hadn't had that kind of sex in years, and that fact alone seemed to boil her blood.

"Yeah, but, it was the wrap party for *Washing Well Wenches*. Being the playwright, well, let's just say I had my choice of ladies." Gavin grinned like congratulations were in order. Twirling his pen between his fingers, he started tapping it on his knee but stopped to adjust a captain's hat complete with shiny black brim, gold cording, and embroidered patches. Cap adjusted, he resumed his pen tapping, mouth open to reveal a startlingly black tongue. Had he been licking a bowling ball?

She wanted to slap him. Hard.

She tapped her desk with her forefinger. "I shouldn't even meet with you. You missed our first conference and you've missed half of this one." She'd awoken at six, fed the kids, made lunches, got the girls to camp, and taught a class all while this little shit was finishing a beer. She hated him. Hated his youth. His freedom. Hated how he brought a bucket of chicken to class and how he compared every story they read to a scene in a movie. Hated how she hadn't been promoted to full professor while her male counterparts and novel-ed newbies flew up the ranks.

"Yeah. But I'm here now." His eyes were so red they looked painful. "Hey," he said, pen frozen mid-air, "that shirt's … *nice*."

"You're drunk."

His smile flattened and he bunched his lips to one side. "No. I'm. Not."

"Yes. You are."

He pouted, Shirley Temple-like, all innocence and knitted eyebrows. "No. I'm not."

She pointed to the door. "Out."

He threw up his hands as if deflecting a punch, a lopsided grin smeared across his face. "Come on. You party, right?"

"No. Actually. I don't *party*."

That sobered him. "Really? That's so *sad*."

"Look. We're not here to discuss me. We're here to discuss your writing."

His asinine grin softened. "It was really great to see you the other night."

She could have told him, calmly and rationally, to get out. She could have led him to the door and shut it coolly behind him. Could have. But didn't. This kid had been making her life a living hell since he'd walked into her classroom with his cool, arrogant nonchalance. The entire class loved him. Looked up to him. Wrote like him. Wrote *for* him.

She felt out of sync, outdated. She was last year's Atari. A limping Chevette. Platform shoes. Neon. Scrunch socks, feathered hair, and Aqua Net. She and Jackie hadn't spoken since the night of the Faire and this, coupled with the shocking realization that Jackie and her father had been lovers, had nearly crushed her.

Instead, she opened his folder of work and began, "Let's see … here's a piece about a homeless guy smoking …" She flipped to the next piece, "And, oh, here's another piece about a hobo smoking … and, this next one? Well, here's a change. Three homeless guys smoking."

He nodded, eyes glazed like he'd glimpsed paradise.

"What's with all the homeless people?"

He tipped his head back like they were having a serious conversation, "They're just so … pure. They really *know* what's going on."

She couldn't stop the eye roll. "That's debatable. But, in your work they don't *do* anything. There's no scene here, Gavin. No story."

He pressed the space between them with both palms. "I'm buildin' to that."

"To what?"

"I don't want to give it all away on the first page. My theater experience has taught me that." He smirked and pointed to his cap. "I got it all up here. Rate of reveal."

Louise rubbed her temples and stared at him while he explained how these homeless guys were knights of some new-age round table, how they judged the righteous by gifts of booze and tobacco and money. Blah, blah, blah.

She felt sapped. Useless and weak, unmoored. This was what it had come to? Listening to some kid wax on about knighted, homeless guys? He kept talking and talking and she seemed unable to stop him. He was so earnest. So excited. His face glowed.

The more excited he became, the angrier she felt. Twenty years, two kids, a sham marriage, and two rejected novels ago, she had been him. Something vulnerable and delicate inside her chest tightened, threatened to snap. She grabbed her shirt with both hands and pressed, so sure that something would explode, unravel into an unalterable scene.

Gavin stopped. "You okay?"

And then it just came out. "That's inane."

"What?"

"That idea. It's idiotic. And the rest of your work—and I use that term loosely—is insipid and sophomoric."

"What do you mean?"

"You heard me." She shoved his folder at him, "Your time's up."

He'd morphed, in that aperture of time, into a sober, skinny, hurt kid. All the bravado gone, shoulders slumped, head cocked like a dog waiting for the next kick.

"Why'd you say that?"

She realized she'd gone too far. She rounded her desk to stand next to him. "I—"

"You're, like, my *favorite* teacher. This is my *favorite* class. I want to *be* a writer."

Her face burned. She leaned against her bookcase.

"I thought you *got* me. I thought you were one of the cool teachers."

"I'm not," she managed.

"Clearly." He grabbed his backpack, violently stuffed his notebook inside and, suddenly, became very still. Then his shoulders began to shake.

"I had a—" he took a great gulp of air like he was about to go underwater, "crush on you."

Louise found herself kneeling next to him, her hand hovering above his shoulder. "I shouldn't have said that."

"Did you mean it?"

"I shouldn't have said it."

"But you meant it!" He sat up, enraged. "Who are you, anyway? You're not even *published*. You're what?

Ancient? Like thirty or *forty*, even? Why should I even listen to you? I should have taken Professor Heller. At least he published that stupid memoir about his dog."

He was right. Who was she, anyway? She just couldn't seem to conjure a good answer to this key question. Hell. That, above all things, was something she'd like to find out.

Tangled Elements

During his tenure, Superintendent Gerald had successfully fired only one person: a cafeteria lunch lady (whose English repertoire included *yes, no,* and *no problem*) after complaints of her dandruff falling into students' meals became too numerous to ignore. After the deed, he broke out in welts that lasted two months. And now this. Just thinking about confronting Coach Haney made bumps bubble up under his collar. He read the police report again but, any way he read it, the fact remained that Haney'd been busted having sex—with a man—in a rest area stall.

Gerald had spent his entire career avoiding confrontation. He didn't like admitting that he'd slid into the superintendent's job because of a lack of suitable candidates and, it couldn't be overlooked, his wife's parents' school board connections. When it came right down to it, Haney intimidated the hell out of Gerald. In fact, Haney intimidated most everyone. It wasn't just Haney's imposing build—the massive, square head, thick neck, and boulder-like shoulders—but his offhand demeanor. It said: *I don't have time for you. In fact, you barely exist in my world.* Whenever Gerald came within ten feet of Haney, his round, cherub cheeks flushed while perspiration scored his temples.

The night before, noting Gerald's reticence to fire Haney, school board president Ed Tremaine had advised Gerald to *grow a pair.* He also insinuated that Gerald was expendable. That's how Tremaine, with his gold cufflinks and perfect smile, had put it: *expendable.* It made Gerald feel like a worn pair of socks. The time had passed, Tremaine said, when they could let this kind of nonsense go unpunished and, even though Haney had been the most successful football coach in New Canaan's history, he wouldn't stand by and let *some homo coach our boys.*

By the time Haney sauntered into Gerald's office twenty minutes late—tucking his T-shirt into Adidas sweat pants, patting the sides of his slicked back hair with an open palm—Gerald's entire neck and chest prickled with welts.

Settling himself in the chair across from Gerald's desk, arms draped over the seat back Haney said, simply, "What's up?"

Gerald cleared his throat and in one, quick breath announced, "It has come to my attention that you were arrested for public sexual acts—specifically sodomy—and, as you know, we can't allow this kind of behavior—"

Haney started shaking his head as soon as Gerald opened his mouth, "It's crazy."

"What? What's crazy?"

"I'm taking a dump and those fags are in there doing—" and, here, he stopped purposefully to look suspiciously at Gerald, "whatever they do." Gerald looked down quickly as Haney continued, "Can you believe my timing? One in a million. I mean, shoulda played the lottery."

Gerald had the fleeting sensation that an enormous weight had been lifted from his shoulders. *This was all a mistake! An absurd mistake!* Then he remembered hearing lurid rumors about Haney. And, too, he held the police report.

"But—"

"Disgusting. Those animals. Pigs. Hell, if I'd known what was going on in there I'd have held it until I got home."

"So, you're saying—"

"Yeah. Go figure." Haney smiled and pushed himself up as if readying to leave.

Remembering Ed Tremaine's threat, Gerald held up his hand. He pushed forward, "But what were you doing—"

"Huh?"

Gerald swallowed with such difficulty that he nearly choked. "What were you doing at a rest area at two in the morning?"

Haney looked from the row of state championship banners on his left to the windows on his right. Gerald followed his gaze. Thick gray clouds, from morning storms, piled on the horizon. "Coming home from meeting some MSU scouts. Had a few beers afterward. Why?"

"Scouts usually visit in the fall."

Haney looked down at his fingernails as if it pained him to explain the obvious, "How d'ya think I get scouts to come here in the fall?"

Gerald's heart pounded. A wave of embarrassment caused his scalp to prickle. "Right. Right."

"So, we done here?"

Sweat dripped down Gerald's chest. He took a deep breath and employed the furrowed brow he'd practiced earlier that morning, "Actually, I've been instructed to give you your notice."

"What notice?"

"Your notice of dismissal."

"From who? Who instructed you?"

"The school board president."

"Tremaine? Really." Haney leaned forward. His jaw tightened and he flexed his hands in front of his chest as if readying to lift a great weight.

Gerald sat motionless under Haney's gaze.

"You remember what Tremaine's son—and the Mansour and Henderson boys—did to Caroline Godrich? You remember when Billy Vance and I told you?"

When Gerald didn't respond, Haney stood abruptly and planted his palms on Haney's desk, upsetting family photos and knocking over a lopsided paperweight given to him by his son on Father's Day. "You remember that, don't you? You ever tell Tremaine his son raped a fifteen-year-old?"

Gerald had shoved the incident so far back, had even forgotten the Godrich girl's first name, that when Haney said it, he had to unfold the memory like an intricate work of origami. But, once he did, once the names and events bloomed, he realized his predicament.

When Gerald didn't answer, Haney continued, "Yeah. Only reason I didn't take it to the police was because that poor girl made me promise. Said it would kill her grandpa."

Sweat poured down Gerald's temples so that he had to dab his entire face with a hankie. He'd resisted bringing it out of his suit coat pocket—his wife said it made him look weak. But here he was, swabbing away like someone had dumped a bucket of water over his head.

"Rape is a felony, Gerald. And aiding and abetting is a crime."

"Yes, well—"

"Yes, well—" Haney leaned so close that Gerald could smell the coach's minty mouthwash. "You sonsabitches take *that* into consideration. And if I hear you told *anyone* about this, you'll be sorry." He straightened but kept his eyes on Gerald, "I have a class to teach."

•

Gerald's head felt ready to explode. He'd spent all morning talking to Principal Bunch trying to resolve what to do about Haney's threat when his secretary, an efficient Presbyterian, walked into his office to inform him that even she had heard the rumor about Coach Haney. Since she wasn't inclined to engage in small talk (and with this, she gazed at the framed portrait of Gerald's wife), if she'd heard it, she admitted with some relish, no doubt everyone else had, too.

Sadly, Gerald had made the unfortunate miscalculation of sharing the details of Haney's arrest with his wife. And, sadly, again, what Sandra Gerald lacked in intellect, she made up in enthusiasm. As the typing teacher and pom squad coach, she'd found Haney's constant digs unbearable (*Women have Title Nine and this is what you do with it? Is it disco or cheerleading?*). Not only that but the cocky so-and-so always found it funny to slap her husband on the back so hard that the poor dear clenched his teeth in pain.

She did not like Haney.

She also disliked disorder. And weakness. And people who made her life appear disorderly and weak, two things Haney could accomplish with a sidelong glance. And now this! Haney, the most macho guy in town, a homosexual! She whispered it to Mr. Hanks, a notorious busybody, and by noon, whether they cared or not, every teacher at New Canaan High had heard the news.

•

Gerald called Sandra into his office. She sat dutifully across from him in the same chair Haney had occupied earlier. Her head and neck bobbed above a blazer with ridiculously large shoulder pads, her wide cheeks flushed with excitement.

After a weak reprimand, Gerald rubbed his temples, "I specifically asked you to keep this under your hat."

"Look," Sandra whispered (she suspected the Presbyterian of listening to their conversations), "if you think Haney will take it to the police, we need a diversion. Something dangerous. Something juicy. Something big."

•

She considered exposing the mayor's illegitimate child, but the kid was still in utero and the mother wouldn't talk. Plus, she needed to sink her teeth into something fast. The sheriff, town treasurer, and board members were all octogenarians with lives less eventful than hers. Rumors still floated about Orion Jones and the Miracal girl, but those were never confirmed—she'd already graduated and even Sandra opted to avoid hitting a family when they were down.

She turned her attention to Father Silver, but even the priest's alcoholism couldn't tarnish his reputation. And then, voila! After only a minimal amount of meddling, she discovered that a young man was living in Father Silver's parish house—a very gaunt, very ill young man who suffered from something called AIDS.

She'd heard about the disease—about homosexuals and monkeys and Canadian flight attendants. It was all tantalizingly strange. After a few visits to the library to read up on it, she found some articles in *The New York Times*. One about a child with AIDS causing a furor in his NYC school, that of the one thousand and eleven families attending the infected child's school, nine hundred and forty-four of them protested by keeping their child home after learning about the disease.

In the breakroom, Mr. Hanks nervously hovering over her shoulder, Sandra read the article loud enough so that a few other teachers intent on ignoring her could hear, "A New York State Assemblyman concerned about his constituents burst out, 'There is no medical authority who can say that AIDS cannot be transmitted in school. What about somebody sneezing in the classroom? What about the water fountain? What about kids who get in a fight with a bloody nose? They don't know!' "

Mr. Hanks, a failed poet, tapped his lips with his index finger and wanted to know if he should be concerned. "Well," Sandra responded, "That's just it. We don't know, do we? We've got an infected man right in our midst! He's taken Communion—same cup as the rest of us—you've seen it, I've seen it, we've all seen it! We could all be at risk!"

•

A swift, spinning vortex of misinformation and outright lies about the disease began consuming the country and New Canaan was suddenly and unceremoniously thrust into the storm. The buzz about Haney's arrest faded and Father Silver's "guest," as the town referred to him, became the glowing ember. Rumors morphed and shifted like flocks of birds.

In her fervor, Sandra found her calling. She'd always known that she'd been underestimated and this was her time to shine. Maybe she wasn't the best typing teacher (dismally low words-per-minute) or pom squad coach (she'd always hated dancing) but it was up to her to save the town from this scourge. Sure, in the past she'd been shunned by her fellow teachers and, yes, the only thing keeping her from standing in the unemployment line were her family ties, but she took this entire event as a sign from God.

And she didn't intend on screwing it up.

She gnawed city leaders' ears off, requested Father Silver's parish house be quarantined, distributed mimeographed fliers with bullet points detailing the threat New Canaan faced.

DID YOU KNOW?
- There's a man living in Father Maurice Silver's parish house with Acquired Immune Deficiency (AIDS)!

- AIDS is a deadly disease! There is no known cure for AIDS!

- AIDS could infect our entire town! We are warning people to avoid drinking from the Holy Family drinking fountain or taking Communion! Do not, under any circumstances, get near the infected man!

Holy Family must be quarantined!
- In New York City, a child with AIDS infected his entire school!

- In NYC, over 100 people have died from AIDS!

She made signs and a banner, and enlisted student protesters by promising them service credits. Her core group included members of the pom squad, football and baseball players, marching band members, and the entire bowling team. She borrowed a bullhorn and made up slogans: "NO KNOWN CURE! HE'S UNPURE!" and "QUARANTINE! THAT'S WHAT WE MEAN!"

•

On a sticky Monday morning, with long shadows crawling across the lawn and the smell of lilacs in the air, Father Silver opened his front door. Attendance at Mass had been dismally low and he didn't know if it was because of his defrocking troubles, the protesters, or (and he guessed this was the case) a combination of both. As he descended his porch steps, he greeted each protester by name. He then commended them for exercising their first amendment right and asked who organized the rally.

A member of the bowling team quickly pointed to Sandra. Now, it was already established that Sandra's intelligence was subpar at best and, because of this, she had not prepared for a confrontation with Father Silver.

He'd just taken a cool shower, shaved, and combed his gray mane into a neat wave above his forehead. His eyes were red-rimmed and swollen. Watching a row of cars pass slowly on Saginaw Street, he sighed, "What's all this about, Sandra?"

While Sandra panicked, the kids behind her dug their toes into the grass and looked away when Father Silver tried to meet their eyes. She'd known Father Silver for years, nodded during his sermons, and prayed with him. But she had a job to do. Even though she stood only a few steps from him, she raised her bullhorn, "WE'RE PROTESTING."

"I'm right here, Sandra." Father Silver gently pushed the bullhorn's bell out of his face. "I think you might not have all the facts."

Sandra let the bullhorn fall. "Does he have AIDS or not?"

"He does have AIDS and he's gravely ill but the doctors assure me it is not spread through casual contact."

Sandra tugged the waistline of her acid-washed jeans. "I've heard you gave him Communion. He might have drunk out of the parish school's water fountains—"

"It's not spread that way."

"How's it spread?" Sandra suddenly felt bold.

"As far as they know—"

"As far as they know? In New York parents kept their kids away from an infected child."

"Yes but—"

"I want one hundred percent certainty!"

"*Nothing* is certain. You know that."

"So, how is it spread?"

"Through sexual contact."

"*Homo*-sexual contact."

"True. But not always. It's been spread by blood transfusions and heterosexual relations, too."

"So, it is true, we are *all* at risk!" With this, Sandra brought her hand around to indicate her little flock.

"Well, yes, if you have sex with him."

Sandra gasped, narrowed her eyes, and raised the bullhorn.

"Sandra, please."

"QUARANTINE! THAT'S WHAT WE MEAN!"

And, with that, the little group resumed their unenthusiastic dirge, chanting the poorly written lines they'd been fed by their most unlikely leader.

●

The protest had been going on over a week when Eric, the hood of his sweatshirt pulled up and jeans cinched with a belt, walked out the back door of Father Silver's parish house, over the cobblestone path leading to the front yard, and tucked himself into the protest line behind a girl with hair so blonde it reflected the late-morning sun. Father Silver had left early that morning for another inquiry; one of the last, he'd said, before his defrocking.

No one chanted. They just walked, drearily, in a circle worn in the lawn like ponies do at a carnival. Someone handed Eric a sign with "AIDS" crossed out by a red line. He rested it on his shoulder, but the wooden dowel felt anvil-heavy and he deposited it on a bush. The ragtag group looked like they needed a line of coke, but he doubted anyone in this town had a reliable source. For some reason, walking in a circle settled his nerves. He'd been inside, with the fan on high to drown out those ridiculous slogans.

Since Father Silver had taken him in and a dozen or so parishioners had quietly cared for him, bathed him, cooked for him, his most debilitating symptoms had eased slightly—the mouth sores and fevers and diarrhea—and he'd actually had a bit of a recovery, a jolt of energy, and perhaps even an anemic rekindling of his faith in humanity.

Even this group gave him a twisted kind of joy.

He spotted Astrid's Monte Carlo coming up Saginaw Street. She and Caroline brought him lunch most days. He waved as Astrid turned into Father Silver's driveway and cracked a smile when the girls craned their necks in disbelief.

He must have stopped walking though because, just then, someone stepped on the back of his sneaker. When Eric tripped, a chain reaction left people in a pile around him. As they untangled themselves, laughing and rolling on the grass, Eric remained on his side. His hoodie had fallen off his head to reveal a nearly bald skull, skeletal neck, and drawn face. On his palm, blood bloomed around a small pink triangle of granite.

He lay there for a moment, concentrating on the pink shard of granite and the frill of blood surrounding it. He'd begged the doctors to simply transfuse new blood into him. Wouldn't that work? Why not? *Just pump me full of new blood*, he'd begged. But they'd only shaken their heads and tried to explain the science behind it. After a while, Eric drowned out their doom and gloom. The set of their mouths—those grim, straight lines—told him everything he needed to know: his situation was hopeless. The damage had been done.

As the group of protesters surrounded him, he brought his palm in front of his face and laid his head on the cool grass. Without warning, his blood ribboned out of the tiny cut in a voracious crimson stream, blowing and jerking in the breeze, up and up into the sky. He watched it ruffle out of him like a kite string heading higher and until it lassoed the sky. Who knew you could lasso the sky? And so beautiful! Inside the imagined rope, with his skin peeled back to expose the sinewy muscles beneath, Max appeared. He spread his arms up to grab the lasso and balanced his big feet on the bottom of the arc. He knew it was Max because Max's only option—after what had happened to him—was heaven. Because, when you waste away, when your body simply gives up, what choice does God have but to take you?

And he loved Max so very much, so much more than himself. He loved Max as much as he'd loved his mother and father and little brothers. He'd loved Max and he'd stayed with him until the end when Max's parents came into the hospital room and asked him who he was and he'd said, stoically, *We worked together*, and when they said, *Oh, at the firm?* because, God knew, he didn't want them learning that their son loved *him*, a *dancer*, of all things, didn't want to let the homo cat out of the bag at Max's death-bed, couldn't let them know he'd loved their son as deeply as they had. Perhaps keeping all that information under wraps had been his single, crowning achievement.

Everyone suddenly stopped to stare at Eric. Or maybe they'd been staring for a long time. Eric couldn't tell. But their eyes looked down on him the way he'd looked down on Max, in those last days, the way you look down on someone who has no earthly hope and you say things you'd never imagined yourself saying. All lies! You say idiotic things, cheery things, stupid things like, *You'll get better* and *Have faith*—and the words pass like acid across your lips.

Someone whispered, *Is it him?* And, at the same time, Astrid and Caroline ran to Eric and knelt on either side of him, to protect or help him up, they weren't quite sure. They hadn't seen him fall, didn't know if he'd been pushed or punched or kicked, so they were fierce and ready and tense with the complete knowledge that nothing they could do would protect him.

And, just then, Sandra collected herself. She'd been staring at the young man, thinking he looked like the baby sparrow she'd found fallen from its nest—the prominent, bulging eyes, purple veins, bones poking through skin, broken neck, curled claws, the promise of budding feathers. She pushed the image out of her mind because this young man had long legs and arms, wasted now, but even so, she imagined that he'd once been heart-wrenchingly lovely because his eyes were very blue and his skin was very pale and the hair that was left was very blond. Something about the look on his face, like he'd been caught doing something wrong, softened her toward him, reminded her of her own sons, and she found herself wondering at his predicament, wondering about his parents—*Why weren't they here? Why wasn't he with them?* She suddenly wanted to throw down her bullhorn and wrap him in her arms but then someone said, "Is it *him?*"

That's when she snapped to and remembered what she was about and what was at stake.

Sandra nodded. "He's the one—" she began, but stopped. She didn't know what to say, what to do, how to rally her troops, but sensed that this confrontation might shift the situation out of neutral.

As Caroline and Astrid helped Eric to his feet, Sandra realized who the girls were. *Why on earth was the Godrich girl here?* Her imagination—never too grounded to begin with—began wildly unraveling. *Had she come to reveal the cover-up? What was going on?*

As Astrid and Caroline positioned themselves on either side of Eric, wrapping their arms around his back and gripping his forearms, Sandra readjusted her scowl and positioned herself between them and the front door, "Aren't you the Godrich girl?"

Caroline looked confused but nodded quickly.

"Well? What's going on? What are you doing?"

Astrid snapped, "What does it look like we're doing?" Much later in life, Astrid would identify Sandra's actions as desperate. Now, however, she simply registered her as dangerous—not only to Eric but, for some strange reason, to Caroline—and she simply wanted to get Eric and Caroline away from her.

"Don't get smart with me, young lady."

"Her walnut-size brain can't handle smart," Eric muttered.

"What did you say?"

"I said, 'Your acorn-size brain can't handle smart.' "

"Excuse me?"

"Your pea-sized—"

"That's enough!" Sandra's voice pitched, "You dirty, filthy boy, you—"

Sandra's lips kept moving, telling him how awful and sickening and dirty and nasty he was but Eric concentrated on the red lipstick seeping into the perpendicular cracks spoking off her lips and the glimpses of white teeth and crimson tongue and flecks of spit hitting his skin.

"Nasty, godless boy—"

Eric could feel the sharp piece of granite piercing his palm, blood leaking out under the stone. He wanted, very badly, for her to shut up so he raised his bleeding hand and closed his eyes. When he opened them, her mouth became his father's mouth and he became so full of despair that he couldn't resist the urge to stop the words. So, he did. He pressed his injured palm over Sandra's mouth. The stone connected with her front teeth and, for a split second, rested on her tongue before she spit it to the ground.

Sandra began scraping her fingernails across her tongue, wiping the blood and saliva on her parachute pants, whimpering now, shaking, her fingers digging into the soft skin of her mouth until she wasn't sure if she scooped out her own blood or his.

Spectacular Diversions

Lou Tremaine walked into the spring night oblivious to the sky bright with stars, the hum of cicadas, the moon waning yet fiercely bright, but feeling very keenly the ghostly touch of the man's hands lingering on his body. The memory filled him with a twisted joy. He pushed the key into the ignition but stopped to remove his baseball cap and ruffle his bristled crew. It was then, with his chin tilted into the rearview, that he saw the line of squad cars exiting I-69, swift as a dream, lights off, hopping the curbs to surround the low-slung rest area. He tried to turn the key in the ignition but froze, stunned, heart pounding, until the cops flicked on their lights and the brick building, with its flat top extending like a great cement cape, lit up. There was a moment of complete silence before a bullhorn voice ordered everyone out of the building and men began crawling out of the rectangular crank windows above every stall. The windows' hardware snapped and popped followed by baseball-capped heads, shoulders, and arms. But the cops were there, waiting, angling their flashlights into their eyes, knowing the stakes for these guys, that they'd be desperate, that they'd do damn near anything to get out of that place without getting caught. Some men jumped the eight feet onto the sidewalk and were tackled by cops. Others, realizing their fate, slid back into the building and exited the front entrance, hands shielding their eyes from the lights' glare.

Only then, with the commotion of bullhorns and lights, did Lou manage to fire up the Camaro and drive. His hands shook and his heart pounded the way it always did when he nearly got caught, but this time was different. This time, the anger and disgust he usually reserved for himself bled into disdain for the rest of them. He'd gotten away, but those assholes? *They'd* gotten caught. He'd escaped, just barely, so many times. Masked his desires so well and for so long, slipped out of cars and houses at just the right moment, run through woods and subdivisions, through cornfields and down highways putting distance between himself, an impending scene, and who he was. When he was in high school, certain he was different, he'd orchestrated elaborate diversions—sneaking his buddies into titty bars, tallies of how many virgins he'd popped. Later, as an adult, he talked constantly about the women he'd bagged. At bachelor parties, his ability to produce hookers was legend. His appetite seemed unquenchable.

His hands still shook as he plugged *Machine Head* into the eight-track. When the music started, he pounded his open palm on the dash in time to "Smoke on the Water." When he rolled down the windows, he suddenly realized he was slick with sweat. It trickled down his temples and chest, made the gold necklace with the heavy Berlinetta fob feel like a chunk of ice against his heart.

•

On the edge of town, Lou turned into the Bad Habit, a squat, rectangular building set way off the road, not nestled under trees but plunked unceremoniously in the middle of a potholed, gravel parking lot. It was busy for a weekday at two a.m. The owner had commissioned some high school kids to spruce up the cinder block front with a mural of the American flag. Somehow, they'd painted it with the star field in the top right instead of the top left.

One huge mercury vapor lamp hung high on a pole in the middle of the parking lot, bleaching everything like a camera flash. Its stark light accompanied Lou as he entered the dim, windowless interior. The regulars playing pool glanced up quickly at Lou and returned to their game.

A huddle of men sat at one end of the simple, maple-topped bar so Lou took a seat at the other end, between a constantly rolling twelve-inch black and white TV pushed up against the wall and a thin guy with a bald head and dark little eyes set deep in his skull. Lou had seen him here before. Same spot. He usually sat alone or, if he did sit next to another guy, the conversation never lasted long.

The guy straddled the corner to Lou's left, bounced his leg on the bar rail, and constantly cleared his throat as if he was about to begin a conversation. The bartender brought Lou two whiskeys and a beer chaser, his usual, and leaned on the bar to watch a rerun of *The Gong Show*. A tuxedoed Rex Reed, his black hair slicked back off his smugly handsome face, sat between Elke Sommer and a boa-wrapped Phyllis Diller while a woman dressed like a mutant ladybug, fake insect arms flopping at her sides, tap-danced ungracefully to "Tea for Two." Rex Reed leaned on his open palm, bored to tears.

When the celebrity guests announced the scores, the guy on the corner lifted his chin, "Fuckin' faggot."

Lou's senses still hummed from his earlier escape and he froze until he realized the guy referred to Rex Reed. He steadied his hand around his whiskey and nodded.

Next, a guy whose act consisted of a medley of distorted faces was dramatically gonged. As soon as Rex opened his mouth, the guy on the corner added, "Fruit."

Lou swallowed the whiskey like a shot. He usually jumped on the chance to bash someone who wasn't sufficiently macho, but he didn't have the stomach for it tonight. When the guy stared at him a beat too long, though, Lou recognized his role and shook his head in disgust. "Faggots, man—"

"Damn right. They say Hollywood's full of 'em."

Lou nodded in agreement.

"They say you can't get a role in Hollywood unless you're a butt-buddy."

The bartender looked at the guy. "What's it to ya?"

"What?" the guy bristled, "You like faggots?"

"They don't bother me, I don't bother them." The bartender brought Lou another whiskey before pulling more drafts for the guys at the other end of the bar.

The guy leaned in. "Get this. My buddy says there's a faggot living in Father Silver's place."

Lou's stomach clenched as he downed the whiskey. The sound of a cue ball breaking the pack sounded like shattering glass.

"You think that's *right*? Some faggot living in the Holy Family parish house?"

Lou shook his head. "Don't know about that—"

"But if you did know? That's bullshit, right?"

Lou raised his eyebrows.

"Damn right it's bullshit." He paused, "Art." Lou looked confused so the guy smiled. "Name's Art."

"Lou."

Art cocked his head. "Take off that ball cap."

Lou did.

"Hell, I thought that was you! I bought my pickup from your dad's dealership."

Lou sipped his beer.

"I gotta tell ya … I've been sitting here all night trying to think of a way to get rid of that faggot."

On *The Gong Show*, a family of dancers dressed entirely in white leotards danced in a crooked line. Lou dug in his back pocket to grab his cigarettes.

The guy leaned over his beer. His oversized front teeth reminded Lou of a horse. "And get this. This faggot's sick with something they say only fruits get. They get it from having sex with monkeys and elephants and shit."

Lou sat forward and Art took this as encouragement. "They say faggots put hamsters up. Their. Asses."

Lou hadn't eaten since dinner and the booze started working on him. The fluttering in his chest eased and his hands relaxed. "I used to have a hamster."

"Who didn't? Point is, guy's taking Communion." He paused. "You Catholic?"

Lou shook his head.

"Well, maybe you don't have to worry but I take Communion most Sundays and I sure as shit don't want that faggot contaminating me." Art leaned in, "Look, man, he's right next to the parish school. He could infect every one of those little kids."

Lou downed his beer and lit a cigarette. "Father Silver's a good guy, though. I don't think—"

"You don't think what?"

"I was just gonna say—"

"Look, Lou. It's Lou, right?"

Lou nodded.

"Lou, man, you can't just assume this guy isn't going to *fag recruit*. That's what they do, man. Fags recruit like the fucking army. They find unsuspecting kids, promise them shit, *make* them faggots."

No one had recruited Lou. He'd just always known. Same way he'd been convinced that his desire was shameful and wrong. And, even though Art wasn't making any sense, Lou nodded as if he did.

"Pisses me off, too, man." Art shook his head slowly. "Pisses the shit out of me."

The last guest on *The Gong Show* juggled flaming torches. Lou watched as the torches arced end-over-end, the throats landing gracefully in the juggler's waiting hands. The act ended when the juggler buried the flame down his throat.

Art leaned forward and pointed to the TV. His arms were long and skinny and so white that the veins in his forearms merged like rivers on a map. "Now that's an act. Damn. Wish I knew how to make money doing *that.*

Lou ordered another whiskey and beer and those went down so easily that Art started to amuse him. When he was sober, Lou found most people revolting, but when he got a few drinks in him, their sharp edges fell away. This Art guy wasn't so bad. He hated faggots and so did Lou.

The bartender announced last call. By this time, the scene at the rest area seemed like a story Lou had read about in the newspaper. It seemed distant and fuzzy—something you heard about and could shake your head at because it was so far removed from your own experience. This was the way it had always been. He'd be with a guy and it would end, suddenly—because of a girlfriend or wife or, who knew, really—and Lou would go back to his life as if nothing had ever happened. But it *had* happened and he didn't have any way to resolve it except to find the next guy and the next and, damn, he was getting so tired of it, of all of it, so tired of separating the truth from the lies and he knew that if he only wanted to enough, he could rearrange his desire and become the man his dad expected him to be. His dad had been a basketball star, a successful businessman, and a family man, and his son would be the same. It was all about *expectations*.

His dad had never failed to make those expectations clear. When Lou was thirteen, filthy from a day of running through scrub forest and plunging down sand dunes with the gang of kids whose cottages surrounded theirs, his mother had found a tick burrowed just below his hairline at the base of his neck. His dad lit a cigarette and pressed it onto the tick. Lou remembered the smell of his own singed hair and skin, the way he clenched his teeth and fists, the way his dad promised it wouldn't hurt, the way he tried hard not to cry, but he couldn't help it. Once he started crying he couldn't stop. Dad got sore, wanted to know what the fuss was about.

The cigarette burn hurt like hell, but there was something else Lou couldn't explain at the time: he'd wished that the feelings he'd been having, feelings he couldn't even admit to himself, feelings he'd tested on other boys only to be flatly refused, could be burned out of him, too, so he could get on with the life everyone expected.

He watched the flame juggler's encore but suddenly felt exhausted. Laying his head on his folded arms, he slurred, "Damn … wish I could burn it out."

"What?"

"Burnitout …"

Art leaned in, close enough for Lou to smell his meaty breath, "Now, that's the best idea I've heard all night. You and me—a couple a flame throwers, huh?"

Lou nodded as he closed his eyes.

Art poked Lou's shoulder. "Hey, man, wake up. We'll be like that guy, like that flame-thrower dude, right?"

Lou nodded absently.

"Well, then." Art threw a wad of crumpled bills on the bar, grabbed Lou's shoulder, and with a finality Lou couldn't refuse, commanded, "Let's go."

What Will Crush You

Watching Father Silver's home go up in flames reminded me that you can't measure the depth of people's meanness. It might be delicate as spider silk or thick and jagged, but it runs vein-like and deep and nothing can erase it—not regret, nor good deeds, nor gulps from the cup of salvation. It's always there, crouched and waiting.

I walk all night. Can't sleep. Never could. So, that early spring morning before the sun rose I found myself down the street from Father Silver's modest parish house. Next to it, Holy Family's spires disappeared in the dusky smear of twilight. Streetlights flickered, songbirds chattered, and I ambled past ACE Hardware, Sew Fabrics, over the train tracks, past the Depot Diner, Crossbow Inn, Palace Jewelers, the donut and auto shops, until I was directly across from Father Silver's. That's when something caught my attention. It was a flash of orange from the row of yews lining the side of the house. At first I thought it might be a firefly, but it was too big and too early in the season. I almost wrote it off, too, because the dark had been playing tricks on my mind and I'd been imagining things that simply weren't there— bugs the size of baseballs skittering up my walls and other things, scarier things, of people long dead but standing right there in front of me.

Then I saw it again. I knew it didn't belong so I crouched behind a pine tree and stayed very still. A burglar? But I couldn't remember the last burglary in New Canaan. And why steal from a man who lived as simply as Father Silver?

Hidden behind the pine's bows, their aroma filling my head, I saw the spark again, and watched as a flame arced through the air. Then the sparkling sound of shattering glass filled the night and, simultaneously, a wave of flame licked out the side window. Two hooded figures ran behind the house. Then I heard another window breaking, the back kitchen window this time, I imagined, followed by two more I couldn't see.

A light went on upstairs as the first floor became a glowing lantern. The sky's bruise-colored tint didn't reveal faces but I saw two figures scramble back to the yews, pushing them back and forth, as if they'd lost something in the branches. One of the figures yanked the other's arm as if to say, *Let's get out of here*, and, with that, they disappeared into the neighborhood behind the church. Then two car doors slammed, tires peeled, and an engine's rumble faded into the distance.

I crossed the street, my heart racing and hands shaking and, as soon as I stepped onto the front yard, Father Silver's head appeared in his open bedroom window. He took a great gulp of air and disappeared. Every business was closed, of course, so I moved as fast as I could to the yards backing up to the lit house and banged on doors until neighbors hauled out ladders. They leaned them beneath windows but the heat and smoke thwarted the effort. A few men tried crawling in through the kitchen window but the smoke turned them back and, by then, the fire department had arrived.

Once the firemen took over, the neighbors and I huddled together to watch. The flames lit our faces, washed us all in the same orange glow, so that even I looked like I belonged.

Few people knew my history. Father Silver was one of them. He knew that my father, Billy Durant, founded and ran General Motors. Ever heard the name? Probably not. That's par for the course, here, too. People don't pay attention to history, not even their own. They ranted and raved about General Motors pulling out of Flint but no one remembered that GM ruined my father, too. He pulled Flint out of the muck and pioneered the auto industry before those bastard bankers wrenched control from him and ruined it. And they could thank him for the library, too, because just a fraction of his fortune built that. But it's all gone now, except for the little pieces he left me, his biggest secret, his illegitimate daughter.

Most people saw me scuttling down Saginaw Street with my cart full to bursting, my white hair wild about my head, but they didn't really *see* me.

But I knew *them*. I knew where and when that Miracal man met his women. And that Dr. Rupert talked to his sister when he planted petunias around her grave. That Father Silver started drinking after Leila Miracal's death. The days Mae Shaheen met that butcher she'd taken up with. That the Goynes boy saved that poor white dog, the dog that, for years, had been abused, chained, left unprotected and starving outside the liquor store. That the Miracal girl raced her father's Corvette on clear, calm nights. That Godrich's daughter was a heroin addict before she disappeared for good.

I knew other things, too, unbelievably dark things I wish I didn't. I knew that those boys raped Caroline Godrich. It was me who spotted them under the bleachers during that football game. I thought they were drinking or smoking dope. They huddled around something, their backs to me, and didn't hear me over the crowd's roar so, when I walked right up to see them pushing the mouth of a beer bottle between her legs, I nearly lost my mind. I cracked that Tremaine boy right over the back with my walking stick. They ran like hell when I cocked my arm to swing again. She'd passed out, poor thing, bled from between her legs, her bra ripped right off her body. I pulled that beer bottle from between her legs very gently, covered her with my coat, got the custodian, and we helped clean her up.

That memory won't disappear—it's a misery that keeps after me. I don't know how someone in their right mind could drown something like that horror out. Some people can, I suppose, but not me.

Regardless, I couldn't stay still. I was restless because I missed my calling. As a child, I rarely spoke.

It was as if the words that came out of my mouth had no relation to what I meant to say. Or, perhaps, people simply interpreted them wrong. I don't know.

The way I remember, my window of opportunity closed so slowly that I didn't realize what was happening. One day, I woke up with no career, no mother, no father, no siblings … at least none who would recognize me. Father promised to send me to college but he lost his fortune just before I graduated from high school and, even though his two legitimate children had the best of everything, there was nothing left for me. The checks stopped coming and Mama—who was only twenty-one when she had me, who'd been kicked out of her parents home for having a bastard child—never too focused or energetic in the first place, became sick with grief. At eighteen, I ended up cashiering at Mitchell's Finer Foods to pay the bills. For some reason that even I can't explain, I just never left this place.

•

I'd been reading to the sick boy. To hear Sandra Gerald talk, you'd think the entire town had lost its mind and turned against that poor, sweet Eric. But there were dozens of women, and even a few men, caring for him. They never once expressed concern for their own health. We organized into twenty-four-hour shifts of caretaking and food preparation. Father Silver called us the Florence Nightingale Brigade.

The others bathed and fed him but, I liked to think, it was me who fed his soul. He liked Michael

Crichton best but some days I read him the good stuff: London, Melville, Dickinson, or Austen. I kept as many books with me as I could carry. That way, Eric could choose what he wanted to hear. When I read Dickinson's "I Never Saw a Moor," he cried so pitifully that I held his hand until he settled down.

•

They found Father Silver and Eric on the upstairs landing. They say Father tried carrying Eric out of the spare bedroom but was overcome by smoke and, when he passed out, he landed on top of Eric. They say Eric just didn't have the strength to push him off and that Father Silver's weight probably smothered him.

They say Father Silver will be *okay*, that he'll recover nicely from the concussion, smoke inhalation, and burns to his left hand and arm.

They say lots of things. Things, I believe, that have little to do with reality.

•

After the cops and insurance men finished investigating and most everyone had driven by to gawk at the wreckage, I went to the row of trees where I saw the first flash. Those yews, at least fifteen feet high, stretch the depth of the yard, shooting up like green rockets. They were Father Silver's favorite Easter egg hiding place. They're packed tightly against each other and the earth beneath them has been swept smooth by their boughs.

Pushing my hands into them, I opened my fingers to run them through their foliage the way my mother used to look for tangles in my thick auburn hair. The day was hot and muggy. Spring had suddenly turned to summer, and a deathly charred scent filled the air. It reminded me of the Maxwell House coffee can Mama used as an ashtray. She filled the bottom with sand and, when it rained, it smelled of soaked cardboard and spent tobacco. Behind me, the top floor of the house had crushed the first, two-by-fours lay like pick-up sticks, the entire side of the house had disappeared and part of the roof angled into the kitchen. Only Father Silver's dining room table looked eerily undisturbed with wet piles of folders drying in the sun.

I ran my hands through every branch and stick, feeling tenacious but silly, like I was pretending at being a detective, like I was someone who might influence something, not really expecting to find anything. When I'd finished, I decided to double-check from the other side and, sure enough, halfway down the row, something metallic brushed my palm.

Parting the yew's branches with both hands, I spotted what I had already touched caught on an inner branch: a chain with a circular fob. Untangling it from the branch, I suddenly felt murderous. I knew the logo even before I saw the gold script raised out of the cherry-red background.

Berlinetta.

It looked like twenty-four karat gold. It looked like a tchotchke a Chevy dealer might scoff at before tossing it to his no-good son who deserved nothing but got damn near everything.

•

The next morning, I visited Father Silver at St. Joseph's. Same hospital where I was born, same hospital where Mother and Father died. He sat upright, propped by pillows, everything starched and white, including the gauze wrapping his left hand and arm. A tall, gaunt priest with sad eyes started when I walked in.

"Adelaide, please, come in." Father Silver's eyes were swollen but he waved me in and wrapped my hand in his good one. No one except Father Silver called me by my first name and few touched me. His touch and my name on his voice felt like presents.

I recognized the other man, Bishop Connor, from newspaper articles. Through it all, he'd defended Maurice. Worn and pale, he greeted me and, turning back to Maurice, he shook his head, "I'm sorry about this—all of it. I've done all I could do."

Maurice nodded as the Bishop turned to leave.

His left eyebrow and the hair above his temple had been singed. It threw off the balance of his handsome face. The pink skin shone beneath a layer of Vaseline. I couldn't help staring.

"Well, Adelaide, that was the last nail in the coffin."

I told him I figured as much.

He stared at me for a long moment, as if he wanted me to explain a very important point that would solve his dilemma. His chest strained the hospital gown and there were still black smudges of ash on his earlobe and neck. He gazed out the window. "I didn't know about Eric—they didn't tell me—until this morning." He bit his lip and tried to regain his composure. "I thought I'd saved him."

He suddenly looked like a child, tears scoring his red cheeks, snot dripping, chest shaking.

He looked so broken that I stood and put my palm on his cheek. He shook his head, "He was right beneath me, that whole time, dying under my weight."

•

I left Father Silver without telling him about the chain I'd found. He looked so broken that I simply couldn't add to his agony. It's awful to see great people come down and, even though I'd steeled myself against the memories, on the bus ride home, I thought about my own father.

It was the mid-1920s and, while Mrs. Durant was away, Father arranged a train trip for me to visit him at his estate on the New Jersey Shore. You can't imagine the splendor of it! They called it Raymere and it was the most elegant place on earth. When the chauffeur pulled up, I couldn't believe my eyes. Mama and I lived in a modest little house he'd bought us—but this! A stone drive led to a cream limestone façade that matched the crushed seashell paths winding to the beach. Every bush and tree and plant had been trimmed to perfection. Servants padded noiselessly over spotless floors. Chandeliers, bigger than our kitchen table, lit rooms the size of our entire house. Tablecloths, silver, flowers, crystal, paintings, sculpture, everything glistened and gleamed. It was a shock to know that my father, the person whose driver delivered an envelope of cash on birthdays and holidays, lived in such splendor.

The morning after I arrived, Father asked me to join him for some fresh air. He and I are the same: compact, light on our feet, quick-bodied and quick-minded. The skin of his temples crinkled when he smiled. He was and remains the gentlest man I've ever known. He walked briskly, hands clasped behind his back, along the crushed-shell path toward shore as I tried to keep up with him. The sharp, broken pieces poked through the thin soles of my sandals. When I commented on how beautiful it was, he stopped as if considering it for the very first time, *This? Yes, well Mrs. Durant loves it. But it will soon be gone. All of it.*

He went on to tell me how he'd lost everything. I didn't understand how he could *lose* an entire institution like General Motors. It wasn't, after all, a pocket watch with a broken chain. We sat in lounge chairs facing the water. It was spring, with a brisk breeze coming off the water and towering clouds hopscotching the sky. My jacket was thin and I started to shiver, but I tried to hide it. I didn't want anything to distract him. He never looked at me, kept his eyes on the horizon, as he explained how he'd built GM from nothing, yes, but business was complicated, his partners had betrayed him, bankers had gotten involved, he'd *overextended*, he feared for what would happen to his people. I understood very little of the specifics but I knew by the tone of his voice, his situation seemed dire.

It was my first time to the ocean and, as he talked, its power and magnitude filled me with dread. I imagined it suddenly breaching the shore to swallow us whole. I wanted to care about what he was saying, about what would be lost. So I listened. I'd been taught, from a very young age, that Father was a very important man not to be bothered or interrupted. I coveted him the way I kept one of his expensive gifts on a shelf and never played with it. I wanted to love him the way other kids loved their fathers—fully and without reserve—but I wasn't allowed to talk about him outside of our home and once, when I did, my teacher reprimanded me for telling lies.

I tried to concentrate on what he was saying, I really did, but what I wanted to know was this, *Why hadn't I been important enough to share in his life?* Not this glittering side of him, but just *this*. Just sitting next to him, hearing him talk.

And it just came out. I was eighteen, impulsive, and the words tumbled out hot and raw. He looked at me, then, for a very long time, before he took my ice-cold hands in his and pressed them to his suddenly wet cheeks. "I was having so much *fun*, Adelaide. For so many years. It wasn't just you. Even my other children. I missed even them. And here you are, now, grown. I do love you, I just never stopped long enough to mention it."

He'd never made promises he couldn't keep. He'd never lied. And, so, having so little to go on, I had to believe him.

•

I put the fob and broken chain in a pouch around my neck, tucked it under my shirt, and walked through town to Tremaine's Chevy dealership determined to tell Ed what I'd found. The sky bulged with storm clouds and the wind came hard out of the northeast. On the way, I kept thinking about that poor little Godrich girl and, now, Eric.

As I approached the massive steel and glass-fronted building, I stood for a moment under the fluttering red, white, and blue flags strung across the lot. Above the flags, Ed and that shit of a son, their faces huge, hair slicked back, handsome in an intimidating kind of way, appeared on a billboard accompanied by the slogan: **"Tremaine-dous Deals! We Can Not Tell A Lie!"**

I doubted both claims as I pushed through the glass doors and walked straight to the receptionist's desk in the center of the building. I could see Ed in his floor-to-ceiling glass office, feet propped on his desk, a young couple mesmerized by whatever it was he was telling them. The receptionist, a good woman from church, one who had been helping with Eric, held up one perfectly manicured finger as she finished a call. She pushed her foam earpiece back and smiled, "Hello, Miss Durant."

"Hello, Edith. I'd like to see Ed."

She raised her chin, just slightly, and narrowed her eyes before nodding, "He just started in there and it might be a while—"

"I'll wait." I settled myself in a chair just outside his office.

With Tremaine Senior at the center, a half-dozen smaller, glass-walled offices surrounded his in a perfect semicircle. It must have been a good day because they were filled with buyers scouring paper-work and, in the showroom, a dozen would-be buyers opened doors, adjusted themselves behind steering wheels, weighing their desire, no doubt, against the money in their bank accounts.

It took an hour and seventeen minutes for that couple to complete their paperwork and for Ed to push the keys dramatically across his desk. When they were done, I heard Edith telling him that I was waiting to see him.

He sauntered out a few minutes later and stood in front of me, smiling so that his perfect teeth, which charmed most people, were on full display. He was a tall man, a former basketball star, very aware of his height and the awe it commanded. "Are you," he asked, fully aware that it was a ridiculous question, "ready to buy a car, Miss Durant?"

When I shook my head, he glanced at his watch distractedly, "I'm late for a meeting."

"This won't take long," I said, fumbling in the pouch to retrieve the chain and fob. He started walking away. I caught up with him to tug his sleeve. He stopped abruptly and turned to me. He had a habit of pursing his lips and he did that now as I raised the chain to eye level, "I wanted to return this. Figured it was yours."

He barely concealed an eye roll, "It's Lou's. Loves that Berlinetta. Great, great." He motioned to take it from me, "Thanks. Now—"

I stepped back, out of his reach, "I found it."

By this time, a few customers had gathered to see what the crazy lady with layered vests and plaid shorts had to say. "You're Presbyterian, right?"

He addressed me like I was a very young child. "Very good, Miss Durant. My family *is* Presbyterian. Gold star—" Again, he reached for the fob and I pulled it just out of reach.

"I'm sure there were only a few of these given out. It's twenty-four karat. Something corporate awards dealers for high sales. Am I right?"

There was something mildly sinister about him. He was the kind of man whose anger simmered just below a façade of affability. I knew this, I *felt* the danger of him tingling up my spine, but I didn't back down.

"Yes. Right. Great. I really have to go, Miss Durant. Thanks for returning Lou's necklace." When I didn't give it to him, he pointed to Edith over his shoulder as he walked to the doors, "Just leave it—"

I raised my voice. "The people who threw those firebombs hid in the bushes next to Father Silver's house. I saw them."

He stopped abruptly before pushing through the front doors, turning and closing the distance separating us in three giant strides.

"I found this in those bushes."

"What are you saying?"

"I'm saying that your son's necklace was in those bushes. I'm saying that he started the fire."

Ed glanced quickly around the showroom, smiled nervously, and pointed to Edith, "Get Lou out here to clear this up."

Lou emerged from his office. He was the spitting image of his father, but his shoulders and chest seemed less powerfully built. He was only five years older than the day I found him kneeling over the Godrich girl, but his face looked puffy, his eyes unfocused. He walked with a lurching gait, like he'd never quite figured out how to move that big frame as elegantly as his father, his shoulders dipping with each step.

I raised the chain in front of him like a hypnotist. Lou's eyes widened in acknowledgment; he took a step toward me but his father's arm straightened to stop him.

The senior Tremaine's eyes narrowed. Between clenched teeth, he managed, "Let's go outside."

Lou glared at me as we walked out the side door. A cold rain had begun and, with the wind, the drops felt needle sharp on my skin. Ed turned a corner, out of sight of the showroom, and stopped to face his son. "Miss Durant found that necklace in the bushes next to Father Silver's place. We were the only dealer in Michigan that sold enough Camaros to earn it. Now, where's your necklace?"

Lou couldn't meet his father's eyes. "At home."

"Get it."

"Dad," Lou pleaded, "can we talk?"

"Get it. Now. And bring it back."

Lou turned but immediately walked back, "I can't."

"Why?"

Lou closed his eyes tightly the way a little kid does when he knows he's been caught in a lie.

"Tell me the truth."

"I lost it, okay?"

With that, Ed slapped Lou with such ferocity that it knocked him off his feet to send him sprawling onto the concrete.

He leaned over his son. "You lost it?"

Lou nodded quickly. He tried pushing himself backward but stopped when his back hit a brick wall. Ed matched Lou's retreat, reached over, grabbed him by his suit coat, lifted and slammed him against the wall. "You think I'll get you out of this, too? You think I'll—"

I didn't stick around to hear what Ed thought his son might think. I walked toward town, trying to tune out the sound of Ed's voice rising above the wind and the roar of my own beating heart.

Ectopistes Migratorious

"Men still live who, in their youth, remember pigeons; trees still live who, in their youth, were shaken by a living wind. But a few decades hence only the oldest oaks will remember, and at long last only the hills will know."
—Aldo Leopold, *"On a Monument to the Pigeon,"* 1947

The morning of the final laicization hearing was magnificently bright, but the breeze brought the scent of sewage from the Detroit River. Before entering St. Anne's where his colleagues waited in judgment, Father Silver looked up to see thousands of long-winged birds, their underbodies iridescent against the rising sun, circling the steeples. While this seemed somewhat odd, he was too distracted by his worries to think much of it.

The room's limestone appeared translucent, the marble polished to a high sheen, the ceilings barreled and inlaid with intricate mosaics, the windows stretching from floor to four-story ceiling. The bishops, in their clerical suitcoats, filled both sides of a long mahogany table. They quivered with excitement. The archbishop entered wearing a long black cassock and quietly situated himself at the far end of the table, opposite from where Father Silver sat.

Blood dripped from their beaks.

The memory of those birds circling the steeples seized him and, simultaneously, Father Silver remembered his fascination, as a young boy, with the extinction of the *Ectopistes Migratorius*, the passenger pigeon, once the most common bird in the Northern Hemisphere. When he was young, his grandfather told him how, up until the late 1800s, millions, perhaps billions of them, darkened the skies. Their flocks were so dense that when they flew overhead they blotted out the sun and sent people into cold shivers. But humans went at them hard and without mercy. Cut them down with rifles, nets, raided their nesting areas, preyed on the squabs.

The Archbishop cleared his throat, called the hearing to order.

"Father Silver," he began, his fine white skin and feminine features practically glowing in the morning light, "let me get right to the point ..." He prattled on, throwing out words and phrases like *heresy* and *breaking of canon law* and *ecclesiastical discipline* until Father Silver whirred with rage.

Through the window, Father Silver watched the sky darken. It became a living thing—shifting, flapping, pounding—until the glass shattered and millions of brightly colored pigeons poured through the opening. They had wedge-shaped tails, long pointed wings, shining metallic bronze, green, and purple necks, rose-colored breasts, bright red irides.

The men surrounding the table, suddenly huge and vulturous, flapped their enormous wings, breaking the necks of thousands of pigeons. Regardless, they poured in by the thousands. By sheer number, they overpowered the vultures, pecked out their eyes, and as quickly as they entered, left carrying every last vulture out the window, gripped in their fierce talons.

Father Silver stood unsteadily, and gently nudged aside the fallen pigeon carcasses as he moved to the shattered window through which his enemies had been taken. He stood there for a long time, lost in thought, until a woman, surprisingly similar in stature to Leila, walked in with sharp little heels, each step puncturing a bird's body.

"Coffee, Father Silver?" Her irides glowed bright red. Her arm swooped to reveal two porcelain cups, a small pitcher of milk, sugar cubes in a bowl.

"Why, thank you," he nodded, wiping a bright white dropping off his coat sleeve, "wouldn't that be just lovely."

Swarm Suppression

When the queen bee senses that her colony has outgrown their hive, she moves them out. Thwarting the queen's natural instincts by blocking her departure could kill the entire colony. Paulie knew this because his great-grandfather brought one thing with him to this country: an egg-shaped sun hive, handwoven from rye, split horizontally to open like a clamshell. One of Paulie's first memories was standing on a crate, watching his grandfather remove the hives' golden frames dripping with honey.

Paulie treated Astrid the same way he treated his bees: gently, patiently, with respect and enduring love. He'd given her room. The fact that both the bees and Astrid had injured him made him bracingly alert to their whims. A few stings could send his heart beating wildly and, simultaneously, wrap him in a wet fog of impending doom.

It had been a year since the *boat incident,* as he referred to it, and Astrid had called because she'd heard Mrs. Ehrlich was laid up after surgery. It was the first time she'd contacted Paulie and she made it clear that she was coming over to make his mom's favorite dish, something Leila used to send over with Astrid: kibbeh nayeh.

Astrid's Monte Carlo was in the shop so, the next day, Paulie picked her up at eight in the morning, drove her to the butcher shop, and stood next to her while she instructed the butcher how to grind the eye of round—three times with clean blades—and to spread the ground meat thinly so it wouldn't turn brown in the middle. Astrid stood on tiptoe, her eye on the butcher, to make sure he did everything just so. They drove back to Paulie's house where they pureed sweet onions, soaked fine bulgur, kneaded the wheat into the raw meat. She added pinches of ice water—just enough to make the mixture soft but not mushy—and seasoned it with salt, pepper, cayenne, cinnamon.

Astrid stood across from Paulie at the Ehrlich's big wooden table. She wore a sleeveless shirt made from red bandana material and she'd pulled her hair back in a ponytail. The humidity bullied the baby hairs around her forehead into tight ringlets.

She kept her eyes down, looking at an index card covered in her mother's elegant cursive. Astrid dipped her fingers into the ice water and said, absent-mindedly, "I love her handwriting."

Paulie picked up the recipe and mentally compared it to his mother's worn and stained recipe cards. "It looks brand new."

"Yeah. She never used recipes. She just *made* stuff like it was part of her DNA or something."

"So …" But Paulie stopped himself.

"She left a recipe box full of her mother's recipes. For that garlic dip, remember it? And fatayer and tabouli and pickles and talami. I guess she wanted me to have them. I never really paid attention the way I should have. But she knew how much I loved it, I guess."

"Man, I loved her food."

"She loved how you ate, Paulie. She said she'd never seen anyone eat like you. She lived for that. She *loved* that about you."

"She was always so nice to me. Your dad, though—"

"Yeah. He never liked you."

They laughed.

"Come here." Astrid moved aside and motioned for Paulie to stand next to her, "Take it out and shape it into an oval on the platter."

Paulie's hands were the most beautiful things Astrid had ever seen. His knuckles were smooth and his fingers long and tapered and, even though they were powerful, moved delicately when he set his mind to a task. Astrid noticed them years ago when he'd introduced her to his bees. It was their first date and he'd brought her to the edge of the strawberry field to show her the stacked hives he'd started for 4-H. He never wore a beekeeper suit, just moved very slowly and methodically, cooing and talking to the bees when they got agitated.

When he'd finished, Astrid pressed her index finger into the oval to make a cross. Then Astrid drizzled the dish with olive oil, topped it with chopped onions, and served it to Mrs. Ehrlich with pita and labneh.

When the three of them finished, Mrs. Ehrlich looked at Paulie and Astrid with a combination of understanding and pity and asked, "You getting along okay?"

"As well as expected, I guess." Astrid missed Mrs. Ehrlich's direct ways.

After Astrid and Paulie cleaned up, they walked slowly out to the gazebo, soaking up the heat, the gauzy violet sky, and lay side-by-side, an arm's length apart on the worn plank floors. His great-grandfather had built the gazebo and christened it the *Bien House* because, he'd said, without the bees, the land would be nothing. The strawberry fields to the west and apple orchards to the east, the thick clumps of meadows and forest, none of it would be possible without the bees. And, without the demands of the hive, the bees, too, would be nothing more than irritating pests.

Paulie's great, tree-trunk arms stuck out like wings behind his head, hands cradling his crew cut, as he stared at the azure beams and yellow, orange, and red roof panels. The sun hives, with their woven bulbs topped by brightly painted wooden boxes, hung off the rafters like great, bulbous lanterns. It was a still, humid day and the sound of the bees' industrious buzzing filled his head. A red-winged blackbird scolded something in the meadow.

Astrid smelled of the cinnamon she'd spilled on the counter and on her shorts, and when she pointed up to one of the hives to ask a question, he could see it, red and powdery, staining her fingers. He wanted to kiss the tips of them, bury his face in her hands, let her hold him but knew he couldn't, knew Astrid wouldn't allow it. He kept his gaze at the panels that met in a multifaceted point and not at Astrid because, if he did, if he looked at her, he wasn't sure he could control his desire to wrap her in his arms.

So he focused on choosing the right words to express how he'd been bettering himself. In the time they'd spent apart, Paulie had tried, desperately, to expand himself, to change, to become more intro- spective and appealing to Astrid's intellect. After they broke up, he pulled *The Art of Survival* off his broth- er's shelf, devoured it, and marooned himself on an island up north for an entire week with nothing but a pack of matches, *The Great Gatsby*, and a bottle of water. At college, where football fans asked him for his autograph, he spent all of his non-training time studying just to keep his C average. He went to a few plays, too, for good measure, because Astrid loved theater.

He tried to keep up because, in her letters, Astrid went on and on about her new interests—she seemed very concerned about rivers, had learned the guitar, fancied herself a *social advocate*—and, although she explained all of this the best she could, it was diffi- cult for Paulie to process. He figured that it was just Astrid's way of filling the wake left in her mother's absence and was convinced that she was drifting, unmoored. If she hadn't pushed him away, he would have saved her, could still save her.

He couldn't find a way to say all this because she'd developed a kind but thick layer of protection against him. It didn't matter, though; just her presence, just that, nothing else, filled him with a joy he hadn't felt since they'd been together. And, he believed, if he just bided his time, she'd come around.

He'd tried dating other girls but they all seemed too eager to please, flat and tasteless. They didn't know his history. They only knew his present. And although he could still throw a football, Astrid had torn the life out of him.

She was talking about some river that needed saving out east, about wearing waders and gloves and plucking out thousands of pounds of junk people had been throwing into the river for hundreds of years and natural filtration and ... Paulie propped himself on his elbow to listen. He tried desperately to process what she was saying, but he couldn't stop looking at her. She had changed, somehow, and he couldn't put his finger on it. It was as if she'd become more of *herself* in the time she'd been away from him. Her widow's peak still fanned right above her left eye and she'd taken her hair out of the ponytail so that her black curls fell below her shoulders. Her skin looked very fine and pale and her dark eyelashes framed her hazel eyes.

She sat up, talking with her hands, the way she did when she got excited. She stopped, "Paulie?"

"Yeah?"

"You listening?"

"Yeah."

"What was I talking about?"

He bit his lower lip which meant he was scrambling. "The river."

"What about it?"

He'd been listening at some level, thank God. "Cleaning it up. And designing new infrastructures—"

Astrid nodded, "Good save."

"Give me a little credit."

She smirked, "I do."

"A little or a lot?"

"Enough, all right?"

He swallowed hard because he wanted to know how much credit, ask her if she still thought about him, spill everything he'd been thinking, tell her he still loved her, proclaim that he'd worked on controlling his anger, that he hadn't hit anyone since the *boat incident*, share everything out loud that he'd been holding back. He wanted to tell her about the girl who'd come to his room one night and crawled into bed with him—he'd imagined it was Astrid just to get through it. He wanted her to hear that he sobbed after that girl left. He didn't want Astrid's pity. He just wanted her to *know*.

He sat up and turned to her. "Astrid, I—"

She shifted and sat cross-legged, attentive, a few feet away from him and waited. When she broke it off with him, she'd detailed, ad nauseam, her reasons. But things change, right? He'd changed. He pressed his lips firmly together. The words wouldn't come. So he looked at her, hard, without meaning to, until she stood and lifted her gaze to the hives. "I miss them."

Paulie sighed. "Yeah?"

"Yeah. It's crazy how much."

Paulie had taught her everything he knew about bees.

"Your grandpa would be proud of the way you take care of them."

"First thing he did, when he got to Michigan, was make more of them. All those years while he saved up to buy this land, he worked on them every night when he got home from the factory."

While Paulie had trouble expressing his feelings, he could talk all day about his bees. Walking through the fields, back to the house, he told her that his granddad spoke German, Russian, and English and insisted that this ability, above all else, led to the happiness of his colonies. The bees respond to vibration, he'd told Paulie, and certain vibrations calmed or infuriated them. Certain words, too. He used a combination of all three languages and his hives thrived.

He was a Volga German, an old Kraut from Russia, fiercely proud with a quick temper and even quicker fists. At Catherine the Great's request, his family and others left Germany to colonize the Steppe region of Russia. They had been there nearly a century when the Russians decided they were no longer welcome. So they packed up and moved here without his bees. He had mourned those hives left back in Russia until the day he died. Said that leaving those bees was, quite possibly, the saddest day of his life.

•

It had been raining for a week, a cool and dreary end to summer, and Paulie felt panicked. Since they'd made lunch for his mom, Astrid flatly refused to spend time with him. His plan had been to win her back this summer. It was a plan without strategy, though, a dream, really, and now, with the summer winding down and thoughts of returning to college early for full-time training nagging him, he fell into a funk.

That morning, exhausted after a grueling workout, he mixed sugar and water in a gallon jug and took his time walking through the now dormant strawberry fields, past the apple orchard nearly ready to harvest to the east, out to his stacks at the edge of the meadow. These were *his* stacks—he'd started them with queens from the sun hives and, although he lost more bees in these conventional stacks, they produced enough honey to keep him in spending money during the school year. A light rain coated his face, caught in his eyelashes, and blurred his vision. He could have taken the truck, but he wanted to think. His boots sank in the mud and, by the time he made it to the hives, the bottoms of his jeans hung heavy with mud.

He knelt next to one of his hives and watched the workers coming and going. The cool weather and rain made them sluggish. A worker crawled onto his index finger and he held it up to eye level. After all of this time, they still amazed him, were still the most perfect things he'd ever seen: powerful, light, focused, fast. No matter what they did—whether they were guards, workers, house bees, honey, or wax makers—they performed beautifully. They were flexible and diligent and determined. After they emerged, momentarily awkward as a baby deer, they spent a few days eating pollen from nearby cells in preparation to incubate and nurse young larvae, then moved on to produce wax, process honey into nectar, control the hive's temperature, remove debris and dead bees from the hive.

All spring and summer, Paulie watched them hover over strawberry, chestnut, apple, and wildflower blossoms, up and down, sideways and back. He got to the point where he could anticipate their moves. That's how he was on the field, too. He'd trained himself to get inside the defensemen's heads, move faster than them, do exactly the opposite of what they expected. For him these things seemed innate. It was other stuff that tripped him up.

He removed the cap of one stack, pulled out a feeder frame, and filled it. The workers would exhaust themselves to a certain death for the next few weeks. The emerging workers would live slightly longer because their workload would be lighter during the winter months.

By the time he'd finished filling the last feeder frame, he'd decided that his job—to win back Astrid—was not finished. He needed to go to Astrid, find her, today, immediately, and tell her everything. With this decision firmly in place, he suddenly felt buoyant, nearly giddy. He would get her back. He would win. It's what he did.

•

He changed into clean clothes and drove to Astrid's house, but she wasn't home so he drove around town looking for the Monte Carlo. He distinguished this kind of stalking from the stalking he'd done when they were dating because, after all, this was *not* stalking. This was search and rescue. Search and recovery. Search and restore.

Gray clouds compressed the world into an extended black and white celluloid frame. Everything looked waterlogged, dull, and lifeless. Driving into town, up Saginaw, he passed the cement slab where Father Silver's house once stood. They'd razed it shortly after the fire and it remained a knocked-out tooth in New Canaan's perfect facade. He pulled his old Chevy pickup past the lunchtime parking lots of Big Boy, Crossbow Inn, A&W, past the library, ACE, Burger Depot, and, finally, he spotted Astrid's Monte at Angelo's Coney Island.

He pulled his hand through his hair, straightened the collar of his freshly pressed button down and got out. As he'd pulled into Angelo's, the rain intensified and bubbling black puddles filled potholes. He hopped one puddle but didn't anticipate the depth of another and soaked his loafer and jeans. He hardly felt it, though, because his heart pounded in anticipation of seeing Astrid, of finally winning her back.

A bored cashier with bangs Aqua-netted into a nest above her forehead slouched behind the cash register reading the *Flint Journal*. She followed all six-foot-four of Paulie as he moved past her and into the dining area. He didn't see Astrid at first, but finally spotted her in the far corner booth. She sat facing Paulie, across from a guy so wide that he nearly blocked Paulie's view of her laughing face. The guy's thick neck and meaty shoulders cleared the red leather booth by nearly a foot.

A familiar humming sensation began to fill Paulie. Of course she'd been seeing someone. That's why she'd kept her distance. At this realization, every other distraction fell away—the clink of forks, the polite conversation, the waitresses asking *What'llyahave?*, the cooks' *Order up!*, the cash register's ching. And with the old buzz of anger so fierce that it surprised even him, he launched himself toward Astrid and stood, breathing heavily, at the end of the booth.

Astrid had been laughing, her head thrown back the way she did when something genuinely amused her. But when she leaned forward and saw Paulie, she tensed immediately, took a sharp breath and held up her hand as if to say, *It's not what you think*, but Paulie already had that look on his face, that crazy-eyed look, that look that said, *Astrid's mine and you damn well better know it*. As Astrid's palm moved toward Paulie, the guy across from her thought Astrid was introducing him to Paulie so he offered his right hand. Paulie grasped the outstretched palm in both of his and pulled the guy nearly out of the booth toward him.

The guy, taken totally off guard, pressed his free hand against Paulie's chest.

"Paulie!" Astrid pushed herself out of the booth, put one hand on Paulie's shoulder, the other on his back, just as a young woman appeared at Paulie's other side, "This is Pete, a coworker of my dad's and—" She shoved Paulie's shoulder toward the young woman, "this is his fiancé, Diane. They've just this week moved here."

The situation might have been salvageable if Paulie had let go of Pete's hand. But he didn't. It took a few uncomfortable beats for the fear and surprise and anger to drain away and by then it was too late.

Paulie felt Astrid's nails digging into his shoulder. She hissed, "Outside."

The rain fell harder now, pinging off the hoods of cars, exploding into puddles and, when Astrid stepped out into it, Paulie thought he saw tiny puffs of steam coming off her. Her face, that beautiful face that he cherished and wanted to protect, twisted into something he barely recognized. She stood on tiptoe, right up in his grill, right there in the rain outside the entrance, with her lips moving and her eyes bulging and her hands gripping his button down so that he thought she might rip it right off him.

"—the hell are you thinking? *Do* you think? Has nothing registered with you? Those are my dad's friends. He asked me to meet Diane because she's new in town. I can't take it anymore, Paulie. I've changed. I've—I'm not your girlfriend anymore. I'm nothing to you. Why can't you understand that?"

When she let go of him, Paulie didn't move, just stood with his feet submerged in a puddle. They were both soaked when Astrid finally stopped screaming and leaned against the diner's slick aluminum facade. "I thought you'd changed, Paulie. I thought you'd give me some room."

Paulie leaned over, elbows on his thighs, palms together as if praying. He watched the raindrops exploding all around him because he couldn't bear Astrid's face, "I'm sorry. God, Astrid. I'm so sorry. Please believe me. I came here to tell you how much I love you. I can't live without you. I can't—"

"You're gonna have to."

Paulie looked up.

"I'm not that person, Paulie. I'm just not her."

•

Paulie drove home in a daze. He choked the steering wheel, white-knuckled, staring straight ahead. He didn't remember stopping at lights or swerving to avoid a stalled car or blowing the stop signs on the county roads leading to the farm. He drove past the house where his mother sat, one hand on a calculator balancing the books, over the U-Pick fields to the road that led to the back fields and his stacks. The old Chevy fishtailed and nearly got stuck a few times before Paulie stopped fifty feet from the stacks.

The bees would be hunkered down now, contentedly dry, sipping the sugar water he'd fed them earlier that morning. The workers would be wrapping up their summer season of building cells, incubating larvae, nursing young and older larvae, making wax, controlling the temperature, handling food, guarding the entrance, cleaning up debris. The drones would be dancing around the virgin queens or being fed by the workers. The queen might have just laid her daily quota of two thousand eggs and settled in for a well-deserved rest. Long ago, he'd calculated that each frame held about twenty-two hundred bees per frame, ten frames per box equaled twenty-two thousand bees per box, two boxes per hive equaled forty-four thousand bees.

Give or take a thousand. But only one queen.

He revved the engine and flexed his fingers. The windshield wiper blades needed replacing and their crescent journey produced an irritating, high-pitched noise that set his teeth on edge. He switched them off and gripped the steering wheel with both hands until he thought it might snap in half. The stacks looked abandoned, unprotected, at the edge of the field. He knew better, though. Inside they audibly vibrated full of life.

He shifted into DRIVE, eased up on the brake, and pressed hard on the accelerator.

This Is How Accidents Happen

Dear Father Silver,

I want you to know that, on more than one occasion, the burden of what I am about to tell you has nearly sunk me. I do realize that to confess this now, so many years after you lost not only Leila but also your career, may seem particularly vicious. Please believe me when I say that I never intended you harm; that I only wanted to protect Leila. But I feel I must tell you the truth. It's been weighing on me so heavily that I simply must confess: I told your superiors about you and Leila.

At one time, I was proud and self-righteous. After losing Leila—my cousin and best friend—and what followed, I see that I was wrong. But before you judge me, please let me explain.

Leila never told you that she confided in me. I kept her secret until I wrote that letter. I was angry with you long before you ever laid a hand on her. In your sermons, you spoke of so many foolish things: the rights of homosexuals, the ordination of women, abortion. I'm not saying that I now agree with you. I do now see that there was, at the very least, room for discussion.

After losing her, my world became unrecognizable. We'd been friends, as you probably know, from the beginning. Cousins, of course, but also dear friends. Like sisters, people said, but I never had a sister so I wouldn't know. All I knew was that she was a very significant part of me. Our mothers, new to this country from their native Lebanon, raised us together. My most vivid childhood memory was of Leila biting me on the shoulder, me tattling, our mothers descending upon her, her crying. From that moment on, we learned to keep things between us.

In high school, when her depression became apparent, I protected her as fiercely as I could. Even then, her beauty attracted boys. They flocked to her. We'd been so sheltered, our parents forbade us to date, and so refusing their advances caused boys to lash out at her. They spread rumors. They said she was stuck up. A bitch. You know how boys can be. Everyone says girls can be mean but, in my experience, boys' retaliation has always struck me as worse, as unspeakably brutal.

We went to college together. I met Robert and got married. Not long after that, Leila met Luke. I didn't like Luke from the get-go. It wasn't only that he was older—although that was part of it—but I couldn't abide his arrogance, his wandering eye, the way he treated Leila. I told her all of this. I begged her not to marry him.

But she didn't listen.

Luke's infidelities were apparent even before Leila got pregnant. After having Astrid, Leila's postpartum triggered deeper bouts of depression. I would come to her house to find her screaming, little Astrid in a corner with her hands covering her ears. Leila's sister and I would alternate staying at their house during her darkest periods.

You might be wondering why I am telling you this. Bear with me.

I filled my life with motherhood and my marriage. And Leila. So when Louise left for college, and after Robert became District Attorney, I finally had time to think. After years of caring for everyone else, I felt that I'd been merely sleepwalking through life and, more significantly, that I was running out of time. I felt frantic. It was ridiculous, I know, but it's just how it was with me then.

And then Leila told me about you.

As I did with Luke and for obvious reasons, I warned her against you. But she didn't listen. This would be the second time she hadn't listened to me about a man and I was furious. We didn't speak for months. That's when I wrote the letter to your superiors.

In the time we'd spent apart, she found a new doctor who tried a different combination of medications on her with some positive results. And, not insignificantly, she had you. I see, now, that you were good for her. You were wonderful for her, really, and I hadn't seen her this content in years. She'd grown into herself, somehow. She seemed happy and at peace.

Perhaps, because of this, I made a rash decision. A few weeks before our fortieth anniversary, sitting across from each other at dinner, watching the sun set over the golf course, I suddenly said to Robert, "Instead of giving each other gifts for our anniversary, we should give each other passes to see anyone we want for a full year."

Robert stopped, his fork halfway to his mouth, and looked up at me. He cocked his head and asked, "What's this about?"

Looking back on it, I should have realized that he thought I knew he'd been fooling around. He must have thought I was about to launch into him for it. Oh, sure, I knew something was afoot but, unless I saw it with my own eyes, it didn't exist.

Our arrangement worked splendidly until I met Wallace. I ruined everything. Not Robert.

I had just turned sixty; Robert was five years my senior. Until the last few years, Robert hadn't strayed. And me? Well, you know what a prude I was! I thought I was so superior. Above it all. And I did, I do, genuinely care for Robert. I love him. I just didn't know how much.

My first dalliance, let's call him Number One, turned out to be less emotionally developed than an adolescent. It was as if he'd regressed into adulthood. He'd been an admirer of mine in college and I think we went to a dance or two until I met Robert. We met at a dark Italian restaurant that smelled faintly of fish. He opened with an awkward compliment about how I looked twenty years younger than his ex-wife and didn't stop talking until the moment we left the restaurant. I barely got a word in edgewise. His repertoire included golf handicaps, medical supply sales, and golf handicaps. In that order. But he had a dimple in his chin and a dimple can be a powerful distraction. Even though he blew his nose in the cloth napkin, I agreed when he invited me back to his place. But his lovemaking was as selfish as his conversation. I actually rolled out from under him and announced, You're not doing it right, gathered my things and left.

I didn't see him after that.

Number Two and Number Three were no better and I began to doubt whether our agreement had been a good one. I also started appreciating Robert all over again; the little things he did like unloading the dishwasher every other Wednesday, cutting the nettles out of the dog's coat, hanging that mirror in the hallway after three months of nagging.

And that's when I met Wallace.

Let me back up a bit. You're probably wondering why a relatively happy sixty-year-old would want to engage in an *extramarital affair (or two) after forty years of monogamy. After all, most people see me and Robert walking together and, simultaneously, have the fleeting image of swans swimming into the sunset. I don't blame them. We did, after all, start to look alike. We were both olive-skinned and (in our youth) dark-haired. But that's where the resemblance stopped. Robert had a large, slightly hooked nose and walnut-dark eyes (that I loved) and I had the straightest of straight noses and the wolfish gray eyes of my mother. My parents, first generation and unwilling to step outside conventions, insisted that their only daughter marry a Lebanese man, saying that even though he might stray, he would always come back. He was tall and thickly built and I was as slim as I am now. I mention this because even though I have aged gracefully, as everyone says, it isn't easy for a woman known for her beauty to slide easily into her sixties. I went kicking and screaming with expensive creams clenched in my fist, a strict vitamin regimen, and tennis every Tuesday and Thursday.*

Where was I? Wallace. Right.

We met at the farmer's market on an overcast August morning. It was my habit to go early, just as the vendors put out their produce. That morning, I bought some lovely little koosa squash, tomatoes, parsley, and those knob onions I liked to slice over salad. I needed some ground lamb and, after pulling my number at the butcher shop, turned to bump right into him.

Let me be more specific: the heel of my pump skewered a shoe. I started and turned to see a much younger man smiling at me.

"Pardon me. Did I hurt you?"

"Didn't feel a thing—" He cocked his head as if he recognized me or knew me. I couldn't decide which.

"You must have! My heel came right down on your toe."

He smiled, leaned over and tapped his ankle, "Prosthetic. Really. I didn't feel a thing."

I tried to hide my surprise. "Good thing. I've maimed men with much less."

He nodded, still with that grin, and I turned back to the meat case to wonder if I'd offended him by using maim. *I thought our exchange was over when he stepped next to me. "What are you ordering?"*

"Lamb. Ground," I said without looking at him. But I could feel his shoulder too close to mine. The way he whispered in my ear felt conspiratorial.

"The ground lamb here is cull grade."

I'd been ordering lamb from this shop since he'd been in diapers. I turned to look at him. He studied the price chart above the butcher's head with his chin tilted slightly up and away from me. He was a full head taller than me, which is saying something, with dark hair cut very close on the sides and curls on top. His skin was very pale as if he hadn't been out all summer. "You don't say?"

"I do say."

"So why are you here?"

"Checking out the competition."

"You're a butcher?"

He turned to me. "Opened my shop a few months ago. Wallace Fine Meats. I'm Wallace Fine."

I'd heard of it. "I hear you're pricey."

"Yes, well," he scratched his chin with his thumb, "much better meat. Why don't you stop by? I just ran over here to pick up some produce and do a little snooping. Going back now. Give you the lamb on the house. How's that sound?"

"I'll think about it."

"Nothing to think about. It's a no-brainer." He turned but stopped. "Wait. You didn't tell me your name."

I cut my eyes at him.

After a pause, he nodded, "Okay." He looked hurt but studied my face as if still waiting for an answer. "A free pound of lamb to the customer with no name. The best you've ever tasted. Guaranteed."

Wallace Fine was right, of course. That night, I made the tastiest koosa ever (and I could write a cookbook with what I know so I don't say that lightly). Everything about his shop was superior. It was immaculate. Brightly lit. It smelled of blood and sawed bone and spices. His suppliers were small farmers who raised their own animals. Not corporate farms. He could go on and on about the differences as I stood there staring into his eyes that were darkly girlish with long, thick lashes. How cliché! Falling in love with a young, gorgeous butcher! As if the other women waiting patiently with paper numbers clenched in their paws hadn't been thinking the same thing.

Every time I left, he would say, "Thank you. See you next week," until I said, finally, Mae, and handed him a note beneath my cash inviting him to meet me for a drink.

It was a gutsy move. After all, I'd never asked a man out in my life. And because I'd always been the rule-follower, the good child, this bold move took months of agonizing indecision. Had I misread the way he leaned on the counter to look at me when I ordered? His compliments? What if he was a charmer? Saw me as merely a sweet old lady? I watched, closely, to see how he treated his other customers and found that he was businesslike and friendly but not focused the way he was with me. I agonized over that letter for days before handing it to him with payment for shish kabob beef. He carefully put the cash in the drawer with his nicked and scarred hands, opened the note, looked at me and nodded, "Thank you, Mae. That'll be just fine."

Wallace took Tuesday mornings off and, after a brief courtship, we'd spend entire mornings in bed. Louise was in Chicago then and Robert worked obsessively so I had all the time in the world. It was strange. All those months going to his shop, him behind the cool, curved glass of the cases, moving with only the slightest hitch, that I'd nearly forgotten his imperfection.

His bungalow was as neat and organized as his shop. He'd inherited it from his grandparents, both deceased, and I teased him about the worn camelback couch and wingback chairs, framed needlepoint and floral sheets. That day, though, when I poked him about his decorating, he merely shrugged, pinned me against the front door, outlined my body with his hands as if he'd forgotten how I felt and kissed me until I kicked his wooden shin. It didn't matter how hard I kicked because he would only challenge me to kick harder, which I did, and he would brag that any normal man would be in tears. That's when I teasingly pushed him. He wasn't expecting it, though, and stumbled backward to land on his butt. I leaned over to help him, afraid he'd be ashamed or mad, apologizing, but he started laughing and pulled me onto him. I unclipped the buckles of the prosthetic to run my cool hands over the part of his leg just above where his knee would have been, where his leg met the felt.

"What happened?"

He raised himself onto his shoulders. "I never told you?"

"You said it was an accident."

"Yeah. Well, my grandparents had a place on Saginaw Bay and we—my family, my aunts and uncles and cousins—spent nearly every summer weekend up there. My cousins and I always took the boat out to Charity Island to goof off without parents, you know—cover ourselves in mud, have rock fights, build forts. It was a blast. This one time, though, we all swam back out to the boat—Charity has a rocky shore so we would anchor the boat in deep water—and since I was the youngest,

I was always the last to climb on. Everyone was prodding me and for some reason I decided to climb up between the two big Yamaha outboards instead of the ladder. My cousin didn't see me when he turned the key in the ignition."

Wallace put his open palm on his other shin. "It caught my lower leg."

"How old were you?"

"Ten. It took them a long time to get my leg out. It got caught, horizontally, between the two propellers."

"And they couldn't save it?"

"They tried. I had twenty-two surgeries. In the end, though, it was an infection that sealed the deal."

Because I didn't know what else to do or say, I kissed him then and Wallace reciprocated by kissing me ten times in rhythm to the grandfather clock's gong. It's a small detail but one I connected once I returned home to listen to my answering machine. At exactly ten that morning, Leila left her first message on my answering machine. She said that they'd started laicization proceedings. After that, she left ten more frantic messages. In them, she kept saying that she needed me to do something. Eventually, her thoughts rambled. She became increasingly erratic. Her speech slurred. She must have held the phone in the crook of her shoulder as she rummaged through the drawer to find a razor or prescription bottles. The last few calls were nearly unintelligible except for the distinct request to watch over Astrid. In her last call, she told me how much she loved me.

That afternoon, when I returned home, the answering machine's frantic blinking caught my eye. I didn't need to listen to the end of the first message. As soon as I heard Leila's voice, so pained and desperate, I immediately jumped in the car and drove to her house. It was so cold that day. Remember? It was also the day that the hostage crisis ended and we learned that Will Goynes would be coming home. But I didn't think about that. I only thought about getting to Leila. Really, though, I knew it was too late. I knew as well as I'd known anything in my life.

I ran into her house and everything felt dark and still. Walter Cronkite's voice, much too loud, filled the emptiness and a trail of blood led from the family room, through the kitchen, past the living room, through her bedroom, to her master bath. And that's where I found her. Her head rested against the shower glass at an odd, terrifying angle. The phone lay beside her left hand and beneath her right, on her chest, was a letter. I knelt beside her to feel for a pulse and, as I did, I looked into her open eyes. The combination of her lifeless eyes and the stillness of her body conspired to crush me and I fell back against the wall where I began shaking uncontrollably because, in that instant, I realized that all this was my fault. Had I not written that letter, none of this would have happened.

This is where the truth becomes too much to bear. I could have touched her cheek, called an ambulance, tried CPR, held her until help arrived. I could have.

Instead, I moved her right hand to see your name, written in her lovely cursive, on the envelope. I slid the letter from beneath her hand and held it for a long time. I couldn't stand so I crawled out of the bathroom, through her bedroom. The thought of Astrid coming home from ski practice to find me crawling down her hallway struck me and it was then that I found my strength, got up, and ran out of the house.

That evening, instead of checking on Astrid, I repeatedly listened to Leila's frantic messages, removed the tape from the answering machine, wrapped it in a linen handkerchief and hid it and the letter in a joist above the furnace where no one would find it.

One night, not long after Leila's death, Wallace asked me to spend the night at his place, said he wanted to wake up next to me. Certain he would never check up on me, I told Robert I'd be with a cousin who'd fallen ill and needed help. Looking back on it, I'm not sure what I thought I was doing with a man twenty years my junior. Had I thought about the future, I would have realized what a fool I was being. But I wasn't thinking about the future.

While Wallace was at work I stayed at his place all day cooking and, by the time he closed shop and got home, I'd made a feast: tabouli, kibbeh nayeh, fül medames. I even rolled grape leaves. When he'd finished eating and raving about my cooking, he leaned back. "I have a question."

I raised my eyebrows.

"Why do you think Leila killed herself?"

The question irritated me not only because, up until that moment, I'd been enjoying myself but because I'd never told him—or anyone—the truth. "I'm not sure."

He shook his head. "So, she was your best friend but you don't know why she killed herself?"

"How can anyone know why another person does anything? Especially that."

"She didn't leave a note?"

"Why would she leave a note?"

He shrugged his shoulders. "It just seems like—"

"It just seems like what?" I snapped.

He looked hurt. "Like you would have some idea."

"Well I don't," I lied.

Wallace held up his hands. "Okay."

"I don't know why you brought it up!" I stood, walked beside him, snatched his plate and slammed it on the counter. I steadied myself on the sink's cool porcelain edge, my back to him, while the thoughts I'd tamped down hard kept rising to the top: if I hadn't sent that letter, if I had been home to answer her calls.

I'd used Wallace to take my mind off my mistakes. One sin masking the other. My sins ballooned in front of me and I couldn't control my emotions. I lashed out with lies. Told him I'd noticed him looking at other women. Accused him of growing tired of me. I went on and on. I kept it up until I looked up to see him crying.

"I thought this was what couples did," he managed.

"What?" I snapped, still angry.

"Talked."

That stopped me.

"We never talk. I mean. I love you and I want to know you."

And right then, I realized that we'd fallen in love. I'd broken my agreement with Robert. The future spooled out in front of me and what did I see? Messiness? A divorce? Wallace and me living happily? No. I saw me and Robert. Only Robert and me.

"You love me? Really? Will you love me in ten years? In twenty?"

Wallace nodded, "Yes. I will. What makes you think I won't?"

"Because you're young. And foolish."

"Jesus, Mae, what is this?"

He meant, Why are you acting this way? I knew that. But I fanned my hand between us, "This is sex. This is an affair. What did you think it was?"

Wallace shook his head as if trying to clear away the ugliness. "Mae? What's wrong?"

"What's wrong? I don't know why Leila did what she did, okay?"

"Okay." He tried covering his trembling lips with an open palm, but his cheeks were wet with tears.

"I make you this dinner and you ask me why my best friend killed herself!? For God sakes, Wallace—"

I was being ridiculous, but I couldn't stop. I gathered my things and left him crying at his kitchen table.

It was nine o'clock by the time I pulled into our driveway, still shaking, wiping mascara off my cheeks, hoping Robert had turned in early. The house was dark. Good sign, I thought, as I moved up the stairs to our bedroom. Just as I reached the top stair, I heard a familiar laugh. For a moment, I thought Louise was upstairs with Jackie because it was, unmistakably, Jackie's deep, throaty laugh. She'd practically grown up with us, after all, and I knew her laugh as well as I knew Louise's. I stopped and heard it again. Then I heard Robert's voice. I stopped on the top stair before crossing the hallway to our bedroom where I stood just outside the door for a very long time listening to the two of them in our bed.

As I turned to leave, I marveled at how the things that scar us forever happen so swiftly, but we remember them in such long, excruciating detail.

Sincerely,

Mae Shaheen

P.S. Enclosed you will find Leila's letter addressed to you. I have never opened it. I hope it brings you comfort.

ACKNOWLEDGMENTS

Over the years, many people have nurtured me and supported my work. Thanks to my mom, Sadie Maul, for your encouragement and fierce and unconditional love, and to my father for teaching me that forgiveness is possible even when it's least expected. Thanks to David for your enduring love and for making me laugh. To Lillie and Ella: you inspire and amaze me and make me want to be a better person. To my mentors John Schultz, Betty Shiflett, Randall Albers, Anne Hemenway, and Patricia Ann McNair: thank you for encouraging and supporting me, and for your careful reading of my work.

Huge thanks to University of Hell publisher Greg Gerding for bravely publishing innovative work and for believing in *Swarm Theory* and to University of Hell editor Eve Connell for her energy, spot-on editorial prowess, and her deep intuitive understanding of my work.

Thanks to editors René Steinke and Minna Proctor at the *Literary Review* for publishing "Exacting Revenge," Paul Hanstedt at the *Roanoke Review* for publishing "Undesirable Interruptions," Sahar Mustafah and Anita Dellaria at *Bird's Thumb* for publishing "Known Issues," Rima Rantisi at *Rusted Radishes* for publishing "Atmospheric Disturbances," and Abigail Shaeffer at *Chicago Literati* for publishing "Ectopistes Migratorious." And thanks to In Print Writers Organization for awarding "The Art of Breaking Away" First Place in your 2013 Fiction Writing Contest.

All kinds of gratitude to Julia Borcherts (Kaye Publicity) for believing in *Swarm Theory* and helping guide it into the world.

To my fearless, innovative, and talented colleagues (you know who you are) at Columbia College Chicago: you are my people.

ABOUT THE AUTHOR

Christine Rice's stories have been published in Roanoke College's *Roanoke Review*, American University of Beirut's *Rusted Radishes*, Farleigh Dickinson University's *The Literary Review*, and online at *Chicago Literati* and *Bird's Thumb*. Her writing has appeared in the *Chicago Tribune*, Detroit *Metro Times*, *The Good Men Project*, *The Urbaness.com*, *CellStories.net*, *F Magazine* and her radio essays have been produced by WBEZ Chicago. Christine is the managing editor of *Hypertext Magazine* and the director of Hypertext Studio Writing Center. She also teaches in the Department of Creative Writing at Columbia College Chicago and is the 2015 recipient of the Ragdale Rubin Fellowship.

THIS BOOK IS ONE OF THE MANY AVAILABLE FROM **UNIVERSITY OF HELL PRESS.** DO YOU HAVE THEM ALL?

by **Tyler Atwood**
an electric sheep jumps to greener pasture

by **John W Barrios**
Here Comes the New Joy

by **Eirean Bradley**
the I in team
the little BIG book of Go Kill Yourself

by **Calvero**
someday i'm going to marry Katy Perry
i want love so great it makes Nicholas Sparks cream in his pants

by **Leah Noble Davidson**
Poetic Scientifica
Door

by **Rory Douglas**
The Most Fun You'll Have at a Cage Fight

by **Brian S. Ellis**
American Dust Revisited
Often Go Awry

by **Greg Gerding**
The Burning Album of Lame
Venue Voyeurisms: Bars of San Diego
Loser Makes Good: Selected Poems 1994
Piss Artist: Selected Poems 1995-1999
The Idiot Parade: Selected Poems 2000-2005

by **Lauren Gilmore**
Outdancing the Universe

by **Robert Duncan Gray**
Immaculate/The Rhododendron and Camellia Year Book (1966)

by **Joseph Edwin Haeger**
Learn to Swim

by **Lindsey Kugler**
HERE.

by **Wryly T. McCutchen**
My Ugly and Other Love Snarls

by **Michael McLaughlin**
Countless Cinemas

by **Johnny No Bueno**
We Were Warriors

by **A.M. O'Malley**
Expecting Something Else